The author, Gerald J. Stalter, comes from a big genealogical-rooted family. In 2012, after the death of his grandmother, Gertrude Rose, he took over her spot in keeping the genealogy going and solving family mysteries along the way. He is most known for his research on his great-great-grandfather Alexander Colash Totten's suicide. He lives in Waverly, Tennessee, with his pug, Bucky, along with his sister, Sarah. Originally from upstate New York (not the city), he was given the gift of using his imagination that leads him to write. Some of the writing of Gerald's comes from experiences from his own life that he poured into his characters throughout his storytelling. Starting small in publications in genealogical-based magazines, Gerald has gained experience to lead to a full-length manuscript. Gerald has a two-year degree in education and hopes to teach more in the future. When not writing, you can find Gerald spending time with his mother who has kidney disease, keeping his fingers crossed for a cure.

Like a rose you can't glue the petals back on when they fall. You have taught me to stand on my feet and when I get knocked down to stand back up, Look at fear in the face, remember not to blink. This book is dedicated to a woman who has given it all to not want in return. Books are her best friend, and she can make a mean peanut butter cookie. Moo-Moo, or as they all know you, Mary J. Stalter-Dragon. This is for you. You will always be that lady on the porch of your doublewide in your curlers, holding a red mixing bowl telling us to get off that four-wheeler. Thank you for letting me plant those candies in your garden instead of flower seeds too. If you didn't know, then I didn't do that. Love you more. – J.

Gerald J. Stalter

WILLIAM

Freddie Series: Book 2

AUSTIN MACAULEY PUBLISHERS™

LONDON • CAMBRIDGE • NEW YORK • SHARJAH

Ordering Information
Quantity sales: special discounts are available on quantity purchases by corporations, associations, and others. For details, contact the publisher at the address below.

Publisher's Cataloging-in-Publication data
Stalter, Gerald J.
William

ISBN 9781645755050 (Paperback)
ISBN 9781645755043 (Hardback)
ISBN 9781645755067 (ePub e-book)

Library of Congress Control Number: 2020918141

www.austinmacauley.com/us

First Published (2020)
Austin Macauley Publishers LLC
40 Wall Street, 28th Floor
New York, NY 10005
USA

mail-usa@austinmacauley.com
+1 (646) 5125767

I would like to thank my mother, who thinks a dedication is not for her as she did not earn it, but she has. Let us wear green for Lorraine to hope for a cure for kidney disease. I am right there in your shoes when it comes to taking care of a loved one 24 hours a day. It's hard to balance everything and take that hit. For all she has given me there is no way that I am turning my back onto her. I have dropped everything for her and forever will. She was my cheerleader, now it's my turn.

Also, I would like to thank the team who helped this book / wounded soldier to get on his feet and those who work for my publisher, Austin Macauley. This company has taken what I said and made it into a reality. It is like when you're collecting vintage president election pins you get so excited when it comes in the mail. Well, I get the same reaction when I get an email from them. Who is having a geek moment right now, not me?

Please donate this book to a charity organization near you so someone who might not be able to buy a copy can read it. If it were not for places like that, I would not be here today, so please pass it forward. Smile on!

March 5, 1944

Yesterday and today was rather cool. It was hard to sleep as last night, the wind was whistling around the building. Sounded like winter but I was not cold.

Chapter 1
Rusted Halo

(William!)

The embryonic Preacher man stood face, clutching his book of statistics with a glisten. Holding the smile as the Photographer asked him to stand still. Humming a sixpence as the frozen moment was captured in upside down glass silhouettes. A dead still photo for the loved one's blessing fold. The best suit he ever owned with penniless shoes. Hands attached to each other, placed just so over the lap one last time like the roses left on the lid his loved ones leave attached with a kiss. Sitting the body in an upright pose watching as the eyes opened like a baby doll. Hand up the back of his suit coat as if he was a puppet just getting the right feet for the ventriloquist. Watered down skin, with a upside down smile adding glass like eyes. Once the photo was done, putting the poor boy back into the wooden box as his eyes closed as they lowered his back onto the fabric. A stranger holding him in the air as he is laid down to rest as flashes of a baby boy without a chance, a boy getting thrown into the water learning to swim, a man who was lowered as he took a wife, an old man sitting on his rocking chair, now a life gone waisted lowered down into a box of pine. With nothing but hands to tie it like a bow from all his year.

"May we bow our heads." I saw all the pretty in your soul boy. Why does it feel like I was just another one of your ghosts? "We gather here to lower William A. Starr into mothers' natures beautiful garden of endless time." I was walking among the frozen field of people when my face turn to listen to the words the preacher man called out. Why did he just say my name? Looking around in the crowd of people that were standing around a coffin. On the other side stands alone my Freddie. The coffin lid was up as I saw myself lying there. Freddie's hand reaches to me on the other side. Why can't I feel? Watching as Edith came to say her goodbyes when it was said.

"Why did he have to commit Suicide?" Looked down at my fingers as blood dripped down to the ground. Lines going crossed my wrist. That is when

I took his hand. It forced me to see my eyes to see a bright light as if it were dots off a Morse code reader. It was just a dream, I found myself on a hospital bed getting transported down the hall. Sat up in my own body sweat and my wrist were wrapped in pink cloth, a nurse pushed me back to lying down. One of them said I coded before. Wait, last thing I remember was counting numbers. How did I die? I must go back to the beginning to make it clear.

Four months earlier!
    3.5 months,
    12 hours,
    46 minutes,
    17 seconds,
    2 milliseconds!

That is how long he has been away. I counted the numbers like it was a recipe I was following. It felt like I was walking around this house with the redness from the rope burn after they took off my noose. Counting down the time until they come and get me to die. Going through the crowds of people, listening to them mock me for what I have done. Watching their faces as I fall to the ground. Now in our new lives they still bully me, but they do not remember what they did to me all those years ago. We live with the ones we known in our past lives. They play different rolls but who says I would not remember to not forgive those.

It felt more like I volunteered to be the canary in the coal mine. Felt more like I was getting dragged into the mine in a cage as I watched my Freddie getting smaller until I could not see him anymore. Just standing there looking like a ghost. He did not think about the thought if I was to come back dead or alive. They had a reward on my wanted poster no matter if I saw his face or not. So, I went to the darkest side of this person that no one ever knew was there. Even a grown man fears the dark. There he was to light it back up.

Dancing with the shadows of memories of yesterday as all I do is sit and think. Moving these penny loafers will not make him come back. Now I catch myself dancing in the shower, singing into the air, and head looking back to see if he would come in and catch me rocking out to a song. Then I place my hands on the walls…

Never asking:

Who: Freddie!

What: I given birth to a stillborn baby boy.

Where: He went to New York, I stayed here. No calls too.

When: Three months ago, last Tuesday.

Why: He never told me the whole story.

How: I drove him away.

Never asking myself these but going over them in my head like a running needle on a vinyl record that was done playing. Just letting the water run off my skin as that leaves me too. Ought to live with his ghost then bring him back.

Just asked me to let him in. You think that the only thing that is darker than your thoughts would be the shadows that seeps into the pages of a secret journal that sits under my pillow.

My brother had to pull out the sack the baby was attached to. Can still feel that cold hand reaching inside me, grasping it. Pulling it out, leaving me to shiver holding the counter of the sink. My jawline shattered as it felt as if he was seeing if this cow was pregnant or not. Walt and I buried the baby with our grandmother. The first thing I do when I become an adult is give my child his final resting place. It made my heart hide when the headstone never read his name. So, if you question my dark thoughts have at it. I have already been kicked while I was down. Just do not forget to return my halo when you are done. Did you know that yesterday was the day you died? How is about all the times that I saw your face letting me get closer for you to bite at me. You were my embalming fluid apple yet there I was letting myself drink you in.

STOP!

You don't want to be in my brain as I was thinking about bathing in a claw foot tub full of someone else's blood surrounding me keeping me warm as I watch my knees bobbing as the rubber duck smiling as he flouts on by. Letting myself go under the substance looking up to a world on fire. Like I said I went to the darkest side of who I was. This photo from your youth in the forties you always had to be in the center for all the attention so all would adore you. I might look like the man in the photo where the edges are scratched and faded it do not mean I have to be him. As the photo leaves my fingers and falls to the bottom of this claw foot tub all I could picture is my fingers around your neck, holding you down in the water hoping for your last breath. Making love to your body later as you could not fight back. Is that too dark of me to say that the water that I picture you in was gasoline and all I had to do before you get out of the wonderland of your mind. Light a match and let you burn like the devil you are. Putting on new clothing as you scream out my name.

Was it bad of me to think that the feeling on the inside of my leg felt good as his knee tried to kick me off him? No, it was better when his hands tried so hard to grasp at my face even thought his fingers were inches from reaching me. Or was it the moment when he saw me smile before I forced my hand over his mouth. The cherry was when I heard him take his last breath. It was as if I was watching my favorite team on the screen just win there game and next

13

week there in Florida to play. Feeling his limbs fall as his life left his physical form. This bed was sure something as it was really comfy after I thought about it. Posed him as if he were asleep the whole time until someone on his side of the law came into the room and found him. It's going to make me laugh at the sight that the person has hope that he might still be living. It was if Mister James himself was willing to pull down his trousers for any man who had a coin to bend, and an eye to wink.

My husband did tell me how the boys were a sickness in his family. I wanted the child to do much, I did not pay mind to that. The hardest thing I had to do was sit there in front of his face and tell him that I lost him. I tried to hide it, but he knew right off. When you take a shower with someone you knew like the face of a coin, you wonder when the person smiling is missing. In my case, there was a ring where the baby was on my back. Even I could do that math. Now he is gone. Said that he could not be with me for now as he did not want to hurt me anymore. Even the raspberries sinking in my tea mock my thoughts. I lost the only thing I had. Tried so hard to keep it, yet there it went in a flash. Now I sit in my brother's house as the clock is the only thing I want to do. So many times, did the bottle call over to me, but I was not its fool. Now the only smile I get is watching the news lady tell the weather. I pray for rain.

"You just going to sit there and let your phone ring?" What if I said yes? All that matters are that spots of sun shining in the window. I watch it from when it comes to be and when it goes away. Walt thought more light was the answer, but I rather be in a spacesuit with a cracked screen in my helmet begging for air. "Before I say who that was you better take a bath." I gave him this look like he just asked me to do something that no one ever wanted to do. The only face I want to see right now would be that Dalmatian you adopted last week. Walton just kept on talking as if I were listening "Well if you're not going to get dressed you can at least come with me." Why? You were looking at me like you hushed my birthday candles, and I was not looking when you did that. "This isn't going to water it down! But seeing something that's not these four walls will do you good." That is what you say, but? "Go get dressed, I gotten you something I put it your room. I leave in fifteen." He keeps doing this thing with his fingers where he points to his eyes then at me. Man, do I wish his fingers would detach when he points at himself. Go shut your door than. As if I was going. That is the thing our new relationship as siblings was talking to the front of that sunshine yellow door of his. Now looks like I must get up and get ready for a night of me reading a book as he tries to cheer me up. "I can hear through these walls and the sofa never made a sound. William do not make me dress you myself, I will. I have done worse." He has, and he means it. When I stood my feet slipped a little from my socks onto this extremality clean wooden floor.

The door opened as the wind was right there to run past me like a child. The child I will never know. The room was colder than my thoughts. Like taking a bath in ice the sting never goes away. The Moon's light shined on my bed as there was nothing there. He told me! The things he does for love. The things I have done for love. Just to get pushed to the side. I never said I was done. I would use the rest of my ration book on him if he just comes back and let me show him a good time on my leave. Yet there you go with it all in your bag. Now I see why you were down here for the year. Too hot to handle. I created something with you, and all you wanted to do was keep it all for yourself. I let you carry my solider identification card from my time in service. Even that is gone. Then why was I here thinking about you still when I should not be. The Mason jar nightlight was drawing my eyes in as the electric razor was telling me to end it. Cut my neck open and let my life spill out to the floor. Then there it was in my head, his face again. There was something else going on here. I was having a push in my vision to seeing what was going to be. Been doing that lately.

"Why did I bring my phone in here?" I whispered!

Last call was from, no! Freddie! I let him slip through my fingers again. I dropped my phone falling to the floor as I rubbed against the cabinet door as if I were dodging the bullets in the trenches. Gotten to the sink as I found out where Freddie was hiding my raiser. The one you must sharpen with a belt. The brush to put on the shaving cream still had that elk carved into the side of the bowl and the head as the handle. This beard I was starting was hitting the sink bed. He hated when I grew one of those. Why didn't I take the calls? Not letting the hair take a ride down the sink as I closed my eyes. Picturing his face as the tears started. Truth is every night for the last three months I sat in my closet crying and screaming. Like I did while I was home with mother. I had to hide it from her. When you are forced to kill another man, you relive those moments every day. Took off my shirt as his humming filled my ears. He was the only one who did not make jokes on my belt inlays on my skin. I loved that, that was the one thing that made me fall for him. Then at the same time, it was first sight.

I was in the backyard hitting baseballs as they came flying at me out of the machine my dad gotten for me. I was trying to be perfect for father. When I heard something coming up the road, I normally did not mind to it, but I had to look this time. The balls were hitting the trees as I was not there. Mud on my skin as the sun was beating down while sweat cascaded over me body, making it look like I had this glowing complexion. My shirt was somewhere

15

on the grass. Breathing very heavy. The rim of my jeans was resting on my hips as the bat was over my shoulder. He passed in his purple truck as I waved with the hand my bat was in. He did not see me, but he was singing at the top of his lungs.

Can still remember that song too, but that is the song I keep playing repeatedly every night as I fall to sleep. That is when I knew. It is as if I could feel his fingers hovering over my ribs as I was getting this winter fresh taste on my tongue. I went to go grasp the imaginary fingers. Wait! I was touching real fingers. "Walt, this isn't funny!" Breathing on the back of my neck. "Walton, stop this!" I did not want to move as I could not see the person behind me. My eyes were closed so I was relying on my hearing.

"Walton isn't here." That voice vibrated off my body like when a bell rings and the metal reacts to the hitting of its walls. I forced my eyes open. Freddie was standing on my back. He was in the mirror. Was I seeing things? This is what I wanted, but he did not have to come. I sat there as my back was pressured on the sink, and Freddie was there in my front. There was not anything new that Walt left in my room, it was something I was looking for. He took my hand in his, never letting it go as it was the body and he was the coffin. "I'm sorry for leaving. I had to go upstate and deal with a few things on my own." I do not understand. You left me, Why? What was this feeling coming about me I was letting him in again as I let my guard fight my thoughts here, I was letting him fight for you now? I was a dirty coward.

"Whatever it was, I could have been there for you." He was not looking at me. Fine, go! If you did not want to be here, then. "You have been gone for three months."

"It was ghost-related, and you would have been killed. At the time, you still had the baby you were carrying, and I could not let them get to you... I love you more to let you give me something like that." I let his hand go and went near the bed. That is the thing you cook up after all this time. Even the dog was able to see through your lies. He should know as I talk for him with a goofy voice as if he understood me. Freckles the dog is a better acter then you think.

I do not know if I can take you back like this. Did I live in a lie? Or was he the forgotten soldier felling the smoothness of the metal to his pocket watch hoping it was a compass? There is just one more thing I needed to know in the back my head I wanted to trust him, but there was something holding me back. Then I had to ask him again! "Did Walton know! Can anyone be trusted? You two gang up on me and me did not know it. Edith, where did she go." He was looking confused.

"She might not be coming back." I was confused now. "That's why you couldn't come with us. Edith is deep in with The Guardians of Time." Oh, now I am looking at you. It felt like the boat just hit ice and I was running trying to get my family safe, so they do not die in the cold waters. Yet I feel as I died when I married a Waters.

"I told you never to go near them. You let her go in there. You know what they are going to do to her? Once my mother finds out that she is in there." This was bad. My mind was thinking of a million little ways she could die.

"Went back in time and saved Howard K. Smith from being killed by who I thought was my father. He's with her." I understand now. You throw out names as if I knew who this man was. Looked to the wall as the frame was empty. There was a First World War soldier sitting outside in a wheel barrel with his hands linked together smiling at the camera. We found in the doctor's cabinet he drugs home. He died from mustard gas in his right lung. He spent months in the field hospital, the photos gone. You do not play around with time.

"Cold, I have been cold this whole time. You had Bradley watching me. Making sure I am safe. Freddie, I can be shot in the head and the bullet come rolling in my mouth like a pin ball. I don't need him to watch me." I am not a kid!

"I know you're not a kid, but I had to make sure everything I love is safe. If that means saving a friend to be with my cousin, then so be it. If that means making sure the only person, I have left in my life that matters the most is safe, then yeah I am going to do it." Was he reading my mind? No! Edith gave her gift to him until this was over. Must be. He was crying some, felt that. Was I ready to take you back? It was like one of the scary movies your date takes you to, knowing you will grab for his arm for safety. The moment when the lady in the hotel room investigates the window and the person to kill her is in the glass reflection. There was not a window, but the mirror from the old hotel they were going to knock down that my brother got in a bid. This whole house was covered in vintage items. Looking rich in a poor house. Why was I the girl this time and Freddie was the man standing behind me. The tension that sat in my muscles made them hurt some like when you dive into water letting out a scream. The air felt like it was going to kill my lungs within a matter of moments. Sitting on the bed thinking, and that was dangerous to do.

"Freddie! Where is Kelly? Your aunt went to live with her cousin in another state. He is not with us. He cannot be with the other two people he knows. Where is your brother?" Why wasn't he worried. His shoes came over to rest near my feet, all he wanted to do was put his hands in his pockets. I did not look at him, but I could feel him. My hand on his arm forcing him to sit.

He did not because he was tearing now, and he did not want me to know. "What is going on?" If you cannot tell me, just go and never come back. I am done waiting. He used the top of my arm to wipe the tears from his eyes. Making me laugh with it. Miss the times when he would watch the blond hairs on my arms shine in the morning. Stop it!

"The Guardians have taken him in time. That is why she asked to go in, so she can follow where they move him. They know to get to me you have to have him, and it's working." No! Now I understand. This is not going to be easy. "The last time he was in was 1683, England. She had to sleep with the king just to find him, but you do what you must for family." She had to sleep with the king who had a chair made of people he sat on every day. This was not right. Freddie's mother dies, now this. That was her test from The Guardians, she is now a member. "Howard, he had to kill a man in Germany during the war, have you ever heard of!" He said a name of a superhero, but I did not know who it was. You mean he just killed a man that was supposed to change the world as we know it and we do not know it now.

"Do we have to worry?" We were next, I knew it.

"You never think your mother is the main person running this thing. My father was her greatest love, so we do not have to worry about me. If anything happened to me, she wouldn't be incredibly happy." I throw my hands in the air.

"Are we related?" He looked at me and laughed but it was so hard he forgotten how to breath.

"No, no nothing like that. They did not see each other until my birthday party. So, we are not, but they are not going to touch the families of the two highest in power. This is going to be hard for you to take, William." I stood and turned to see him sitting there. Hovering my legs over his. Pushing him gently to the bed. Pushing my fingers over the rim of his belt. My knee was placed between his legs on the mattress now, as my lips were over his. After a moment, he licked his lips to taste me while his hand rested on the back of my head as we took in each other's breath. His eyes were in mine right now. What was happing, why was I seeing a man running in his. Was that me? "My…my father is in just like Edith is. He has always been there getting the highest power. Oh, yes, kiss me there again." I was trying to keep him at bay, so he never finished what he said. "William, your mother is the one who is responsible for this." I did not care right now. My hands are down your pants, and my tongue is in your mouth, this is what matters. The clothing on my floor, and nothing but the sheets to cover what we were doing. Walt turning his ear buds to the fullest they can get a workout on his exercise machine. This is what I was waiting for. He was gone for three months. For something that felt like

18

years was forgotten right this moment. Then my thoughts went to the bodies I had to crawl over. All the mother's sons getting left behind. At night before marching on the desperate men letting their souls die a little as they made love to the corps. The poor boy's bodies, the eyes would open, and the head push back as the vocal cords would still hum as they pushed their way in. Their hands forcing the hardness to take. "You're hurting me!" He was whispering as if the people on the television were hearing what we were doing. "Don't bite my lip again." I was not a vampire, liking the way his blood tasted. My face was hovering his body, watching it react to what I was doing to it. Like a wave on the water as the pebble is thrown into it making those rings. There it was I was becoming one of those men. I scared myself as I saw myself running again. Forcing myself off him. Sitting there just hoping this was not happening. "Did you have a vison?" Was that okay? My head said yes.

"Why did I have a vison? I let myself go to the darkest place in my mind." I was going crazy.

"The gift's transferred to you. I gotten Edith's, now you have mine until she takes it back." I do not want it. A door appeared near me as I heard a little girl asking me to play.

"I have to go into this door." I lined the frame with my hands so Freddie, who cannot see it, can see the shape. There is someone on the other side knocking on it. I told Freddie they want me to open it. Why couldn't he see this too? My hands took the knob, yet I was shaking with him looking at me.

"Your eyes are silver like a bullet. Your hair, it is changing to an eggshell color. Your fingernails are turning to metal. Like that mineral in science that came off like dandruff." What was happening. No, I know what is happening right now. Freddie, his gift was mine now and this is how I use it with a Tin Starr ability. Freddie came up behind me, grasping my hand in his. Resting his forehead on the back of mine. "If anyone can do this, it's you!" When the door opened, I went in, like when a hand goes into the bottom of a puppet. You do not know what is inside the fabric until you get in there. For a spilt moment, he could see in here too. "Wow!" was the last thing I heard him say before the door closed. Funny thing is, I still can see him standing behind me. I got you back now I still must let you go.

March 14, 1944

Asked Mom for her cheese bread recipe. Fingers crossed if it comes in her next letter.

Chapter 2
Weathering Thoughts

(Freddie!)

For every minute, a bell would chime it was like he was burning Alabama. His fingers left skin fragments on the handle of the metal every time his person lifted his hand. Even though how does a ghost leaves skin particle? The groves in the body of this bell were like a girl's dress as she twirls. The little metal ball in the middle hitting the insides making a reaction to every time it hit. Yet that was just a sound. Vibration from one's vocal cords. With every chime of the bell, the hairs on his skin would move yet there was no wind. The bell from the town square was being rung as there were no emergencies to attend to, but the sadness in the air. He wanted the town's folk to see the witch that haunt them. I was the witch.

It was a twilight moon as the sky was the coloring of silk, and all the nature-type effects were different shades of dark blue. Pebbles falling as his boots walk crossed the ground. It was like the soles of his boots were made from the candlemaker's heartstring. As one can learn two trades, and all his hard work was around his feet. He was scared to breath as they might hear him. Those size-thirteen boots held his stance, so he did not fall. His socks were long, going up his leg up to his knees. Gray and orange tips on his toes and a little orange on the ankles. It was hot to wear those socks, but it kept him cool at the same time.

Around his hips were baby blue boxers with yellow rabbits on the fabric as he wore navy blue pants over them. The ends of the legs to his boots covering the neck making him look like he was wearing sneakers instead of boots. He was wearing a gray hooded sweatshirt, with a navy-blue coat on top. The hood on his head as his blond hair covered the front of his face. Easter egg dye on his fingertips from the night before. Not knowing he was going to find himself in a strange world tomorrow. He was bent down balancing himself on the pads of his feet. Just one man in the middle of the woods. He felt the ground letting the red clay getting under his nail bed. His eyes were gray as that is how he could see this world. His chin was still covered in hair from not shaving in two days. The veins in his corpus cavernosum let him know that there was a person behind him. He never felt that before as this was new. There was a vibration in the ground that went up his whole body yet that he felt the most. The person from behind him was me. His fingers started to act as if they were treading water, I couldn't see what he was seeing as he couldn't see what I could thus making us on an uneven battlefield. I could feel the whispers around me as it felt like little tiny ants crawling up my legs.

"William, it's Freddie." He heard my breathing very heavy. I was trying not to as he was listening to me as if I were being hunted. He circled me as I stood there. Sniffing the air like a dog. "Tell me what you see?" He saw these people his mom warned us of.

"People, angry people. All dressed in dark and light-colored clothing. In different shades of greys and yellows. They all hide beside things as they are scared that I am here in their world as I am not supposed to be where they are. They can bend light too like I can. There is a boy who is in the corner making me smile." He said there was a girl coming up to him. She had long hair that was parted so it flushed her face. She did not look him in the eyes as she kept her head on the side. She was dressed like a little doll a girl would carry in the eighteen-hundreds. "She's telling me she's happy to see me, Everett King. That is my name over here. Her hand, she was giving me something." Why would they bring his name up? She knew something about my mister Starr that even I did not know it was as if she was playing a game without minds. I had to stop it.

"Don't open her hand. Ask her people's name." So, he did. "William, Everett King, was a boy who rode on a racetrack when I was a kid for soap box cars. He even mowed my grandparents' yard on the side. I looked up to him, he kept me out of trouble." They remembered my thoughts trying to get him to play the role as they were sick in their minds as they were taking my darkest fantasy of sometimes, I wish he were William and using it against me. They wanted him, not me. If I went with him, they would kill me. William was trying not to back away, but his hands kept moving as he was trying not to freak out.

"Her people are called, Before. Just Before as they came before us walking on the planet. They are living another life, but still some of the last life must go somewhere. A lot of people say that they are called shadows. What is it you wish from me?" Good question. He described everything she was doing. Her head turned like an owl as she pointed at me, he said. "You can't have him." I heard his voice slowly turn into an older lady's voice who has been smoking for years. He would cough in mid speech as he spoke her words to me. I wish he wasn't there right now. "Not him, but who follows him." William said her words after she did. "The boy with the red hair shall die if you don't get us the thirteenth nail." Her voice was changing. Everything she was talking about was my brother, Stu, but he killed himself jumping off a building. Wearing a red hood.

William! He told me that her face looked at him. Her eyes went behind her skull. Nothing but seeing the red veins in the back of the balls. Crows were coming all around. Yet I did not see them. William kept holding his head as she was making him live all his past lives all at once. He just yelled out names and things they did. I didn't understand all of them as he talked so quick it was like playing a song very quick. "She is opening her hand. She is pointing at you, Freddie. She's saying, him!" If you stood still you could feel the impact on the ground as Williams hit the ground. She had pushed him to the ground, and he told me she was dragging him by his eyes, but all I saw was her trying to grab at his face. He was being dragged on the ground, kicking for her to let him go. The yelling filled my ears making them bleed. All I saw was blood on my fingertips, and my William getting dragged in the dirt. It wasn't fair that I couldn't see her.

He was screaming for her to stop. I quickly went to grab his legs. As I could not see her, but I looked up to where I thought he was asking her to let him go. He sat there covering his eyes telling me they were gone. She told him that if I give them the one, they seek, they will leave us all alone, but until then, they will kill people off, one at a time. Never knowing when it will be. It will all start when they all fall. Starting with me as I have the power to kill them. William stood to his feet as he stumbled to his knees some. Getting on his feet like a good boy does. Looks at me with this fear on his face like he just ran for a year nonstop, catching his breath like he does after we make love. His face was flushed as he looked at his hands as they were shaking. Ice box cookies wrapped in parchment paper lined his right coat pocket. Made with all the love from his mother's fingers as he knew that even if they got a little old, they would come back to life with a cup of tea. The memory of raspberry's sits in his dried-out taste buds. The bottom of his tongue gets stuck on the dried skin on his bottom lip. The flaps of his helmet hitting the base of his chin as he walked. If he stepped with his left foot the right foot hit his skin if he stepped with his right foot the left would hit the opposite side. Mud splashed over his boots, as the strings were loose. His pant legs were tighter than usual where he was in a rush to get going. Those dog tags of his were pressed on his backside. The three buttons on his underwear were indenting themselves in his skin as he forgotten to fold the top down under his midriff. The coldness was taking heed of his teeth to the point that he wouldn't dare let someone kiss his face as his teeth would hurt. The jolt to the pain wasn't the thing he wished for at this moment. His brain pounded from the stress of getting to where he needs to go that singing a song his mother sang while doing dishes made the headache slowly leave his thoughts. His upper leg numbs to the feel, but he keeps marching on. He stopped after walking miles at none stop. Following the enemy soldiers in their wake wasn't as easy as many think. One wrong sound, or if they see him. This man would be dead. When they made camp, he bedded down like the deer did in the woods in the woods from near where he grew up. Ending up in the cabin in the woods. It was making me worried as William had magical abilities that he never told me about. He can change his cloths now in a blink.

"William! What did she say!" The door creaked open, making him jump. A little tin solider came marching in, stopping in his tracks when his key was done spinning in his back. What was out there is not what I need to know. His eyes looked at the toy, to me, to the toy back again. This went on for a while.

"She told me to bring her the thirteenth nail, if not she will kill you. Hammering in the thirteenth nail will let them control your gift. If I have anything to say about it there will be no thirteenth nail." He looked back to the ground as William took the toy in his hands.

"William, who's he?" He winded up the toy trying not to answer me. Walked over to his side when I took his arm and stopped him from what he was doing.

"The Paper Prince!" William let the toy go as he started to follow it. "He will lead us to him. Come on!" He whispered; it was the two of us who could hear.

"Coming!" Oh, dear! "Where are we going" He was smiling as he was just thinking how cool it was to follow a toy. I yelled out his name as I stopped, he stopped looking back at me, the toy stopped as well, picked up when we started walking again.

"We're going to a place where, well I think, it's another being on this planet that we have to stop. That for a reason whatever they are, they are what your father, my mother, and everyone else come from. They are supposed to be their version of the dead. Were you're half Tin Star, half human gives you the ability to see multiple worlds here on this planet? Your gift going to me gives me the right to see them. Our family is running from their people and started over here in the Amish community, so they were not found. Them wanting all the power, well that's what took them here." This was too much to take in. I had to investigate the trees for their lights as the leaves were shedding the water from their branches. Taking in the smells of natural beauty. "See, if we don't stop them, they will find a way to take us with them until all life here is dead. So, their dead can control our freshly left bodies to get to them." No, now I am not scared to go at all! "Ms. Louise was hunting the three princes. She needs all three to rule all of time and we must stop her. The princes are the descendants of the three founders of time." She said all this.

1. The paper prince, the one who knows all of time.
2. The prince of death, You! Self-explanatory!
3. The prince of magic, now that title is Edith's.

"And what is she doing with them when she gets them." What to say when unexpected questions fly at you.

"If she gets the bottle, the wand, and the diary from all three she can control the universe." That is not good. Later that night he was writing in his journal he has since his time in forty-four. He was putting names on the page. "Names, and things I did in the past lives. Maybe I need to remember them." That scares me even more. "Freddie, there are times I remember getting shot and I stand there holding my head. I feel as if I am in both places at the same time. I feel the dog tags on swaying onto my skin, yet I am wearing a T-shirt and no necklace. Getting split into two different people in the same body" He put the book down as his head was now on my shoulder. "Am I sick" What do I say?

"William, let me ask this. How did you know all that information?" He didn't wasn't to say, but he did it for me.

"I knew that stuff. Just like I remembered all of this." He lifted the book in his hands. Afterward while he slept, I read what he written. Almost all everything.

- I love the smell of old paper that had been stored away or in the basement left in a shoe box. Brings me back to my childhood. Most of you right now will be like he is strange, or why? To me it's better then what your saying is your favorite smell.
- They handed me a blue book to write things down in that I view while I am here. If I write in it what will I gain. They must think that I will not be able to remember anything after I get out of here. Singing up for a three-year tour I knew that there might be a chance at adding more time to our cards. It's just how good of a number you are. Well they added it to our current time.
- Went into town the last three days and man did I get a bad sunburn. Never help in the mess hall by cutting up the carrots while sitting under the sun.

- They had us in forty tents lined up, I was in the twenty-first. There was more noise coming from our tent every night than the others.
- My first day in the army they gave us test after test after test. The next day after that we gotten our cloths. Had to sign a few papers to get them. Never had to sign a receipt to get clothing before.

April 7th, 1944

Gotten to go to a local beach with the guys today. They never said though the locals swim with nothing on. I am starting to like the beaches here.

Chapter 3
Yellow Bell Bush

(William!)

I wore that old reddish hat that was weathered from the sun. You know the one that most of us have that you do not want to throw it away, you can still get some life from it. I think this hat seen me without clothes on more than I have. It was like we were married but I did not need a paper to say to myself I love this thing on my head. It had my last name on it, it was a must buy. Always thought my real father was somehow working for the hatter business. As his son waits for his father's return from his mental breakdown, he will come back for him. Yeah that day has never came, but I am still hopeful. All I get is poked by the pins that were left on the ground after he left me where I grew up. Maybe this cap can now cover up the balding spot on the back of my head. Hope that Freddie don't think anything about it being there. Fingers crossed. No, he is going to know something is up; he has never seen me wear the hat unless I cut the grass. He says that the hat makes the eyelashes pop more, giving my eyes a better feature, making the blue stand out from the darkness of the lashes.

I was one of those odd kids that delivered papers in the morning, out until dad went to work then I went home, poured into my clothing, and hoped the bus lady would wait until I get to the bus. If not, I had to ask Aunt Mary to give me a ride. That is how I found out things about Freddie before I met him. She would tell me things about him as I asked her to. Made the trip go faster. It was as if this hat made the thoughts stay in my head, I have never forgotten the things she told me. When he gets angry with me, I bring those things up, it calms him down. Freddie gets angry and gets to the point that I must get him to calm down, but he is nothing like my parents were in the long run. The hat sits on the back of my head just enough to cover the spot I do not want to be seen. Then the hair grows around the cap like when they say us humans would not be here what would happen to what we left behind. The grass would come up into the blacktop as that is how it was before. Nature will fight man-made items at the end. And the building would be empty.

Freddie always says that if I were to carry a magic wand that it would be in the shape of a pen. I always have one in my pocket. There is something on my mind every moment I blink that I must write it all down. That is what woke me up this morning as the pen rolled over to the door casing. Didn't help the old springs to the mattress. If it is still good, dad never throws anything anyway. When I fell to sleep, he was landing his head on my chest as I felt the coolness to his hair hit my skin. Running the tips of these middle size fingers over the back of his legs. He is ticklish behind his kneecaps. Leave it up to him to get up and never once try to motion me to wake as well. That is his kindness. I never said I love you to him, not yet and I love him the most. I love him even more then my own self be truthful. Thinking about giving it a go. Even asked mother for grandpa's wedding band. Thing is I stop because being gay in the world that I am in gets men like me scared to stay away from that subject. Did I want to put him through that?

What do you think? Too bad when you do read this, if you read this you can't write into the past. These pillows he knows how to place them, so it feels like you are on a cloud. His imprint still lines the fabrics. Outside my window a Christmas bird made her nest, he named her Holly. Saw the dust particles in the sun as it shines down on parts of my arms letting the blonde hairs shine. Looking down to what I could see where I had red rings all up and down my body from the base of my neck down to my well you do not go down that far. Only two people have the code to get into there. Why am I smiling? You know what I talked myself into it. I'm saying it!

Now I knew how a vacuum felt. He made me laugh so hard last night it was worth all these hard kisses that left these rings. His favorite spot is right under my breast where the six-pace connects. Do not really know the name to the muscle as he is the only smart one in the scientifically mathematical equivalents. Sat up on the side of the bed where his clothing sat under my toes. He is still here. Walking around the room trying to find my trousers. I knew they were somewhere I left them on the chair near my bed. Then at the same time I added it up, he is wearing them.

Why is my closet locked?

I can't get to my clothing. He took his pants too. Fine I will trip getting into your boxers and walk through this house I think not. Hearing him singing in the tub means he is in the shower and all my ears can do is guard away. I could hear him sing all day. One day, but he doses do his best in the shower must be why he holds to his name so deemed water for Waters. Last night I still hear the humming as my hands cascade across the rings. That's where the old reddish hat comes into play. As I tiptoed around the house covering myself with it. No one be home, please let no one be home.

"You know your home is the only one with a butler's pantry. You must be the pantry boy." He whispered last night as he danced his fingers on my midriffed. Now I find myself in that very room. He might be right. The bathroom sits attached to this room. No one was about the house, so I pretended to do pushups in front of the door. I was lying on the floor looking through the bottom cracks of the bathroom door. Seeing the gold legs from the tub, and wooden floors from back when. Where was he? The tub was empty as the water was getting emptied. So, I closed my eyes to hear his feet to see in my mind if I could fathom where he was standing. When I went back to look, I was shaking somewhat as his eyes were there to greet mine. He was smiling bigger than I was. Do not know who was louder laughing harder Freddie or me.

"Open the door!" I said!

"No, you will see me with no clothes on." What? Oh, who could say no to that smile. Smile on, go on!

"So, last night was nothing then. I saw nothing. You didn't leave anything on me." He put his fingers to the cracks.

"Give me your hands." So, I let the skin on my hands get scratched up as my knuckles where all red bleeding even, but I had to touch. The skin on the top my hand was rubbing off it stung like a million bees chasing for you. No ice, nor chap-stick will make this sting go away. There was a set of boots on the heels of my feet. All I heard was feet. I stood to mine as I tried to figure out what I could not see. The figure had locked the door in his wake. I could feel fingers grasp the back of my pants as tension settled in. worry ran up my body faster than the settlement. There is something going on here as we should be the only ones here. Freddie got back into the tub to hide his feet from being seen.

"William! William!" The sound of him knocking on the door went through my body as fast as if I got hit with thunder. My father's voice cries out for me. I looked over to my side as my eyes saw this line on the ground. Looking up to seeing a strange young man. He was standing on this door that back in the olden times, it was a root cellar where the family would hide if they had to. He was reacting like I was in fear, but he was trying to hide the door with his feet. His eyes were looking at this hall closet mother still used. Clothing was in there. Thank you, ghost boy! Father came rushing in as I put the shirt over my head. The smell of the laundry pod was still in the fabric.

"In here." He put his head to the door near my face. Made me jump.

"Why is the Waters boy's book bag here near the door?" I had to think twice. The boy motioned for me as he told me what I should say to keep me alive. My father did not know who I was talking to as he could not see him. I was learning Freddie's gift to help him learn. This was a test. Like when I know I am dreaming, and you could tell they do not like it that I know how to control them. Still trying to figure out who they are. Arguing with the floor wasn't healthy.

"Walton took it off the bus by mistake. I still have to bring it to him later." The door opened, I thought it was locked. When I went to go look behind me, he was gone.

"Where you get that royal blue suit coat?" I put it on, so you do not see the rings that Freddie left from the night before dad.

"Freddie let me have it for a date I have later. Edith's one friend finally said yes." He smiled so big thought he was going to break. There was a monster in his eyes every time he gotten mad. He reached trod me pushing me across the room into the mirror on the wall. All I felt was the air and falling backward. Hitting into something that felt like little pins hitting your skin. As I fallen to the floor. He rests his hand on the back of my head. Lifting it in the air. The other hand showed me his phone with a picture of Freddie on top of me in bed. How did he get this? He was filming us last night. The boy was back, and angry with my father. The boy's energy was so strong that my father heard his heavy breathing, but his eyes didn't know where to look.

"Next time you lie to me boy I will kill you. If you bring that bag to his house, you better never come back here. You better hope that cars come up the road and hit you dead. You have two hours to get your stuff and get out." He walked out as Walton walked in to see what was going on while Freddie came out from his hiding area. He just put his hand up for him to stop.

"I will get him ready to go, you get home…get!" Freddie ran!

That is was a year ago today.

Currently here I am standing in line with this hat on my head, and blue jeans with my belt as I want to pop out of these skinny jeans, I wish that wasn't on sale thanks to Freddie always saving a penny, thanks to Freddie I get looks from others even the old lady's when I walk past. Wish he would get lessons on how to starch the rims of these jeans they never move. How much starch do you think the mom of the boy sitting at table four and a half uses? Those pants stand at a point even thought his body's is hunched over the table. His back is tilted yet the rim of his trousers stays standing up like a solider. Even the tail of his shirt, the fabric looks softer than mine. Well yours would be too if you did not have to sit in mud for the last few hours.

Victoriously did my eyes lock with his. Like that was my goal for the day. I just wondered who does his laundry, yet he thinks me looking him up and down for a riddle. Look again, I dare you! Do not start fights here, that is not

34

why you have come Starr-boy. I was sitting in an old-fashioned tea restaurant. It is England's version of an eatery, but every food item hints around the idea of teatime. Rice pudding in a better bowtie then I was wearing. The cheese-Danish was happier to see itself in the reflection then I was. The only warmth sitting in a 1944 building in the English countryside would be placing your fingers around the teapots. They can look but he is the only one who can touch. I hate that rule. You know why, I am going to tell you because he knows better, I will only be his no one else's. Why I gotten that ring on my finger, for a reason that's why! Perfect pants boy was getting too much, walk to the bathroom.

It was the morning that time stood still for. For a change time took a day off and let me have the controls. Why did I want to return like a gift I gotten for holiday being it was the wrong size, and we got lucky that grandmother saved the receipt? I was standing, face right into the mirror. Ten minutes only are all you get with Freddie. He was not here so I gotten more. There I was looking at a boy standing in his jeans with a hat on his head holding his shirt in his fingertips. Letting the fabric softly land on the base of the sink. There was a freckle under my right breast that I have not seen a while. Could still feel his mouth letting his lips induce over that spot, as the moisture from his tongue leaving with a hint of air goes a long way. My Freddie tells me that I was fooling myself as I was a perfect weight. Of course, he has to say that for me to think he still loves me, but then again, he loves every inch on my body. Why do I feel sick every time I gain a pound then lose in the same matter of time? There was something bad in my head going on. The voice telling me that I was still too overweight, that voice talking to me as darkness whispering in my ears and that everyone will not want me around if I were always out of breath and could not catch up. There was a time in the history before I met him that I stopped eating all together thinking I had to get my father's approval. If another boy looked one way I would have to, if they did something, I had to do more. I suffer from the no eating thing. But I know when it comes, I must tell myself to eat. There had to be something behind this mirror thing for a reason because it helps me not looking at myself. Then why does it hurt to cover it up with the fabric of that shirt? I cannot drink if I do, I think I will not come back from that. So, I fill up a spoon full of vinegar and let it slide down until the sting goes away. I know I am somewhat made of tin, but even that bends.

"William!" Freddie was in the mirror behind me as he walked in, he was not supposed to be here. Then why was he? "Can I talk with you about something." I had to take the bitterness now before it melts down to my core. "I told Edith to stop cooking for you. Every night I find the food you took in the garbage. Is there something you need to share with me?" I thought I took those bags to the can before he saw it. How do I turn around and face him? By sitting on the counter facing him and rushing the hair back with my fingers. How did he know where to find me? Can I ever get a little of me time?

"When I was in the seventh grade I was in singing. See before you came here high school started in the eighth grades. I begged my father to come, this was going to be the biggest thing. For me! The teacher said that make sure all your family comes to this. Mom was with Walton with his spelling bee. My dad's sister was able to get off from work and come. Well if she can go so could he. They always had to show off in front of each other." I stopped for he was not supposed to find out I was weak as I was his strength, his protector. He mentioned for me to go on. "He sat there near her. As the other kids gotten all the best awards. I gotten best participation. (All the kids get this one. I came here and had to miss my shows for this. This was a waste of time.) He kept repeating things like that to me. It made me feel like I was an ant he was going to step on. Then they were going to get to the last award. He knew I was not going to get it, and he said I was in trouble for lying to him. The award was the musicianship award given out only to a child in a music field every twenty-five years. It gotten me an award to put on my wall and my picture on the wall with a gold plate under my name if I was going to get it. He kept asking to go before all the other parents for, but I had to hear. The earth science teacher's daughter was called up first, then here I thought it be the other child whose parent held a higher power. Then he said my name. I won! Where was he but walking onto the hallway motioning me in my moment to get out of there. That next morning, I found my award in the fireplace. It couldn't be saved."

"Okay what does this have to do with not eating." I pushed the hair behind my ears. This was it. Time for him to find out.

"He told me that boys don't sing for fun they run outside in a field chasing a ball. Get that award then I be proud of you. Well I weighted in for the football tryouts. I was three pounds over for the team's goal. That is when it happened, I started not eating to get on the teams every year. With every year a new sport was added, singing was dead to me until you came. It gave me the name he wanted, but he didn't think what it was doing to me to catch up to him."

"William, you have to eat. I am not your father and I don't expect you to come home a hero." He held my hands as they were shaking.

"You should! Expect out of me, but you don't so I think I am not doing enough." My eyes started to tear, and I could feel them turn red as it burned. He rested my head on his chest.

"To much pressure on you." There was one more thing.

"Freddie, the morning before you came down here. I was standing on Uncle Harveys front porch. Staring at the door. As the blood dripped down my fingers onto my boots. When your uncle opened the door, he saw I cut my wrist. I tried to kill myself as he was in my head that much. You want me to go see and talk with him, but I can't." I cannot be what I repeated to his ears for ten minutes or so. "Your uncle took me in and saved my life. As I sat there on the sofa. No one else was home. He sat me down and asked me why I did what I done. I told him I was gay. That no boy of Starr man was going to like another man if he lived, so I never saw another way out." My voice shivered as if it was cold in the room and it was not. "I wanted to die." That is when he mentioned Freddie was coming that he did not have room for me yet. It played out nice that we did what we did. Him telling me about him moving here is what made me want to know more about him and live more. We went back to the café to drink some more tea with raspberries in them.

"William you have to go and talk with him. It is the only way to break this cycle." I was getting mad at him as I felt trapped. Why couldn't I go somewhere on my own? He was right. It is time! Grabbed my leather jacket and his keys. Drove down to the jail, but I was frozen from going in there. "Don't play chicken!" Freddie was sitting on his hood. Then you saw Edith waving from her car. Guess I must get in there. She knew where I was too. I go to that tea café way too much.

"Next sixty-nine." The lady behind the window called my number about time it has been an hour, and I was standing near a man who kept farting from nerves, and a lady who sang her feelings. Oh, it got worse! The lady I was now looking at looks like a beaver. Her teeth say it all. "Who are you here to see?" She is genuinely nice. Yet not married. Must have cats? She smells like them.

"Paul?" I did not want to be here, but Freddie said if I did not then I would be able to get my birthday gift tomorrow and I only want one thing from him. And I plan on getting it. He even went out and found gingerbread tasting yeah what happens in the bedroom is not for you to know about. Who am I talking to? The voice in my head talks back but come on now I am losing it. I have not seen father in years. Last time I saw him I was eighteen. She looked at me wanting a last name, I knew it. How many people named Paul are in jail here?

"Sir there are one hundred seventeen Pauls in this place would you like to narrow it down." That's a lot of Pauls for sure. Didn't mean to get you mad lady. You know what's odd here? I can't get over the thought of how the two of them knew where I was. Going from topic to topic was the only thing making sense to me right at this moment. "Okay if there isn't a last name you like to share with me, I will go to the next number that pops up. This is being recorded for insurance purposes and what is said will be able to obtain information for you to better us to help you." Really! This cartoon man on my shirt is really looking at you madder than I am now. He cannot react, so I do it for him. See the eyebrows!

"Paul Abplanalp! He is my father." She looks at me strange. No, she just found out the cafeteria is under construction and she might have to walk across the street to get food and not sit on her butt all day.

"If he is your father then you look nothing like him. Wow, that is odd. He has never had a visit. Why now?" There was so much in my head, but I was too sleepy to even try and tell her them.

"I turned twenty-one today, and I was told I couldn't come to see him without an adult until this birthday. Well here I am." I had a heart that is what got her. I looked over to the skinny man sitting behind the glass near her. He shakes as if he is cold every day even if it is hot out. He is better for her anyway.

"Follow Officer Rose and he will be able to bring you to where you will meet him." That is your last name, I hope. Before walking into the room, I was told to stop at the red line on the floor and put my feet at each end. It was strange when the officer patted me down, standing there like a good soldier letting the field doctors try to find something on me that was questionable. Was it odd to say it felt good like getting a spa visit for free? Got to teach Fred this one.

I walked into this room where the only thing you had was a line of telephone booths lined in a wall each having a thin wall, so you did not look at the person next to you. On the wall was an old turn-style phone. On the other side it was the same just the door was closed. They sat him in front of me. I thought I was going to lose my lunch then I had to think I did not eat yet. He picked up his phone as mine rang. Dropped mine as it passed through my finger as I was not thinking. Saw my fingers shake from my nerves. Say something.

"They gave you a haircut!' He smiled. I licked my lips as he did the same. Strange how he was doing all I was. "I am here to tell you I forgive you! That no matter what I am going to try and understand why you did this." I said it felt good too.

"I did it for the same reason you have that ring on your finger. You look at me and see nothing but the man who killed your mother, and I almost had the pleasure of watching you die. You want to know what I was thinking about. How I was not the one bathing in that tub after she bleed to death in it." Freddie, I do not want to be in his head no more.

"I am nothing like you." I looked to the countertop.

"No, you are me! Just like I wanted something so bad I could taste, you did too. Smile me boy! You need me anyway!" I was looking at him again.

"Need is a strong word for you!" He gotten closer to the glass.

"I got the thirteenth nail!" It was in his fingers. "Tell me something William, do you still have those dreams like you do?" He smiled as he knew.

"You mean the ones I still have. Dreaming of a different way to die each night." He tapped on the glass making me lean in. Seeing my breath on the glass.

"You are me!" No! I will never let that happen. Let the phone hit the floor as I ran out the door. Even my Freddie don't realize that I dream of a different way of dying a night. I am nothing like you sir.

(Freddie!)

"Come on Freddie I didn't mean anything why don't you get down here and we can talk." William never gotten drunk before, so I didn't know if I was able to let him in my head right now or not. The door had swung open as all I heard was the screen door slam again. I didn't want to go to the top of the stairs, but I had to. I saw him looking back at the way it shut as he tried to apologize as he forgot to let the door shut softer than he did. What was I supposed to do let him just lay on the floor until morning? If I had the right mind to it, he would, but I was a better person. He was on his knees standing as he tried to walk that way too. The boots where kicks to different sides of the rooms on the walls sitting as his socks were, well I didn't know where they ended up. "Fly in the morning, fly in the evening sometime, come fly with me at nighttime, come let you sweet bombs fly on by!" Singing he was drunk.

"You're not holding a guitar soldier." As I approached, he was there playing an air guitar with his eyes closed so tight thought the seams were going to rip. His eyes popped open as if he was three thinking I couldn't see the melted popsicle around his lips.

"Freddie, I had been a bad boy!" That smile was something that I couldn't say no too. He reached to the back of his boxers and pulled out his old olive-green cap hat. He placed it in my hands. He looked at me as I saw the glow in his eyes. "You want to play pilot?" I felt the hot air from his lips to the top of my arms. He rested the side of his face to my belly button as his ear covered that area as if he was listing in, in for instructions. He made me laugh.

"Go land your plain soldier I will be up in a minute." He stood all excited when I said that, that he put his sunglasses from the top of his head over his eyes.

"This is Starr Boy is it okay to land, over." He really gets into his characters let me tell you.

"Starr Boy, this is Purple Feather it is okay to land, Over." He ran up the stairs with his arms out like wings on a plain as he flew to the bedroom. When I got to the room, he was lying on the bed faced down looking at the bathroom door. His arms were locked in as they both met at his face. I sat there behind his knees as he laughed when I ran my finger down his spin. He rolled over to let me lay on the spot he was just in so he could see me. He read my face as I laid there.

"I love you; you know!" I cried a little as he was my everything and I didn't really know how to help him in the situation we were in.

"You tired?" He was shaking his head yes as I pushed the hair from his face rubbing his forehead. His eyes slowly closed as I waited to make sure he was in a deep sleep. Sat up running my hands in my hair as that hat cap rested on the nightstand. When I heard him snoring then I was able to stand. Opened the door to the bathroom as there was a scared kid sitting in my clawfoot tub. "You know you can go back and stay with Scott if you like." He looked at me the same way William just did that was odd.

April 8th, 1944

Lost twenty-three good men tonight. Do not know how I was not one of them. This war thing is not a joke.

Chapter 4
Bicycle Planter

(Freddie!)

Example: Water Rooster = Waterooster

I am sorry about the way I write as it come out as it was first thought. Thing is I had this problem the moment I could speak. Did not know I had a problem until I was making the numbers see themselves backward. Instead of 23, I would say 32. You see the words Bear Rug; I see the same words but only one R. To me the R's should be the same letter not different. Every time my grades would come back off, but it was not my fault as the teacher failed me. I was the kid in the special needs class. Nothing wrong with it. I needed more time to learn the same material you were. It was funny how much my mother was in my education life. They told her I was not like the other slow kids that I needed to go to a special school. She stood up and told them that if she heard that said about her son again that the police would be coming in and dealing with these issues. He worked with me some and I gotten to the level the normal kids were at and gotten myself from under their wing. I still write my A, P, and 9's the same. But practice is my goal! I see words different too. Strange the things we remember when facing a loved one passing. Thing is no one died that I knew.

William was woken up by a call. How I did not here it is beyond me. Running out to get the phone at five thirty in the morning. Running his toes into something as he tried to answer. "Hello!" Tonight, he was being a mister twisted two-lips instead of his normal self. He was tired after getting off a double shift. Did not matter what he was wearing as it was for me and he would do anything to make sure I got what I needed. "No this Isn't her son. This is his husband can I take the call?" I heard him talking to the person on the other side of the phone, but I did not know what was going on. Who was hurt? William heard me approach from behind him, but he did not look back. Asking him what was wrong. Thought it was something how he was trying to listen to me and talk to her at the same time. "Thank you for telling me. I will make sure he gets the message." The phone went cold. He walked past me as if he did not know I was there. Could see the bags under his eyes. Grabbed the back of his shirt. He tried to walk in one spot as I was keeping the hold to his fabric. "Freddie, Freddie, Freddie!" With every Freddie he said the louder he gotten as if he was singing yet he never healed the tune. The porch light was blinking every time he went past as if it was a warning for my eyes only or something. You could hear his boots drag as he was complaining about the cigarettes falling out of his socks. Those size thirty-two World War Two boxer shorts of his was all he was wearing as ran the driveway back and forth in front of the house. I just know when I walk him up here to get him to bed and change him that the three buttons are going to indented on his skin near his midriff. "Come on Freddie I didn't mean anything why don't you get down here and we can talk." Poor things don't know I'm right next to him. His eyes glanced over trod me. "Oh, hey there you are. Go get dressed your mother was flown into a hospital. Her request was for you to be there as soon as we could." What was going on? Why was my mother here in the hospital? Here of all places. It was like I was ice just frozen in place. Like someone pulled the trigger at the back of my head and everything went blank.

"WILLIAM!" I yelled out. He did what I needed, his arms around me. "Is my mother dying?" How brittle we are when we are forced to face death. I live with it but even I have this moment. He went to throw on a pair of something as I was already dressed. Images in my mind of her. What was going to be seen? He had to drive as I could not even bother put the key to start it. It was not like her to come here if she needed emergency help. There was something wrong. He took my hand as it was colder than the wheel.

"She's going to be fine Freddie. She is in better hands then we can give her now." My relationship with her was not a good one, but I tried so hard to think of her. Everything was so getting to me. Everyone doing their own thing as if it was another day as I was rushing to get to her. The lady standing in line getting her pumpkin coffee just talking to the other one she was with. The child ran crossed the hall. All I was worried about was her. Nothing else mattered. The fifth floor the second room to the right.

There she was lying on the bed. The television glued to those vet shows she loved so much. "Hey Mom!" Something was wrong. She was not making a sound. "William go get the nurse. NOW! Mom! Wake up please. It's me Freddie." Rubbed her chest to get her to react. This was not right. Her shoulders were shaking. Her eyes were open, all I saw was nothing. Her eyes were like glass. A glass doll lying there waiting for the kid to come get it to play with. Her head came up, and she was sneezing. Telling me that she was coming to get me. Seven nurses and a doctor came running in. One asking for her to wake, the other for lifting her legs in the air. She was turning purple; one told the other lady. The line was now flat. All I could do was stand there and watch. They were attaching medication to her arms. One was breathing for her. She sat up looking around but no one else saw her sitting up. If she should wake and start throwing something, that my brain could handle. The not knowing was the hardest. Only one person was allowed in the room with her, thing is I never got in there. The one in purple was who I spoken to. "Sorry, where was the man I came here with?" She said they were forced to go to the waiting room. She pushed the button to open the unit doors as I followed. I waited for her to turn the corner. The hall was shaking! My legs had all they could do was walk to where my William was. We gotten here too late. There he was on the phone with Edith. His eyes saw me walking as he let her go. I forced myself to sit. Asking repeatedly what was going on. She followed me as she was sitting in the two-person seat with me.

"Tell him! Go ahead I have all the time to wait." I looked at his face instead of hers.

"They called it! 6:36 a.m." My eyes were red I hope by now. Seeing the dead, I do not cry most of the time. Why?

"She died!" I was letting my emotions get the best.

"No! She is singing in the hallway. What else do you think? Man use your brain." William was trying to get me to see the truth, but she was here with us.

She stood as she saw that I was going to be okay. She wanted more time with me that is why she took the gamble to come here. She was smiling wearing that light pinks dress she loved so. Just walking into the light as if all were right. I stood there in the middle of the floor waiting for her to come back, but I knew she was not coming back. "I'm sorry, William I am so sorry for what I have said. I didn't mean it." He got in front of me making the image of her walking into the light go away. She found a way for me to find what I needed to see. He took the phone and put on our song and hummed as that was the only thing he could think of. Taking off his hat in honor of her. Letting me cry and get his shirt all wet. "She was my mother. She was, that is it she was. Now she's no more." The sound of penny loafers was making their way in.

"I'm looking for the family of Sarah Blue! Her maiden name was Blue I didn't know that." William looked over my shoulder answering the man.

"Yes, that's us. Can you give us a moment?" I stopped him from leaving.

"No, talk to me please. What happened?" He did not want to do this as he was in my place before I heard that before.

"She had cancer! She was getting treatment in New York, but she stopped the treatment to come here to start it again. She died shortly after her husband.

45

Bo, he died from a car crash." I was able to find myself to shake his hand. What is my problem? I didn't even know Bo died.

"What kind did she have?" William was able to ask those questions where I could not.

"Female kind! If you need more in depth, I can bring you into my office." Why didn't she tell me? Well I can answer my own question; she did not want me to stop my life for her.

"No, thank you sir!" I had another question.

"When can we get the body?" This time I looked you in the face sir.

"Well we will want to do more tests and examining. No more than forty-eight hours from now." William had him in the hall asking him for a form to get family medical leave. I had to bury my mother after just getting done burying my brother and uncle. The question was why we all are getting sick. Then maybe we are looking at the future the wrong way. William was getting cancer tax taken out of his pay every other week. What next? That leaves Aunt Mary the last one of that group to live. He did not know where I went but I had to get air.

"Call Officer Blue!" No, phone do not call, The Blue Moon Inn. Just punched it in manually. "Officer Blue!" Finally, a voice.

"Freddie, what is wrong?" I laughed little like I did when I was just a kid. "Mom died!" Was the man crying in my ear? What was going on here? Guess through mercury glass you still can see the man cry. That is the thing men must be strong for all the worse times. The lady who cares but do not let us blink. They teach us to be tough, but that's why ladies have boys right so they can grow up and die to protect the next set to come and protect as they grow and learn. So many things we are given to wear to make a gentleman yet here we are never losing that aspect. "Officer Blue are you alright?" Well he was the only family I had left up there why not give him a chance. I can still remember him training to be an officer. All the new boys had to wear a blue armband, so they knew who students were. That is when I was first introduced to him. He was about twenty-one when my father passed away. He took the role of my father when the moment the sheet was lifted, and he had to drag me from the room where his body was. He made sure I was given what it took to be tough. He taught me to fight for what it was. He was trained to go on the streets of New York, the toughest place to practice. You had to be light on your feet but have strength behind you. If it were not for him, I would not have the strength to do half the things that we have done. I was weak but who is not at first. To this day I still have his picture as my bookmark. I was scared for my first day of school, so he gave me a chapter book. I told him I could not read that yet. But he turned it the third chapter. Did I have a clue what a third chapter was,

46

no, but I would have learned it for him. His image that I had a child would never water itself down for the many year I might have. Always remembering him as this young cool person who many thoughts was hard to understand, but he was a big soft teddy bear when it came to me and my brothers. Eighteen and twenty-one is what? He was thirty-nine! He was more like a big brother then my father.

I was standing on the ledge to the rooftop this was not a bother for me. Everything was different now, why! Looking down at all the lonely people, living there lives as if mine didn't matter much. He was just another man, some number that the government just lost. It was as if they could get their hands on the cash in my pockets fast enough. I was dead, I was one of those people not knowing that there was a truth to the other side of things. What mattered now didn't matter then. The thoughts of the world just slipped off my soul those things didn't matter now. Why did it when I was walking amongst them?. I would love to have a basket full of gingerbread men right now. The people on the ground walking would be in wonder there are little gingerbread people dropping out of the sky. Now I want gingerbread cookie. The lights were shinning like a new penny. When we knock on wood to me it is something to have good luck. But if you think about it, when you knock on wood of a coffin it is giving the dead good luck to travel on its journey. If I fall will someone miss me? If I jump would I even dare think twice? My feet balancing on this concrete balance beam. As my shoes are too big for the width of its body structure. I was looking at the cars headlights when I was now still standing there, but I was not looking down to cars moving on the road. A man that looked a lot like me, but he was not me. Officer Blue, that is how I remember him the most from my childhood. Smiling waiting for someone as he smiles when I was walking near him. I could feel my feet not moving in the real world, but I was walking in this vision. Could feel the coldness of the fabric of the jean material that was on my legs and could feel it getting hot as it was cold out as my body was nerves. My eyes went back to looking at the cars, but I was worried as he kept being in my head trying to get me to come to him. He was there if I liked it or not. This to shale pass. Rested my hands in my pockets as my thumbs rested on the outside of my pants. I wanted more time with my mother, but I wasted my time and did not talk with her nor even tried. I just did not! Thing was she did not too. She knew I loved my William and I was where I was supposed to be. She saw that before crossing over. Why was I so important to her? Why me? Survivors guilt was starting to settle in.

"If you jump, I wouldn't tell." I looked in the corner of my eye on my left there she was. Took one foot and balanced with the other. As I stepped backward. Jumping down. "I was hoping to see you flat on the ground." Hey now! She was at a party or something like that. Her hair was curled, and cut short, her dress was layered in pink with beads of different pinks moving about as she moved. Her headband was a ribbon flappers hair piece that had pinkish flowers woven in it. "Scott's sister invited me to a mystery room when I gotten the call. I came right over here." She did not have to. "I know you Freddie. Oh, you don't have to, is what you just thought, but I have to." Her eyes were glowing, and her eyebrows were raised. "Why? Your mother told me she was sick before we left for her wedding and asked me to put the envelope in my wallet every time, I changed it. When she passed to give it to you. I never opened it." She pinched open her bag that she gotten from an antique place downtown. It was a plain white envelope with my name written on the front.

"I don't want to read it now. You read and tell me what it says. It is mine so please go ahead." She made a noise I did not want to hear.

"I walked here in these heels you're going to read this paper. NOW! Peter." Middle name she was mad, no mom told her to say that as that what she did when she gotten madder than I could even imagine. She had it in her hand, as it folded into a bird, and over to me. It hovered over my fist until I opened it. It was cool how she was able to do this. Opened my hand where it flattened out. It was mine if I liked it or not. She leaned near me on the banister. My fingers opened the seal, but it was the hardest thing I did today. I let her die, and this was the hardest. She took out a picture of me when I was four with Officer Blue. He took me to my first baseball game, we told mom it was baseball, but it was a cricket game, he taught me to play.

"My birth records. No! The one I have don't have all this fancy stuff all over it. My mom's name is here, but." The paper falls to the floor.

"Who is your father. It should say Freddie Ennis Waters." He was few but not all. My arms were crossed as I was getting mad. Why did she let me know now?

"The man's name doesn't match the one I have at home." She was confused she thought it would say his name. "Go ahead read the name of the father. I was being a jerk acting like this."

"Halstead Blue!" Her fingers cascaded over her lips. Her maiden name was not Blue, mine was. She changed it after Bo died so it would help me.

"He was my second father growing up. Now he is my father. I don't understand." She was listening. Where in the hell was William?

"Freddie, she told me that she didn't stop you from having him in your life as he was the man who she thought, and you didn't know who he was. You never caught on that you looked a lot like him?" No!

"When you are a kid you think that you look like the man you call dad, not some officer that came to the house. The only picture I have of him was him sitting in her kitchen sitting next to a drunken Santa. I remember that day. He burned the tree down." She knew something was on my mind, but I did not want to let it out. Her heels were making a loud sound as she tried keeping up with me through the halls. I walk amazingly fast. You think someone walked past the doorway, but it looked like a lightning strike. That is me! Officer Blue taught me that. Man, he taught me so much. I was freaking out as I could not find William. We stopped in the last place I saw him in the cafeteria. My mind was spinning as he was not where I left him. My mind was cooking up an image that he might be dead too.

"Freddie calm down. He is here someplace." Looking all over the place feeling as if the walls were closing in, thinking about the worse as my brain was screaming out for some reason, I was picturing him pulling a trigger to a gun in his hands.

"Call his phone! He is in a ditch somewhere and I do not know about it. We will find his body in two to three weeks." YEAH! It was bad, he was all I had besides her, but I could not lose him too. A cartoon theme from the nineteen sixties was filling my ears his ring tone was calling out, but where is he!

"Freddie!" She pointed with her eyes. He was sitting at the booth near the cafeteria. Never thought seeing blond hair was going to be a best thing for me.

"Poor thing! He was so tired when we got the call. Have we been here for all this time it's almost nine at night?" How fast time goes on when you have papers pushed in your face for them to get the right to cut her open right off.

"I'm sorry dear I didn't mean it." There was lady beside Edith standing with a giant smile. "Are the Waters?" I turned around as I hit William to wake up. This day was like walking into a land of wonders everything was just going all over the place.

"Yes ma'am. Freddie, Edith, William!" What if she was the type to kill? Now she knows all our names.

"Freddie! Yes, your name was the one brought up the most." She came over and took my hand. Edith motioned for me to let me know it was okay to do. "She given my little grandson the chance to live. Her kidneys were transferred to him today. I came here to let you know your mother lives in him. That is why she came here. I got to know her very well. She was the best. She came here so he could live longer." My ears were turning red I could feel it. My eyes were tearing. She was brave to the end. Her smile faded as she left us be.

"Can I meet him? What's his name?" She turned back, but her smile never left her face. She sat with us for a while.

"You can't see him now. I cannot until the morning myself. He is an eleven-year-old boy whose imagination is bigger than his math grade." She had a picture he was drawing in the back of her phone case. She had it printed in the plastic. He could draw good for a boy his age. That was me. Freaky it looks real. "He drawn this! Even said it was his imaginary friend. His guardian angel." ME! "He has these dreams that are very descripted. Things a boy his age should not know. He will have these moments where he will tell me mom, I knew this was coming. It could be a small moment where I dropped my phone out of my hand, and he was laughing at the fact I farted when I bent. He always said something happens every time it happened. It was as if something connects you two. Here is his picture." When I saw the screen, his face was the same face to the man I saw in the vision I just had not even twenty minutes ago. I knew that he was going to be okay, yet I did not know she was the one to give him anything.

"Can I ask you something! Who is his father?" She knew but did not want to say.

"You can tell us." Thank goodness for Edith.

"He was a one-night fling. A jerk too, but knowing I was caring him I had to have him. Halstead Blue." We are connected he was my blood brother. I handed her the birth record that I was given.

"Mine too." The look on her face.

"I moved here for him. Looks like we have a lot to talk about." I was glad to hear that. She started to get upset like when you knock over a thing of flowers and the water travels down the floor then the leaves are left to dry up and die off. It is funny how when we die it is when your mission is done, but we find a way for that to extend. No, it is the council's way of keeping you alive so you can fulfill your purpose. "Would someone come sit with me for a while?" Edith and I looked at one another different as if we did not want to, but there were this thing making us want to.

"I will go. You must find William again! Think he ventured to the bathroom. He needs to stop this vanishing off thing." It was nice of herself to get the moment thing where she was willing to sacrifice her own time for another person. This time she was not in it for herself.

This bathroom was fancy from the golden sinks to the littlest shell soaps they put in a crystal bowl in the middle of the two vanities. The door never made a sound; that was odd as it usually always makes a sound. The door to the stall I could see was not in use as the door was swinging open and shut from the breeze from the air conditioning. Could hear a painful sound as if someone touched a bullet hole where it was just fired. Didn't make sound as I put my phone on the camera watching all his movement as the sounds made me wonder. His shirt was sitting in the other sink. He had this cream which he was rubbing on his backside. His eyes went from making water to feeling better as that cream set in.

I felt for him, I wanted to comfort him but then again, he would have not forgiven me if I did. His fingers kept getting in the way. Better be careful the baby is due soon. Man, this room had great marble flooring. There was this giant bite mark on his backside. What happened? The indention each mark went in by an inch. As far as I can see it was done bleeding. His eyes sunk in his head. "Freddie, you can come in." I showed myself, but the light I did not want to stand in it this was his moment not mine. Saw myself in the mirror for second or fifteen. Turned as I could not see myself. This was not the moment to get ready for something nor see my faults. He looked at me strange. The air even hurt him there. "Well you know now I lost the baby." Thing is I thought I knew before as the spot where the child was supposed to be in was not growing. He was able to put his shirt over his head, but it hurt. Took my finger to help him. Is this how it feels to get older?

"Go suck a dick why don't you?" He said and he is not here to even say anything. I know he was British but come on with the words. Did I do something wrong to deserve this?

"I will!" I yelled at him like I was some lion getting mad at his dinner as it would not die in time for my liking. He went over to the door looking back one last time. Crying! Telling me that he knew my mother just died but I should not have come home. He did not want to see my face. Why was he doing this? He went for a kiss like normal this time biting my lip letting it bleed. My mother's death was the calling card of his mother's, and he knew it. "Don't be mad at me! Edith and I had a baby together before we were together. He was born back in forty-four!" His eyes were wet as I did not even know I heard what I heard. "She named him Jeremey! I can't do this anymore." He was leaving the door as I cried out his name. He did not turn around. I think he is just trying to get me to leave him, but I saw through this lie.

(William's side!)

Kept boxing in the frame of the chicken coop. Listening to the animals feed in the grass nearby as they deserve a last request as well. Could feel the wetness between my toes from the socks as these boots were hot. The clouds were in the sky as it sprinkled rain ever so often, so you did not forget that mother nature was watching. Must have walked the path millions of times never noticing as the mud took hold on the ground that there was this little round mirror underneath, the wooden structure. Kneeled trying to get the item unstuck, trying to get it before it broken in my hands, just to find it was already

51

had cracks. That is the right William in this little round item looking back with many different pieces to put him together, but then I had to think and leave it parallel with the wood and just pull out trod me. The one side was mirror like, but it was broken before I got to it. Four pieces as the fifth was missing. On the other side a photo of a man kneeling in front of his barn with his two hunting dogs. He was so happy as he was young and just starting a fresh new adventure with his pups. Must have been his wife's. This coop was the old owners that we just started using. Never thought to look for things like these. Gotten on my feet as I heard the screen door shut, putting the object in my pocket.

Better hide this or Edith might get second thoughts. She has been getting small packages left to right in the mail. Finally, figured that she has a jewelry tree near her bed on her nightstand. Each man a different time, a different war, a different smile. All handsome, dashing. Each locket gets hung on the tree. There is one whose glass is broken right down the middle. Every night there would be a whisper coming from her room. So, I used one of Walton's glass minutes, an item you wear on your wrist that make you invisible for ten minutes. She took her wand and pulled the man from his frame into her room. Taking him from time. Watching as he willingly undresses for her slowly, each night after a different man from another locket. She says it her way of finding out who the man is and learn more about what history was though their eyes. Yet another woman is still wearing that man on her cloth waiting for him to return in some year. She was slowly turning into my mom in likeness. My mother takes them from their photos eating their groin so she could live the years they were until she killed them.

"He went to New York!" He, He who? I left him at the hospital after his mother died as I knew he was in trouble, but I was worried for him. Jeremy said he would keep him safe for me.

"He, Freddie!" Turned as he through a backpack at me. Made a sound as it landed in my arms from the weight. Bounced to the ground, picking it up with two fingers like a bag of chicken feed.

"She started her attack. If we are to stay alive then, we need to split up." He said as he put on his pack too. He just started to take off. No goodbyes, no good morning to you.

"Walt, I can't do this on my own." He stopped as he came back. Took my jaw line in his hands. This might be the last time I feel the warmth of his hands.

"Now, I know that you know more than you think. You can hunt. We know you can get a deer in the heart with a single bow. Remember when dad didn't drink for a week because you missed and got his favorite can he had sitting in his hands." I laughed! I was weak and I did not like it much. "You know to reserve everything and use it to do other things like the days in war. You know how to live off the land from Freddie's family teaching you the Amish ways. Spending that time in Pennsylvania, use what they taught you. You know the woods and know how to stay alive. Do not worry about me. Here takes this bow. I will take yours. I hid things in the stonewalls that line the woods. Look for the bluebottles." He gave me this tin bow as the stirring was horsehair. He gotten my wooden one.

"There are no arrows." He let turned once more. Smiled as I saw the chill on his breath.

"It's my glass bow. Countless arrows. Just pull the string, point, and it will hit the things you are looking at. They will not see a bow as its clear." The tornado whistle went off as it scared him. "Go, run!" He ran as I was running in the opposite direction. I stopped my boots. As I watched his legs run up the little hill near our house. My hair gathering in my face as I started to run. I forgot!

"Walt, how do we keep in touch?" He rolled his eyes I could feel it in the pit of my stomach. He walked back trod me watching the birds as if they were after him. His feet gotten an inch from mine when something made a sound in the woods.

"I forgotten to tell you. July 16th, 1920 you died in 1981. You must write as if it was code. You have to make them think your someone different" He hands me this book looking thing. "This was grandfather's navy seaman identification passport. You are George W. Spurr writing to his brother Bob. I'll be Jennifer his sister." He was using grandfather as a hiding point. Those are my grandparent's names. His discharge date was my birthdate just the last two numbers were switched. He heard noise. "Go!" Thing was I remember helping George write these letters on his mess kit with the candlelight.

The tornado whistle was now being used as a warning for an attack from those we cannot see. Each day someone else goes missing. It is like they were eating them alive or something like it. Only came out at twilight, they did. Our population went from five hundred and four to now twenty-two. We are told not to live in our homes no more as we are to remain in the woods. Writing him by candlelight, leaning on my mess kit like I was taught. We were safer there, in the woods. The last thing my fingers touched was our letters I carved in the tree behind my father's house, as I heard the warning go off, I cut my fingertip open on the bark of the F.W. of yours. The world's task now was to protect you, and make sure that I get to the city. I had to end this before we all were killed off. Your purple flannel shirt and my skinny jeans kept me worm, as your bottle was around my neck. Must remember the boy scout ways as I march on. Just think it all started the morning the alarm went off at 5:09.

(William!)

Last night I fallen to sleep counting the times the owl nearby as he made his noble knightly sound as he protected the night from the troubles of the next day to come. We happened to stumble onto this old house that was left in the middle of the woods. They do not make these kinds of houses anymore. Stones walls and real tall windows. This house does not hold a stone to the one that was in the woods behind the house when we were kids, but I guess it will do. There were no doors on any frame in the place even the front door was missing. One ear was listing to Freddie's heart beating with my left ear as the other one was counting trying not to feel the coldness that was kissing my skin from the cool off the surface of this claw foot tube. Can something this delicate kiss at your skin? Don't see why not it sees you naked who knows what it would do if it wasn't a tub. The room was dark. The only light was a candle that Freddie had in his back pocket. I didn't ask why he had candlesticks back there, but something tells me this was planned. I missed a lot of time as I was out of time trying to get answers. Starting in the future going backward with everything I saw. My fingers hovered over the sticking on my skin, shaking as I thought about it. After a while there was no way I was sleeping, so my eyes ventured up to the bottom of his jaw. Watching his eyes roll as he was dreaming. My toes felt the insides of my shoes as I would push myself up to get closer to him to hope to get warmer.

Every night we take turns watching out for people that may not be welcomed. With the war of my mother's getting closer with ever step we take we need to be on guard. With the tap of two fingers of the back of your shoulder means that it your time to go to work. It was my turn as Edith wanted to sleep. Fingers grasping the sides of this tub not letting go as my feet rested on each side of Freddie's legs. I didn't want to leave him, but she insured me he was going to be fine. When I went to the front porch, I came upon her one-night call. As I had to hide my eyes. My fingers opening, you think I wouldn't try. He wanted to talk, but I was waiting for him to leave. He was trying so hard here is how the talk went.

William: So, which one are you?

Person: Billy Kiraly! (The young man started to button up the sides of his trousers as his fingers kept getting in the way.)

William: What makes you so, Key for her fancy task? (He had this glow on his face as if it was natural to be there.)

Billy: I died the hour after that picture was taken. I didn't have any family. So, I get best of both world when I get out of this locket. Her love, and a historical attribute. (He winks at me as if he was looking over a pin up. I think

54

not. I find myself covering my chest in embarrassment as his eyes look me over.).

William: Billy, Billy K. from the next road over. You can't be the same one. I signed up because of you. You were the bravest boy in the whole town.

Billy: I smile because, I was the reason you signed up for that mission that your still on. (Tension sat in my body as I hope there are frown lines on my face as I looked at him now.)

William: Oh, what would that mission that be?

Billy: You do not remember Project Waters! Three men walk into the mission only one walks out the winner. Each man had a different place they were placed but had the same mission. To kill Freddie Waters. (He licked his lips as he knew he had said way too much.) Looks like you chose what role you would play. You like to know more go to Ann Street in London. In the underground bunker look for the door with a number missing. You will know more. It might get you what you wish to know, but beware. (He then touched the locket that was has a photo with no man in it. he turned into a big ball of light that made me close my eyes. He was there smiling at the person looking at him once more.

"WHAT, is this? Where did you get this locket? I want to know why you have been not only sleeping with this man to get him to talk, but why you couldn't let a dead man be that way?" The only other time I get made like this is when Freddie fills the tub with nothing but hot water. Edith was sitting with her back trod the tub. I was so loud that Freddie woken. His eyes were cracked open as if he were a dusty book that no one had read for years. Edith was on her feet as I could see it on her face that she knew that she was in the wrong. Placed the locket in her hands. "Edith, you are no longer needed. Please go!" Her face was as if you turned it into stone. It frozen in place.

"William, don't say anything you don't mean." Freddie noted as he wiped his face from the tiredness.

"I mean this. As of the morning I take all the responsibility of Freddie, and I will make sure this war is won. You got Billy to keep you warm." I just walked off as I heard him try to calm her down. I just left him there to clean up my mess once again. When will I learn? As I walked away through the field of green grass there was something in the back of my mind telling me to look back again. I could feel the metal from the pipes in the house. It was as if I could feel the bones of the house as the pipes were shattering in the walls. Standing guard now is a read metal knight. A real Tin Star. It doesn't matter if I was here or not. I wasn't needed. I didn't think, I did what I do best run. I gotten so far into the woods that I didn't know where I was. Breathing extraordinarily strong looking at my surroundings. Had to look twice as there was this driveway in the middle of the woods. Went in deep too, as I followed it there were old flowers that only my mother could name off on the sides. Huckleberry bushes for almost a mile. At the end was another old house. This one was the same as the last one on the outside, but this time there was an old car on cinderblocks from the fifties. Still had that baby blue paint job in it, but it was weathered with the sun, couldn't see the plate on it as Freddie somehow got here before it did. I was smiling as he can't run for anything, and yet here he was to get the problem resolved. Just tried to catch my breath thought the pain of the laughing and tried so hard to place my hands on my hips without talking with them instead.

"My mind always thought your knees would look cuter if they were under the water in that claw foot tub, not getting pushed forward that's to the rusted bumper." I smile, he got me. "How? No, don't even answer me. She needed these purple cone flowers to break it down to make into a tea for a transporting spell. To get us from one place to the other." He uncrossed his arms as he tried so hard not to pick sides.

"Edith don't know anything about what he said to you. He is just her onetime thing. Well many times as all her lockets were turned to ash when your mother was trying to kill us first. You were too busy trying to get my grandfather down your pants." I looked at him the moment he saw me. "Oh, so it's okay for you, but not her?" You're going to play that card, fine.

"That's great now you think I cheated on you." I was getting emotional as this was too much for one person to take.

"What I am trying to say, I get all the information before running your mouth to the only person not trying to murder you." I never saw that look on his face until now. The one with bitterness. "Why do you think we are going to all these houses for in the middle of the woods? Not going after your mother. There is a locket at each place that holds another man that you knew from your mission. She does what she has to for the answers that you're going to need."

"She doesn't have to sleep with them all you know." He let out somewhat of a smile.

"Most of them want her to listen." I wanted this talk over with. I needed to see her soon, but not just yet I had an old car with my husband attached to it.

"Do you know this house? I knew it the moment I saw it. It is the passing bell house. Every house is the same, this one was the only one with parallel windows on each side. Saw it in the lighting from the sunrise. Cuts though the house like a blade. This was their car too." He let me step closer to him.

"You care why?" It didn't matter who was talking, I was walking trod him anyway. Did I hint an upper vocal when he spoke each word?

"Why don't I care?" My right knee was now between his lets as he smiled when he took off my reddish hat and put it on his head. "Laughing are we!" he took my shirt with both hands.

"I'm not mad at you!" His hands pushed me backward as he ran to the car. I heard the door shut as my eyes saw a flash. When I started to run there was this man walking trod me from the right side of the house. He put his gun up, as he asked me in his native tongue to lay on the ground. It was German as I knew what he was saying.

"There's no bullets!" I said back. When my hand rubbed against the doorknob to the car he was gone. I let it go as many it was a time step that Freddie told me about. Where we all are still walking amongst each other, but the earth vibrates at different rates, so we don't see each other.

(William, Three years later!)

"For every birth they take another!" I was spinning in my room on my heals as the cold wind was dancing alongside them. The wind coming from the outside under the door. I still see his fingers trying to reach to mind whenever I see any door. The Silver Leaf Society had stopped there killings. Only if the Before stopped theirs. The only rule was that if a Tin Star ever had a child on this planet that another person in the family must be chosen to die. It didn't stop there. For every child born After that of a Tin Star in the given year of that birth shall sacrifice a sibling or closest cousins' child at the end of that year to fight in a fight to the death until one of each gender is standing. At the end of the fight the two winners vow to merry only the ones who won beside them. If we didn't want them to stop killing, they wanted us to kill each other. Thing is when the peace was talked about, they spilt the planet. The Before, they have the planet where Freddie and all the others are. Walt, and I were on the other side while the talks were being held and we are here in London. No communication with the other side of the planet at all. It is forbidden. Think I was the only Tin Star that I knew about. Yet, they are getting ready for the kill. Tin Stars have been surfacing since the signing. Don't know why I was the only one willing to show his face. The Society members are the rulers of this side of the planet. As I was spinning, the only thing that helps me think anymore. The door opened. Could feel the rush of the color on my face as the light was presenting an old-fashioned photo of a person standing in the modern room.

"Nice to see you are enjoying yourself." Mother was Queen. She came in every day an hour before the last meal of the day was to be given as she needed to know if I was still in this room. If I was to run and join Freddie the war would be back on and the planet would have no more life on it. "We have the rarest of treats tonight. The Orm leader has asked to join our tea." Went over to the dresser as my fingers danced on this toy, she kept all these years from my childhood. I remembered this toy yet why she was so fixed onto it so much. She was going to dress me into this tight clothing to sit at a table as the man on the other side spoke words I don't understand and tell my mother how young I look for another aged. Today only came once a year and so far, it's been three years. "I will meet you downstairs." I had eight men watch me dress myself. They all had a different part of me to watch to make sure no harm gets to me. Each body part had a price on it. It made me feel like a slab of meat getting ready to be smoked on the grill. First each one takes there turn bathing the body part they are paid to protect. All those hands all over your body, you walk to the table as if there were bugs crawling all over you. That's how I feel.

(William, present day!)

She had a Prince doll in her hands. Whispering something under her breath as she walked in a circle backward. Her pink hood over her hair let a little spring blow in the wind. "Edith what are you doing?" Freddie asked as he was watching the food that was heating over a live fire. My eyes watched his as I didn't want to miss a moment of my time, I had left with him. I knew this much that no matter what people try to tell me I knew my mothers' heart was darker then her secrets. Thing is my secrets are darker than my heart. Placed my head on his shoulders where he gave a kiss on the top of my head. "Do you ever wonder what it be like if you stayed in forty-four?" Yes, I have had many ties to that moment in time like he had in his grandfather's death. His spirit chose his own grandson to put the family back together and there are many pieces to gather. Freddie feels him there, but he can't see them.

"Someone has to protect us while we sleep, so I am putting a circle around us to make us invisible to the naked eye. Freddie points to the middle of the circle. Right to my side. I will have forgotten about her being nearby after that question he asked.

"There is a man in his nightgown on a mattress that is screaming in pain with no legs as they had to saw them off after getting hit with bullet. I told him he can stay so keep that in mind." All I did was move in closer to Freddie's side. His eyes must have been looking down at me as he gave off a chuckle. "Scared of a little ghost?" He looked up as if he could see the blueprints of a house. His eyes lined the floor as my eyes followed. "This was a field hospital back during the Civil War. Upstairs in the broom closet there is a young lady from a rich house you can tell as she is wearing a hoop skirt. One of the men talked her into sleeping with him. The things that are still here yet the house does not stand no more. Their ghost can't move on as they don't know they are dead." I had to ask something that I didn't want to know the result to.

"This was a two floored house that burned down. Two people survived it." Edith is always a bookworm.

"Between the three of us can someone tell me what Walton is protecting? By now his health condition gotten better, but he is still weak. What is it that my brother is guarding?" Edith put the doll back into her bag as Freddie was taking off his boot. "Fine I will…just go and figure it out me if it comes down to it." I started to stand when I knew that was a trigger for Edith.

"He's going to find out sometime anyway." You two had a secret without me. This was something new. "Scott, he is protecting him." I ran my fingers on the rim of my chin.

"Scott is dead!" Please, don't let me be the only one talking about now.

"He is one of us. A person that can-do things others can't. his soul can leave his body and travel time where he can show himself as human if he is in the past. His body remains here, so Walton is protecting him as he is protecting you." I was getting worried about my safety now. The air was thin, so he had broken the ice.

"All the ghosts are wondering how you're not dead. All the witches are supposed to be dead, right?" Did you just throw that hot apple piece in your mouth and say that too? Freddie unscrewed the bottle from his necklace as you could hear the echo from the glass as the bullet rolled into it. He throws some cooked apples into my bowl. Guess, Walton knew how to survive in the woods more than I did.

"Are we going to just run from them, and live in the woods until we die off one at a time?" I asked, but Freddie made a strange noise as he did not know the answer. Took hold of one of the buttons on Freddie's shirt as I looked at it in depth. "I have been thinking about dying you know. How this button means something to you as it is your button on your shirt. Then at the end of it all when we are standing up from our bodies that is just a button. A thing that was there for you during your mission was now going to be something for someone else. Sometimes the soul is good at keeping to the item until it's in the hands they need it to be, but then again." I stood as I did not want to hear any more of this. Took off my clothing in front of the two of them like they have not seen it before. Walked out of the circle as I heard them say.

"Where are you going?" Edith said!

"The river! I stink!" We were feet from the water as Edith always had a way to tend to her last name. When I said that I smelt my arm pits. Do not really smell, but then again, I shaved them last week. Got to my knees into the water before it got too cold for me to stand. It did not matter; this running water was better than sitting where I was. Started to splash some water against my breast, then my face.

"One of the men is in there with you by the way." Freddie!

"Great, I am now shaking in my boots." It was not extremely hard to shake as the water was freezing. He did not deserve my voice sounding like this too. "You wish to tell me why you left the circle?" I splashed the water hard.

"You wish to tell me why She of all the girls we know is in that Society? Why my brother was in the past? Why you knew about Bernard the way you did, and made him treat my brother's health condition?" I wasn't looking at him as I didn't want to see the expression he was leaving on his face."

"We needed to put her in there to get answers that we don't have here. If we brought him to a modern hospital, then he be dead. Cannot trust anyone remember. I didn't know who else to trust." Twirled to see him standing there with clothing. I walked trod him as I heard a sound I did not like. Slowed my breath to hear. With metal woven into my skin the water does not stay so I was dry in seconds. Thrown on the clothing on which he was holding. A pink cardigan, where have I seen this before? Took Freddie's hand like I did when I dreamt of him on the other end of my coffin. The treetops were swaying sounding like a deer when it's scared. Mother's call. We ran to the circle, but I do not think we will make it. Freddie stopped in his tracks as hard as he could look up to a light sky of fire.

"Dragon!" He yelled, Yes, I see that!

(Freddie's back!)

Today I was tested by both of Williams personalities. I didn't know which one to trust as they were both in the same person.

"Freddie!" He is here meaning your listing as you brought him to me. He was standing there with a bloodied lip where I hit him. Redness on his face from the scares I gave him too. I am not giving into you. No sir not this time. "This was the only spot I didn't think to look. I was going crazy trying to find you. Edith said to try the graveyard." I will have to block her from reading my mind later. I looked to the ground watching the ants crawling on the blades of grass. Could hear those size ten shoes cut through the grass up to me. Those fingers each one felt them hitting my knees like each finger was typing on my skin with a typewriter. No, not this time. I will not look up to your face. "What if I said it was mine?" What if it was?

"What if you do say yes?" Fine I will give in you are my husband.

"At least your talking to me." Well I was not going to. Even though I am not looking at him he still rested his head on mine. I am not a rabbit this will not go away with a forehead apology. He took the blood dripping off my face

60

drawing a smile over his lips connecting his ears. That is when I knew it that is not really him.

"I'm not going to hurt you. But I will tell you this. I am on your side, and there's too. There coming Freddie! I have to act like this being, I am playing both sides." I did not know if I should as if I turn my back will he try something fishy? "Bradley had the idea to draw the blood on my face if you gave me my nose then you trust me. You don't touch something you not sure of." I can trust you. I was going to use you like you used my William.

"What is coming? Who are they?" He needs to tell me.

"The Guardians of Time, they are planning an attack. Freddie, they have two leaders. Your person you thought was your father, and William's mother. Telling you this they might know that I am talking. I have to go!" He handed me the compass for William to have again. This was all to protect me. He mentioned Bradley. Just like when the girl went into the teapot, she dressed down in the same fabric she came there with. I am still standing in a graveyard at night still madder than I can think of at the real William. Then how do I get to him? Living in a ghost world can be puzzling at times.

"Freddie!" That clown was on my side. William was standing on the hilltop. I ran, ran as fast as I could. "I'm sorry!" His arms wide open as my prayer is always answered by him. It is like the person listening to what I was saying sends him to answer for them. Did not know I could hug someone harder than I did at that moment. "Okay, what happened while I was gone? You're so happy!" Is that a sin? "What is going on? Why did I get a text to say to come here?" I never sent that. Clown! Got my phone while he was trying to put his moves on me.

"William, I need to tell you something." Put my hands in my back pockets. I was nerves like I was when I first kissed him. "The Guardians are planning a war."

"The Dark Fantasy War! The other William this makes sense. You don't misspell my name ever." He knew why not he knew their metal was the rarest in all the stars. "Bradley tried so hard to not involve you, but here we are. He knew the prize was you. Freddie you let me have a baby. Never happened but you know how close this has come. You are their threat. You are the prince to Greenwood, Earth, the living, and the dead! You're a triple threat." I took his hand as he tried to tell me, but I saw it on his face he did not know how to.

"How do I stop this war before it starts?" He knew the answer before I could speak.

"There is only two ways you can stop all of this." He did not want me to know the steps.

61

"William!" I needed him to stop watching the tree line. He was getting on edge. "William, I am going to end this. Tell me." I jumped! Man!

"Tell him what?" Edith, how did you get behind me? Why was she still in that 1920's outfit? Is that a new dress from that time period? It goes with the hair accessories that is why she changed to match it. She was looking at herself in her pocket mirror with the powder in it. There was a vintage married couple in between the glass on the mirror and they were moving in the photo as if it were just being taken. Then she gotten a sower look. "William, you're not thinking about telling him how to stop this war. Why aren't you. Why have blood on your hands when this all can be done?" Why were they hiding things from me while I am standing right here?

"I don't want him to die!" He was running his hand over his head ending them at the top of his ears. "This time I can't bring you back." I went over behind him.

"If I want to drive down the road with your feet on my dash again then I need to do this." Took the back of his suspenders where they meet in the middle. Pulling him near me more. I could feel his skin like the thorns on the rose bush. "Please!" If I love you will you turn around and say it. He turned after a while, but I was able to say the right thing to him. He took the back of my head putting our foreheads together.

"If I tell you then you need to promise me that when it's all over you meet me right here if I lose you." I promised, but I do not know if I can keep it. I might not be able to. Yet I was not telling him that. "First, we get to my mother. If we can get into her head, then she will call off her troops. Then second." He could not but he started he had to finish. "You must face your father alone. Killing him for good." I have tried that before. This was not going to be an act of justice.

"How are we supposed to do that? We have tried that before." This was the hardest thing to do. Even harder than the time I had to pass that dollar in quarters Walton dared me to eat.

"This stays with the three of us. We need to right now make it a pact that we three will go together, and not involve the others. They do not need to be in the fire of this all. Edith has been finding away for you to see the ghost as I do, but it's hard as she needs to test it when she can't see them too." Edith kicked her heels in the rocks she was standing on.

"Freddie, we can run all we want, it doesn't face the fact that we have to get your father out of the picture." She did not know. Yet!

"We need to go back to the past." I am sorry Stu! I was letting you go finally. Please forgive me.

"You're saying to stop your grandfather from having him. Stu! You wouldn't have him back then." Wait! This was bigger than the people they were saying that must be taken out. If I kill that man then I miss out on having that side of me in my life, if I do not then who knows what will happen.

"This isn't my father. He was walking in the path of someone else. This goes back further then my father. The Guardians of Time are not a pack of ghosts coming after us. They are a society of people that indeed still think witches walk among them."

"You are right! There are still descendants of those who were the accusers that think their family members were telling the truth and think they walk among them. No, this goes beyond them. We really don't know." Edith was the last witch of her line, she would know.

"Then we will learn from them. My mother, Your father! Go back to them and tell them we want to join them. You cannot Freddie, but I can. They will think something if I go." Well!

"Then I will go in." There is a voice and I cannot figure it out where it was coming from.

"Walton, no! They know you're in our team." His hands were in an odd posture.

"Do we have any other takers." Yes!

"Edith! Your dress gives me a thought. My father was young in the thirty's, can you go and get a dress from around then. A good one not one where it was your Sunday's best and you live in a box in the city. My father or should I say grandfather, he played both roles for me when I needed it. See he was down more skirts then he was working as his first job was being a call-boy. I think I still have those dance cards he kept in a shoebox under my bed. They thought the thirties was going to be the end for them never seeing a light at the end because as soon as the light came the war started. You can talk him up." She smiled as she was on board.

"I am not sleeping with him, and how dare you think I will live in the city." Think funny.

"But you would live in a box?" She thought about it. "We need a hideout; my mother's house was passed to me. Think that would be perfect."

"We need to look out for the barcodes! You cannot travel time without them, they are like the time police if you will. They are men who are chosen after death who are young soldiers who are printed with a barcode on their backs. When they live again they are our soldiers." There born to die for us.

"How do we know who they are?" Edith good question.

"There eyes are blue. Sky Blue! And their fingernails have a blueish tint to them." I had a problem with this.

63

"Walton you just described yourself to us." Well I did and I had to say it. There is are even things about him we did not even know. He was a person out of time too.

"I am one of them, but I was given the right to choose as Freddie made me his Glass Knight that title was taken away for good. It was supposed to go to William, but Freddie feel in love with him making him his protector. I am a protector, but I can't get as far near you are, he did." I Knew it. We all stood in a circle, but we never asked Edith if we throw her to the wolves if she would be able to take it.

"Edith is this alright? Can you do this if not." She stopped me!

"For you I will do anything. Going down his pants, no! but the thought it to stop him. We have to try." She was doing it more for her father as his death was left unsolved onto who killed him still.

"Alright then we need to get to New York then." Edith had this in a bag. No, she did.

"Don't go anywhere! Freddie, I knew William told you about our son. You think he is lying. Well! He is not. We didn't know if William was going to die or not." It took a lot of courage for her to say that. "We never really loved each other."

"Things are better left unsaid. You love me William!" He responded amazingly fast.

"But of course!" Nothing more needed to be said tonight.

In her Purse she had chocolate shaped dragons. When she put them in our hands, they stood on our palms acting like a dragon would. Its scared Walton, but they were cute. "Eat them, they will not bite. Think where you want to go, and they will take you there." Walton's face when he went first. Just eat blink and you are there. Walton was not okay with traveling this way. He burped out some fire but that was an after effect. She slapped him on the back. "Just don't go near any gas right now. If you fart, then well." She took her hands off him after she said that. Did not think I was going to be again. Never say never.

(Freddie looking back!)

I know we keep saying how we first met. There is only one real way William and I met. I was a new kid to a new school, new town. It was the forties where all the men in the town were off fighting some war that most did not came back from. It was a something when the boys in this town had to keep it going. I remember my mother getting ready for work so that way the boys had things to fight with. I remember going down and melting down my toys, so I thought I was helping. I remember looking at a car with my father when I got my license. I remember when wearing clothing like they did then was a fashion statement and you did not get judged if you do it now a days. I remember when they say this building is old when it was new.

He was in gym class playing basketball with the other students. Wearing his shirts with a big wet stain in the middle of his chest. The lady who sat in front of the principal's office took me around the school telling all who I was. William was running in the hall as he had forgotten to get his books before class. I was walking and did not pay mind to it as much, but William ran into me. Knocking my books out my hands. When he bent to help me pick them up, our locked eyes. He gotten scared off as he ran back the other way.

At the time, my world was different. I was a perfect person with my hair combed back and all the works you can say. No television and only a radio took over your ears at night. You wanted a singing carrier you went for it the hard way and nothing was going to stop you. No voting. And the only way to call someone was having another lady on the other end listening to all you had to say. They all were just playing their game as I thought it was cool how the stage was in the gym as well. Big windows lined the walls as the record was playing. The teacher stopped the music as he wanted the boys to be at the end. William went and put his hands on his hips as he was catching air. His body was like it was when we first met in Tennessee. The shirt he was wearing was belled out from him using it so much. His eyes popped out as he saw I was there.

"Boys, I will like you all to meet a new boy who is going to join our class starting next week." He pointed his hand my way. William turned as he kept his face down looking at his shoes. Moving his feet so he did not have to look. "Now you're the new kids you pick a boy here that will, and I mean will show you the ropes." I did not have to say a thing. He was like the quiet puppy that stands out and that is the first one you want as he was different. My feet came inches from his as he looked from the tip of my toes up to my eyes, smiling with his hands on his hips. I turned as his eyes were different. He looked at me like do I have to. I turned to see the teacher.

"I will find my way on my own. Thank you, anyway." I was used to never having a friend why start now.

"Hey, hey you!" He started walking behind me, matching my steps with his own. I put my hand to my chest. "Oh, are you talking to me? If you are, then I didn't hear you from that smile. Don't worry I'm fine." I was not but I wanted him to want me to be his friend.

"I'm William Starr!" He gave me his hand to, do what with again. Took his hand but not all the way I took it like a dirty sock you throw into the wash. Gave him the same goofy smile he gave me.

"You not going to even give me a shot." I now I turned to talk with you.

"A shot, to means a date." His jaw looked like it was broken yet he was smiling like that. He was now red as he thought I was making a pass for him. Funny how his shorts were so tight his briefs underneath showed when he walked on his legs, now I find it funny how our worlds were changing like that

"Maybe I could be doing that." He was joking right? No one was around, and I was in the locker room. So, I went up to him putting my books on the bench between the lockers. Stood in front of him looking him in the eyes. "I didn't look at you because I liked you. You are my next-door neighbor. I watched you plant your flower bulbs for your mother yesterday. Wishing I was there helping you. Then taking a long cold shower with no one knowing. You know I don't know why I am saying this you don't think like I do, and they all think we have to go out and start a family." He smiled as I told him I did not know they made gym shorts in purple. See my jogging pants came from this moment it happened before it all did but with different people and we both had to grow up again. It is a hot mess.

"So, can you come over later then? History is so puzzling." No, it was not but I did not need him to hear that part. He agreed! He left as I ventured into the hall a girl with red hair was standing there.

"You're not going out with my boy." You're not following me? A question with a question. I stopped as she saw me roll my eyes. I was fighting for him. "Look he don't know I am having his child yet so back off." Oh, I can top it.

"Then why is he dancing the twist with me?" Walk on!

April 10th, 1944

Ladies sang on stage for our entertainment. Sat there pulling apart this compass of mine that was broken. Going to send to mother as a gift with me photo inside it. Cut my thumb open, that is going to leave a scare.

Chapter 5
Chamber Pots

(Freddie!)

I once saw a man with a painted face at the county fair. He did not speak but used his body to tell a story. He looked right at my brother Stu, as he used Stu to get a group of people to watch his act. I took my brother's hand as he looked at me as if why I made him stay. The man went and looked in my eyes where I told him with mine to switch brothers. He looked down to Stu and knew what I meant. That is when he put his pointer finger in my face like a rocket to space pointing up. As he had the other hand as if he were holding a match and he used the side of his face to light the match as he pretended to light the candle. Then he wanted me to make a wish. So, I said it out loud. "I wish for you to say your name." I knew this was going to be something that he could not do. Then he said his name.

"Matthew Pray!" When the crowed made a sound all at once. Do you ever feel like someone who was just there? That you were being used to make someone happy and that's the reason you are here, yet at the same time you know there is more for you to do as this isn't all you were put here. Like when he is sitting next to you on the side of the bed with his different colored jeans on you just want to tell him to put his shirt back on. That all you want to do is go to bed. Him telling you to take it off no matter what as he for some reason I owed my payment and if I did not have money, I had to give in to him. I cannot come in the house no more to put my keys in the bowl near the door without him pulling down my drawers. Once he's done he asks me how it was, and all I can do is put my pants back around my waist line, and run my fingers on the button as I say it was good in a voice he shouldn't like for me to talk in yet he just walks off.

Thing is he is not even using protection anymore as if I did not get anything by now I never will. It does not matter if I even cry a little as it is just the sting of a good time. Just like the man with the painted face using me to get money to get something out of me, so was he. If I say no, then he would hit me until I said yes. Edith said he had an angry side when they were going together well, I know it, I was in her place. If I were out, I would wear long sleeves in the summer. He has been hard onto me so much that I cannot even sit. It feels like sitting on glass every time I move my legs. He would talk to me until I felt so small that nothing was left but nothingness in my head. It does not matter his giant hands just hold my hips down making sure more inches of his bliss get inside of me. It does not matter how long I scream that it hurts it sounds good to him.

Take a ride through the local towns around looking at all the fields of little yellow dots in the grass of butter cups. At least he remembered my favorite flower. Like having a mouthful of tin for years getting to the point you cannot even eat wishing to die to not suffer to never let them see you blink. He changed his mind worse than Edith could change her clothing in an hour. Sometimes I just was not to set his body on fire and watch it burn like a campfire and the kids are in the camper watching old videotapes from your childhood. The orange and the red mixing to make something you wish right now you could smell and take it and put it in a wax to sell on the shelves and call it something like, campfire bliss candles.

"Freddie, I have been waiting for you." There he was in the mirror to the bathroom in the bedroom. I had enough. He was not going to sting me anymore for a boy who likes bees so much I should have seen it from the moment I say the bees on his shirt when he ran past the house the first day I ever was in the state. I am going to roar in your face now as this lion has already played with magic. He came from the restroom with a stick in his hands. In those baby blue boxers with yellow rabbits. He was smiling. "It is positive. Freddie, we are pregnant." He was laughing with happiness. This whole time I was not a waisted space he stuck his little dude in. Wait! Ha! He wanted a baby why didn't he even tell me? Thing is he did not want me to have a say if we have one now or not. Why didn't I catch onto the fact that he was controlling me like a plastic action figure? He was looking at me like I was a man in a vintage photo that he would look at for hours. My eyes just wanted to look the other way.

"We are in a war, and you want a baby. Why didn't you tell me?" He looked at me strange. "I know about you and Bernard were sleeping together while I'm over at Walton's. You forgot his wallet in your pants last night." He did not like this. I got mad at him that I felt invisible.

"Freddie, where did you go?" I was in front of him. I saw myself, yet why was not I am seeing myself in the mirror. I stopped as I hit the wall when there I was again where he could see me. I was becoming a ghost boy, yet why was

I becoming something else then myself? I know my William he would see me if he could not as he always knows where I am. Being in a war he watched his back a lot. Had to test this for myself. Asked my grandma Emma to give me the strength I needed. Walked over to the chimney cupboard where the bowl I put keys in as I took off my wedding ring. She told me to do it for a change I have someone telling me what to do instead of fighting for myself. He heard the metal of the ring hit the glass of the bowl. I could hear him. It does not matter what he did to make me hear him I just heard him.

"I'll be at Edith's if you need me." Put on my coat as he tried to get me to stay.

"I don't know why with good news you don't stay here and be happy with me." He was using different levels with his voice. "What did you tell my brother? He knows everything." I feared him! He came over and took my neck in his hand. "Falling on your sword fool, couldn't keep it in your mouth. The moment you get away you go spilling it to him." He was spitting at my face, but I had it.

"William, you are becoming more like your father every day. I am not going to live with that. You promised me you wouldn't sink that low." He took the bowl and threw it against the wall. Smashing it into pieces. He smiled as I jumped. It was my fear that got him happy. "Hope you and Bernard are very happy together." I had to go; I could not live like this no more. He watched as I crawled on the floor standing to run out the door. Escape, Freddie, escape.

"You can't go out there without me. You will be back." It was like there was a man somewhere playing his violence extremely fast. My heart was breaking with the bowl. "I am nothing like that man." He yelled in my face. Like a lion to his mate. I even seen the yellow stain on his teeth. "Freddie!" Give him a chance. As I turned my face, he hit it with his fist. When I went to the floor gathering myself against the wall sitting. My face was stinging that it did not leave my skin. "You're not going anywhere." He said as he spit in my face. Grandma Emma did not teach me what she did to die to see me not listening to what she said. I am my own person. As he was sweeping up the glass I stood on as I took the bottle off my neck. I had to leave everything of mine behind. I let the string hit the floor near my feet as it rolled down near my toes. When he looked over, I was shutting the door and the only thing left was a bottle of a once was. When he came to the door my purple truck was at the end of the road.

Before I gotten to my truck, I tripped over one of my aunt's lawn gnomes cutting myself on the leg. As he came at me, I ran. When I tried for the door, he would be behind me slamming it shut. Grabbing at me trying to get me on the ground. Getting my pants around my ankles. Tried fighting back yet he was stronger. "Let me go!" I yelled, yet there is no one there to hear me yell. He breath in my face, as he put it in me. I did not want it this time. Like a knife when you get stabbed with it leaving a burning that is all you feel until the rush when you pull out the tip. When he was done, he laughed telling me that I was not going anywhere. I gotten the strength to take my hands and push him to the ground. That is when I got into my truck locking the doors.

My truck was now in her drive. Sitting in my car as every sound I heard made me move as if he was going to hit me. He never did this before. My eye was purple as it stings now. My mouth was dried out as I needed a drink. He made up being with child for me to stay, I guess. I was fooled to what I wanted to me to see. At the end you are always alone but you need to know the people and what role they play for you to be able to get through this life. "Freddie! Open this door!" I put my hands over my face thinking it was his voice I was listening too. I had to lean on my back pulling up my pants as I just left them on my ankles to get away. Anything to get away.

"No! I will not let you hit me again." I yelled at what. I had to get closer to the voice.

"Freddie, it's okay its Edith." My hands went away as I knew I was safe. There she was smiling. "What are you doing here?" Pointing for me to open the door. I let it open as she opened it more. "What is this? Who did this to you?" She doctored my eye.

"William! He's been acting strange." She put her hands in her hair playing with it. "He has been forcing me and hitting me. He might be coming after me now."

"Freddie! William's here he has been here for a few months. I have not seen you as I thought you were in the past. Thing is we can't wake him up." Then who was I living with this whole time. I gotten up from my seat as Edith spoke. "Freddie, where did his compass come from?" What? His compass was spilt in half on the floor of my truck. The William I had was the one I trapped in that compass a year ago today.

"Edith take me to him!" Please! Why look at my chest.

"Where is your bottle? Your being near him will put some of your blood in it. Drinking it will wake him. It will make him stronger and he will take our William's place for good." Man, now I must get the bottle back.

"Oh, someone say bottle! So, you found out I was out of the compass putting your man to sleep until you kill me, that I was having a good time with you this whole time." My necklace was in his hands. My grandfather's picture moving with the wind. He came up to me looking at what he did. My eyes saw the reflection in the bottle. As Edith backed off pretending to be scared. He even saw behind me and did not matter as he was looking at the purple skin on

72

my face. All I did was kneeling as William was there to point fingers at him. Glad he did as now he was dead. Edith ran over to grab the bottle putting back on my neck. Telling me to never take it off again. A baby was crying behind me. As I turned there; he was smiling. The baby that the bad one told me of transformed to my William making it, so we had a baby. This happened fast then at the same time we do not know what he was saying when it was supposed to be said. Fact is there was never any baby just what I wanted to hear.

I was just sitting there now watching the cars go by with William as I counted all the orange cars as he took the silver, he wins every time. "They are fighting back. Thing is they are going after the wrong kind." We are on their side as well and yet they listen to people like his mother. I did not know how to trust him as that evil man looks just like him. William had ice in a bag for my eyes covered in paper towels. I did not know if I could trust him.

"Only a silver bullet can kill them, but that tin you pulled off that guy in front of the gym last year I melted the tin plate down to make bullets, and they kill them." He was humming my song. "Freddie, Bernard died last year. I still don't know how." Why was his wallet on my dresser now? "I saved him before he died, I can't lie to you. he's upstate on a tree farm." I needed to get past this.

"How did you wake up?" He thought about it and said he heard me calling his name it just snapped him from whatever he was in. I stood as I took his hands. "Come no questions Starr boy!" Went to Edith's closet where she still had our old prom outfits.

"Freddie, ah, black suit coat, matching tie with white pants. What's going on?" I needed him to stand there and dance with me. Put on that old song. My ears rested on his bow tie while we circled the floor.

"Get out of here, get out of here. Now!" I let William's hands go as I picked up the gun from the stand nearby, I pointed it at what I thought was Ms. Louise, yet she then became Edith, then Mary. I did not know what to think. When William took the gun from my hands, lowering my hand with his on top of mine. Putting it back from where I gotten it from. Slow dancing again. I was sick right. No, I was becoming myself. I can hide from them now, yet I need to find a way to get it back. Control it if you will. It was two by the time William stopped the music and took me to bed. The real William. My William. The other one died, and the body turned into a seed. That was strange to me. But it was their way of replanting themselves to come back more powerful. Yet I took the seed and put it on top of a candle. Letting it burn. Time to call the stores to put it on the shelves.

Now I need to know why Edith had a gun.

April 11th, 1944

Got a weekend pass to go home. When I came back from it, found out that my Edith was expecting my first child. Now I have something to keep me going.

Chapter 6
Rotting Rocking Horse

(Freddie in the then!)

Funny how when it's cold outside, and the clouds are standing in line as if the queen were changing her dress and no one shall see her form. You can see my breath, and yet there is still a shadow following me. The funny part of all of this is that as I stand tall it bends. The shadow moves without me even having to lift a hand. What next trees will learn how to kill? Here I stand in the middle of the backyard letting myself be a kid like again. Aviator hat on my head as the little pieces of red hair stick out of its coroners. As the wind blows looking flames bouncing off my face. Kelly running with the wind as if he could feel its solid mass. He wanted to play out here today even though I told him he was going to catch a cold if he did, but he wanted to fly. I do not think he really knows what colds are yet.

"Edith's home." He shouted as those little feet ran over to the new pink like car. The things parents buy for you when you graduate higher education.

A: Hey, are you home? Walt.

B: Yeah, what is going on? Fred.

A: Would you like to go see that new superhero film? Walt.

B: Of course! Fred.

A: Just you. Please! Walt.

B: Yes sir! On my way. Fred.

"Hey, there Freddie your Aunt, and I!" Stopped him in midsentence.

"I would like to go with Walton somewhere tonight. Oh no you were going to ask me to stay in." He looked at me as if how did I know what he was thinking. He put his hand on his hip and the other on his chin.

"I was going to ask you to let us have the house. You got to it before I did. Edith's taking Kelly to her friend's house. Stu he is with his friend too, so yeah if you have plans." I smiled as I knew I would see William again. Why that made me smile well I do not know. Did not even take me a moment to get over there. We walked this trail so much that it made a path through the woods. It was our own portal.

B: You home, come down. Fred.

A: Out back, come. Walt.

Guess who invented the new way of knocking on the door without their parents knowing there even there. Oh, they have a camera now as the doorbell. Well there went that idea. My hand was not even inches from the handle to the gate when I heard this yelling. It was like when you make bees mad and they start for you. The person running had no water to jump into.

"You stay out here until you know you can win that next game." The loud voice said. As I walked it gotten worse.

"Maybe I will let the game go this time as I don't have to win all of them to get into a college." As I turned there was William standing, he looks at me as if he didn't know I was coming.

"You do that there will be no more home for you boy." His father was not a nice person. I learned that much.

"Good!" He smiles why did his dad smile. William put his hand for me to stop so his father did not see me nor his hand.

"You want to lose the game. So, you can shake up with that Waters boy." William's eyes grew so wide I did not know they could do that.

"What! I never said that." I wanted to say something so bad.

"I see the way you look at him." I started to leave.

"Wait! Freddie! Freddie is my friend that is all. I do not have many thanks to you I have to borrow Walton's. You already made my lip bleed leave me to my work." His father went into the house to drink some more. William's eyes reacted to the door slamming in his face. He put his hand over his forehead when he spoken again. "Don't hide he knows. That or I think he does. Think the drinking makes him think that. Just because I run past your house, I must be a wall flower. What are you doing here anyway?" He started bouncing the basketball onto the ground, while he found a way to put some jazz hands into the mixture while he was talking. He makes you laugh every time.

"Walton asked me to come over on my phone." He stopped as the ball rolled from him. He was looking at me strange.

"Freddie! Walton he is not here. That was me! He must be reading my text messages too. Man!" He got mad at that.

"So now he knows that we were having phone stuff last night." My world just gotten smaller. "So am I shirts then." Those lips could not hide a smile from me.

"What?" William as I live and breathe you will never understand me.

"Nineteen thirties' gym shorts. Now shirt and long socks. If this is not short shorts, then." He laughed like a lot.

"My dad thinks making me wear his father's shorts from back when it would inspire me. No, it just gave me jock ich instead." Yelling from the front yard now.

"Get your boy out of my yard right now." Yelling that is never good. "They were saying things in secret on the phone last night that they both need to be put away. My boys going to get a licking tonight as the belt will be in my hands. Better think to do the same with yours." William started to shake as his father spoke. He ran to the gate, but I held him there by grabbing his arm.

"I trust my boy. I do not have to spy on him. I know what goes on in all my children's lives." When we ventured to the front yard that is when it hit. "Well if you didn't put your daughter on the street corners every night." Uncle Harvey never made a fist at another man before. I stood in there taking it like a man he thinks I should be. His father just stumbled trod me. "You get in that houseboy." William's father slapped me in the face so hard you heard the echo on the moon. Took William's hair on the back of his head and started by pulling him up the front steps. Could feel his pain through mine. The next time I looked at the porch his father let go of the back of his son's head letting him fall down the stairs like a girl would do to her dolls. William tried to get his grasp and land, so he did not get hurt. He tried to get off the ground, but you could tell he was getting hurt. "That's for last night boys. You will learn from this." I saw that he had little to spare. William's eyes were going dim. No more fight was in him.

"So, being gay is a sickness to you mister Starr. I feel bad for you as your son has a lifetime, he wanted to share with you, and this is the thanks he gets from you." All he did was take a big ball of spit letting it fall from his face onto his son's back. As if I say nothing. William had all he could do was stand but he did. I ran over letting his arm rest over the back of my neck.

"You are no longer my boy." He smiled as the dried-up leaves fell of his skin.

"Good your no longer my father." We started for my house as this was not over yet.

"William your welcome to stay with us as long as you wish." Uncle Harvey said. He grabbed William's baseball bat.

"You can't take him he is my child until he is eighteen." My uncle turned as he was mad as the bat was not shaking.

"William turned that last week. Your beer cans were being sang happy birthday before you sang to him. Think about it." Go, Harvey!

(William in the now!)

My Freddie in the past has told me that there will be a time where your youth dies off like everything else. I laughed it off every time, but I did not realize it that it passed away the moment I pulled down my pants in room eighteen. Here I was standing at the sink bed waiting for him to kick. Every time I brushed my teeth, he would kick. It was as if he was practicing dancing as a ballerina or something the way he kicked at my skin. The toothbrush hit the sink as this kick was the hardest, he has done thus far. So hard that I had to hold the sink's edge. There was this wet substance that was getting the back of my pants wet. There was water on my face, and on my bottom. My water broke. Just think five minutes prior I was singing a song in my head, and I was getting ready to watch my favorite television show from my childhood. How that man gets the news for tomorrow the day before, I do not know. I would keep waking up every hour to see if it would happen for me when I was a kid. It never worked. Oh, boy is he coming.

(Back to you, Freddie!) In London!

There was this brown paper bag sitting near the door. Did not know what it was in, but this I did know it was owned by someone who did not know where he was going. Funny the word owned. You won it until you cannot have it no more. We collect things until we die, use them until we are done with it. Yet we do not care what happens to the items after we're gone. We're gone we cannot use them no more why bother. We spent all this time collecting things like old twenty-seven pins from the fight he had. Yet you are now selling them when they lower me in the ground as they're worth something. Did I do that for a reason? No, you did that for a reason or did I as I knew they be worth something? The tea kettle was yelling again as William gotten up to get the sound. All I can think about was that a bird was going to be in the teapot one day as an old lady buys the pot at a secondhand store. Then hangs it in a tree as her grandchild saw it on a webpage somewhere.

The glow from a giant clock was coming about the window. The window was feet up off the ground yet here was this glow. It was as if the sun was shining and it was nothing but nighttime. Two and three quarters was what was reading on its face. William had left the television on again. Some cop shows from where we were. Everything seemed fogged as I was still sleepy. Could feel my feet reach the toilet, and my hand was wondering where Willie was. Then I heard it. Oh, dear all I was trying to do was go to the bathroom and go back to bed. Now what?

"Police! Show me your hands. Now!" My hands are up, and I am so tired to realize it was the show on the screen in the other room. The waistline meets my skin. The toilet did what it needed to do. As I went to turn off the light. There was a lady in the hotel room. Who is she? Wait why is she walking in here when the door is locked? She worn flat ballerina shoes with a pale pink pants with a red shirt, to top it all she worn a string of pearls around her neck. Brown hair all nice with a clip in her hair in the back. She walked over to the window. As she watches something. She let me come up next to her. She watched the windows as there was a person per window. A man or lady there were even teens. They all one at a time started to fall to the ground. She turned to have her back trod the window. She smiles as the lipstick on her lips moved about her face.

"We all fall down!" She said. I was looking for the button you press for her to say that it was as if she was a toy you pull the string on. Then she stepped back falling out of the window as if the glass were not there. They all then fell. She went to dust before hitting the ground. What was going on here? I stumbled to the side of the bed that William was not taking up. I had fallen like that, but what was going on here. Sitting there and just looking at the wall, playing with my fingers. Every night I scare myself as I start to feel as if I would walk off something making me fall, this was opening old wounds.

"Ah, what's wrong?" Leave it up to him to try and wake himself from a deep sleep to see what is wrong with me. How does he know when I am like this? It was as if it was built into his genetics. My hand was landing on his chest using the hairs like a farmer would to the top of the wheat in his field. He wiped the hair out from the form of his face. His hand then landed on top of mine. "Freddie, Ghost!" I said, yes, but he knew something he knew that something the day I first saw him. He still has not said all of it.

"William… I would like to ask you something. Listen before you start to answer me." Should I bring it up now? There could be many things that can go haywire here. "Why are we in London? Why hide from what?" His tongue licked his lips as he sat up. Took my hand back. "Do we have to put our rings in the back of the dresser drawer for a spell?"

"Never say that again!" He put his feet on the ground, and his back trod me. "Tea!" He was in the little area where there was just a microwave and a few cups. Tell me already, you do not have to hide with me. That or he is going to say it when the tea comes. Is there tea? What kind of tea? Oh, William get in here so we can take that ride in the teacup. He had a flannel shirt hanging on the back of the chair next to myside of the bed. Hot pink with black strips. Stood there buttoning up when… KNOCK! KNOCK! William told me to not get the door. They said they were with the police, but he did not think they were as the real thing was still standing guard outside. "Tea! Freddie, now!" He was frightened, so I let me drink that tea. It tasted worse than socks dipped in dirty water. He placed his forehead on mine, his hands on the back of my neck. "Look at me nothing else but me and listen to my voice nothing but my voice." Why? The bottoms of my feet were touching hard wood slowly now it was wet with sticks underneath them. My feet reacted to the fact that I was standing on a flat surface now to a not so much flat one. He let me let out a yell, but you would go after that tea he gave you. "What do you hear?" Birds, the water hitting the ground off a leaf. I could not tell him that.

"Your voice!" He let his hands go from my head. Breathing heavily when we stepped back. "Why are we in the woods now?" Tell me the truth. Please! I remember if the bark is broken on the trees it meant something in the spring. This time I was asking. "William I would like the truth this time." He stood looking at the woods. This was not the bed to turn your back this time.

"Policeman's helmet...a flower that Edith told me to get. It was hard to find. She gave me a splash of her magic. Use it in a case of emergency. I did!" I stood there trying to figure out where we were.

"I am standing here in a pink flannel shirt, and boxers if I get wet it would show everything underneath that it is trying to hide. You need to tell me now!" I was mad.

"Fact is we are back during the time of the great queen." Oh!

"Which one?" I was laughing like a true hatter now.

"Unknown to you." He started walking as I asked him where we were going. "The Starr farm is not too far from here. It is going to be dark fast. We need to get as far as we can with the light."

"William... Why did we run?" He stopped as I ran into him as I was not looking where I was going.

"My mother is after you. I gotten word from an underground thing that she was in Tennessee looking for you. So, I took you to London. Edith stayed behind to make sure she was distracted. She can control the living as she controls all the timeline. You can control both sides. The living and the dead. She gets you there is no hope for us." He was giving up everything to help me. I just looked at him. "Freddie, my mother gave me a mission, but I failed her." He kept on walking. Finish your line!

"William!" He knew what I was going to say next.

"When I was eighteen...in nineteen forty-four my mother told me, I had a new mission. So, she gave me tea and I would know in the morning what it was. Woken up at the age of four. Remembering everything. She put something in my tea and never told what was in it. I was now being raised by my grandchildren. That's why he hit me as it wasn't meant for me to be there." He sat there on a nearby tree that had fallen. As I sat, he kept speaking. "I was to friend you...get your trust. Lead you to her." I put my hands between my legs.

"What stopped you?" Like I did not know.

"I feel in love with you instead. You are the only person who had not turned their back on me. So, I chose to protect you no matter what." He kept walking. "Better keep moving!" Thus, we did.

"Thank you! I wouldn't be here if it weren't for you." He said something strange next that he is never saw bad this time he was letting it come in his heart for a moment.

"You can thank me by killing her." I stopped near some mushrooms as that did not sound right.

"William Starr, we don't kill." He turned as I saw another person in his eyes.

"If you blink once she will not even think twice as you just done. You need to be ahead of her, and I am trying to teach you that. Freddie if you are thinking twice then I will let her kill you right now you chose." I looked to the ground before saying anything.

"Bow and arrow if you can. That's all I know how to use." He said to me, he could make that work. I was scared at this moment in time for what that working moment was going to initial.

We walked for a good few miles before seeing the smoke coming from the house. There was something off about the house. As if they left it in a hurry for some reason. The chickens were complaining about no breakfast, and the cow was mooing to be milked. The door was wide open. The house was the size of a modern chicken coop. A kitchen and table right next to the bed. Another little one at the end of the master bed for the other one. Their lift was in there. I stood near the horse for William went looked the place over. The horse reacted to the door swinging open. William was dragging a trunk into the barn. Could smell wood. Why?

"What did you do?" Like I did not know he burned the house down.

"The family all had died. Cause of the cold weather they got sick did not know how to shake it. Must burn the cause as it will affect the others if they come by this place. The father's eyes were still open as he held onto his baby girl. This trunk was out in the wagon I think it is still good. No sickness onto it. I also put a spell on it to make sure of it. Your cousin knows her stuff." He said that was I stood in the door frame of the barn. Listening to the crackling of the wood. The father took time to build it for us to just burn it down. He will never be forgotten. "No one survived Freddie. Sorry!" That is the hardest thing to do. He at least told me he closed his eyes. He unlaced the trunk fast. "Get undressed now. They are going to see the smoke and ride out here. We cannot be here. The faster we look like them the better." He handed me long socks that came up to your hips. It was hard to get my leg in this sock as it was tight.

I left my boxers on as I did not feel right not wearing anything. Long nightgown that was gray with buttons in the front. He gave me dark tan pants that looked and felt like a lady's capris, the pants laced in the front.

"William, can you tie me up. Mind yourself mister horse." Scary thing was the horse knew what I was saying and tuned his head. William's fingers shook as it was colder than what we knew. It is just leather strings. "You're not going to hurt me." He was crying as he thought this was his mess we gotten into. I made a sound as he did it too tight. Yet that is the way they worn their clothing. He asked me to close my eyes as I could feel something going around my neck, down my back, and top my head.

"You get the father's cape with a hood. We need to hide your face. The less they know where you are, the better. What, what's wrong with it." Nothing was wrong.

"It's Royal! Who just happens to have a purple cape with a hood? With them little money they had."

"Funny I know this family's farm. They were known for their huckleberries. They would die the fabrics for the royal families. This might be part of that line they were working on at the time." He said it as he put the gown over his head, tucked in the tail as a good duck. As I put the two leather straps in my hands. His eyes widened as I pulled the strings. I took my necklace off. Asked him to close his eyes as I put it over his head.

"You get my necklace. If anything happens to me. Then open it. See what that paper says. Please!" He said yes right off. There were pockets inside the lining of the hood. A paper with their surname on it. As I unfolded the paper, I could not believe my eyes. "William, the family was invited to the queens spring ball."

"Then we go!" Good we need this.

April 23rd, 1944

Edith sent me a list of baby names. Wrote back telling her Jeremy was one I liked after her grandfather's side.

Chapter 7
Falling Bird Feeders

(William!)

The clock struck eight in the afternoon now it is the time for Bernard Conklin to come down from the mountains and have a cold one with me. Each time the old grandfather clock in the living room goes off, there is something in the back of my mind that makes me think of an old family member and what they be doing right now if they were still alive. So, for eight in the afternoon he gets my attention

There was this man who was standing in line in front of me. I was wishing he were gone as he scared me. He had no hair and had a clown smiling tattooed on the back of his head. The face just lingered at me. I was waiting for something to come out and get me or something. When the officer asked him how his day was, he was the nicest person so why have that on your head? He went into the other room, and there was this hope that there were no more clowns that was going to smile at me today. Yet here I was letting myself visit the man I feared so in a way the red nosed thing will still be there to smile at me. There were pictures on the wall behind him of the police station back in the day and the people. It was cool that the man signing me in was a descendant of one of those men. Thing was it was cool he never broke from that line of work. His badge had an elk on it as he was a member of the local elks' lodge. He was middle-aged and was holding one what hair he had left after all these years of balding. Why put yourself through that for nothing? The lady behind you that you hope is going to sleep with is not thinking about sleeping with you. She is thinking about how she is going to ask you to eat the donut on the counter near him. I gave a smile, but he just was looking at me as if he were being troubled. I had on my dark red hood on with my hands in my pockets.

"Aren't you too young son. You have to be eighteen to visit here by yourself." My tongue was feeling the inlay of my mouth as I had to laugh some.

"Here's the thing, I will not tell the fine thing behind you that you want to pull down those size well there is no number after that number as they don't make them any bigger. She's not going to want to see nor want that." Yeah, I get this whole not knowing what to say thing.

"Oh, I get you want her!" Man, she can hear you. I leaned in and made a move with my eyes side to side like those cat clocks.

"Well I'll tell my husband that you said that." He buzzed me in as he wanted me gone.

"Seventeen! He's here to see Seventeen." Thank you! Girl behind him... Your welcome! The room had three chairs at this exceptionally long counter. Each chair sat near this wall with a dial phone attached to the wall. No reason to say more as it was all gray. The officer this one was a girl pointed to the seat near, oh no the clown. My shoes went but I did not want to be here. My hands grasped the back of the chair as he pulled at his pants plucking his manly area so he could sit right. That is what you get for wearing tight jeans. As he was doing that, he looked at me and nodded then winked. All I could do was sit and pull my chair underneath me. Was I giving him a show? Oh dear, did I just cheat on Freddie with him? No, William you have lost it. We were waiting for the third person to get signed in. It was cold as the walls were made from cinder.

"Oliver!" What was that? Oh, he was talking to me. He was looking for my name. I never put my name on these things, my name is! If you don't know by now you never going to.

"Alexander!" Give your middle name. Nice!

He smiled with only one side of his face. "Okay there William, good trick telling me another name." He looked at me strange. Do not make me laugh as I do not know you yet here you know my name. "It will begin when the man flies in the land of ask." What?

"Your part of us! There is no way." Just keep looking to your flection William. There was something I had to know from my father before getting back to Freddie if I can.

"Mary Waters, she sent me here to talk to you. It's okay I can talk to after word." Freddie's aunt sent you. That is odd then at the same time I knew.

"You're the man she killed. They killed!" What was going on here? Can I trust this man with the odd head? I still looked at him as if a gun were being loaded near my face.

"Yes, they never killed a man. They never killed a man. They just let me hide with them. I know your family very well." Say something.

"I'm sorry!" That all you got?

"William I am just here to make sure you're safe. That is all. Not asking you to trust me, but your wellbeing and Freddie's is all I care about." Gun went off outside the door as a scream from that girl behind the counter came in. I stood to my feet faster than I could. He just sat there. The officer put her hand up to stop me. A man in a hood attached to a cape was standing there with his arrow pointed at the officer.

"Walton! Put your arrow to bed brother." He did not want to be called that name. He was with the clown, so I put myself in the middle of them both. For a moment he was going to let it go, but then he saw the man with the clown on his head approach. "Stop! Let her live."

"If you let her live, you're going to have to start running and bring her with you." So, you can talk! He let her go. He hovered his hand over her head. "There she knows everything. He took off his hood as he spoken. He was wearing a masquerade mask that was gold with leaves on the top with two birds in the middle connecting the leaves. He was young.

"What did you kill?" He pointed to the man with the badge. Dale! "I was here to see my father, and this happens." The clown was now talking.

"He died William. Your mother made sure of that last week." What? He was still my uncle slash dad. What gave her the right? They were using him as he thought he was getting something.

"There is one more thing. Follow me." He put his hand out for me to take it. "She will die if you don't." Fine! When I took his hand, I heard Freddie say my name when I turned, I was somewhere else. "A high school that was built in the forties. You want the boy's room." He stood to the side like a butler. My jaw was shaking as I saw what he wanted me to see. Back when this school was first put up it was common for the male bathrooms to have urinals that connected to the floor. There was three here in this restroom. Sitting in the first one was Walton's body.

"No! No! Not you." His wrist was cut the blood ran cold already. His skin was the color of the moons dust. His nipples were now purple. I sat over his lap looking trod him. He was wearing nothing but jeans and his shoes. His jeans were unbuttoned with the zipper down. His eyes were open. Why were they open? My hands went around his head in his hair. I rested my forehead on his. Crying as the tears landed down onto his chest running down his body. His eyes were like two glass eyes. There was nothing there. Looked behind me as I saw what he was looking at, but there was just a wall. "No! you were to be his protector. I still need you." I looked down to his pants. He was sitting in blood. He cut off his own, cannot get the courage to say the word. Could hear his boots land behind me. "Who did this? Tell me." He must.

"They call him Applebottom, but his real name is Landon Starr. See your half-brother. Ms. Louise sent him to kill Freddie and everyone who gets in their way. Well Walton got in his way. You see you must run." I stood leaving his body. Took his arrow and cut off a piece of his hair so I have it for good. I was shaking and looking at him. Before standing I made sure to shut his eyes.

"Where to then?" He just smiled.

"London this time!" I looked at him strange if we run why run from nothing but the police in the thin air as they cannot be seen I didn't know it myself unless it was in front of my own face.

"The moment of anything gone wrong run. Get Freddie then go. The bottom of my boots soaked in the blood of my brother.

"Landon! I know your telling me about yourself. The moment I find the person who really did this you do not have to lie for them. You wanted to tell me the truth then tell it to me. That mask will come off. You chose your side. You are with me...or you are with her. When I leave here you have made the obligation."

"Your right you must know who did this." I was waiting. My heart was torn out.

"Leave I will find out later. Now!" He did not want to leave me, but I had to have my time. I once forced myself to take a bath in all ice. Felt good at first, but you look at it you might think it would hurt. It does not then at the same time whom I to say. Something felt not normal to me as I thought all about those people in the ocean at night after the ship hit that giant piece of cold wilderness bliss. This is how they must have felt. When you put yourself in others shoes it is hard to come back from it all. The smoke from the cubes form around your skin as it dances through the cracks. My hands went from the top of his head to rest against his lower back. For a moment I found myself forcing his body trod mine. Rocking him back and forth like a mother to her babe. If I sing a song will you wake? My tears gathered in his hair as I was not letting him go. If I were to be cold, I would want to be cold with him in this moment. The coloring of the moon was on his skin so be it on mine. The others were out in the hall waiting for me to say it was done and we could get to what they needed.

"Cough!" Why was the body doing that very thing? Blood dripping down my arm like rain to a window. I rested his body against the wall as I was to my feet faster than I could ever hit the opposite wall on the other side of the room. Walton's body his coloring was coming back. Why? He was standing up; no this was not right. My hand went up. I knew this was not the way it is supposed to happen.

"You, you I seen you dead on the floor." He acted as if he was drunk coming back from the dead that is all you can act like.

"You think I would sit myself in the spot where all those men have gone and let them have their way with me body. Not a chance." He was standing what do I do? How do I act?

"You should know brother. I pretended to be dead. That man in the hood cannot be trusted. Why do you think Dale was here? If that Landon, he calls himself is your brother by birthright then. That makes you, Duke of Totten. Freddie being the Price of Death you can't be king, so you get a noble name." He was looking me strange. No, your shirtless body was laying on the ground just then. Ha!

"How did you do it?" I asked.

"I used a rocking horse charm from Edith's kitchen. You sweat out the wood from a rocking horse and it lets you pretend to be dead for a few hours." He handed me a small glass with it inside with a horse sketched in the glass. "Where's Freddie!" I was looking at the glass not you. He asked again thinking I was mad or some sort. "I did this for him, so you think I am not telling the truth now. You came back here to speak to dad to get information on Ms. Louise. I knew so I did this to get them off Freddie's tale."

"Freddie's under the Queen as a footman. Right now, he waits for me to go to ball with him." He did not know how to speak at this point. He warned me about the facts of being gay in the time he was hiding in. I knew so did he, but he had to run. "Funny thing about belts and being gay. If we do live other lives, then as kids to teach us lessons our fathers hit us with a belt. Now in this lifetime. We cannot seem to get away from that. We still must lean over and take it. In a twisted life of wanted to be a bad boy so daddy would hit us. Both getting what they wanted at the end." I thought about that way too much.

"Let's go get him before they hear me talk." I walked in the stall as I stood into the water of the toilet number five. "What are you doing?" I took his hand as he too had to stand here.

"You're not the only one who knows Edith Waters. Dust off a finger from a dead man's pocket. Put it in the water and you get to where you are going. Next step!" He was thinking strange yet again.

"Freddie, here we come." Walton said.

May 13th, 1944

If I exhale my breath onto the pages of this letter, do you think mom can smell the smokes on my breath? So, she knows I indeed got the ones she sent.

Chapter 8

Burning Lanterns

(Freddie!)

There is this new thing now where if you die, you can have your body presented in nothing but your underwear laying on top of the ground. They have body parks now. They call them fancy names, but yeah! They took our class to one of these before graduation. See you think a dead thing on the ground would bring in animals, but no they put something in the bodies under the skin so the animals would not touch them, and it is environmentally friendly. They would only show us a young man. The people with the long white coats wanted us to see someone our age if this happened to us. He looked like a sleeping prince trying to find his princess but failed to find her. See they plant a tree in your mouth and as it grows into the ground it absorbs your body's giving way for the roots. In a way you are giving back. After the tree is grown the grounds keepers, also known as the waterman, who put buckets on your branches to gather the rainwater, so it slows down the water shortage issue.

Is it a good thing to go past a place and just see people lying on the ground? What about the sun, one said? Guess the tree part grows so fast there is not that much sun time for them to have. It does not matter to me much as I am not in there so have at it. I did ask if they had people that were still living have this happened. That why he was shown to us. They all called him the Paper Prince as he was one for the textbooks. They never had something like that happen before. It makes me wonder some why do people forces on the body after were gone and never anything else? Sure, they do, but in the long run they cry over something they cannot help no longer.

William has been gone for a while now. Nothing to do but hide in a barn. That is not all I had done. You try sitting in a spot for so long your brain hurts harder than the wood your back is turned to. Do not go anywhere Freddie as it might make you seen. If Ms. Louise wanted to find me, she would have by now. Right! Or is there something they are not telling me. I only went out once. It was dark but the sun was still out some. Everyone getting ready to eat their final meals not paying no mind to the man in the hood. All I had to eat were apples from the trees out back. Then again, I had to share with the horse. My feet ventured over the burned wood that William had done. There was something about this house he did not like. His family owned it yet left it in a hurry. He knew this information so hard that it did not bother him to burn his history. Ms. Louise always told me about her son. How they had an argument about something that should not have been talked about. He walked out and she never seen him again. She was trying to get information out of me that whole time about where her son was. I did not know him then. If nothing last forever, then, how does she? If she knew the William that I still know to this day, then she would have seen a worm and gentle man. She just wanted everything to fall in place, so she did not have to take off her fancy gloves and spill the teapot. Her goal was to find the one boy or girl who had to the gift I hold. His mission was to find me. Question was, was I supposed to be found? Man, did he try to hide me. Yet I would not let myself hide in the shadows of the unknown. Everyone telling me to run from her. Yet here we are. Standing in the burned house. Just like the Paper Prince giving away to a new. A new what? That up to what every takes it on, but all I know it filled its purpose. When it started to rain it was time for me to get back to the cows. The door locked then there it was. A voice cried out. It was not a voice I thought I hear again.

"Hello there, stranger!" Edith! As I turned, I could help but think why she was here. Her hands held a stick as she was dressed to the hills for this time period. She looked me over said I could be wearing these cloths. With her stick she pointed said something I could not understand and then I was in new clothing myself. She left the hood, however. "I turned eighteen last week. My mom thought it be something if I had something to control my power not just my hands. I got to choose so I came up with this. My dad made this hiking stick for my doll when I was a kid. So, it means he is always with me." I was glad to see her no matter what. I did not have the heart to tell her it was a wand.

"How did you find me?" If she could who else can? This was a scary situation.

"William told me where he was taking you. Just in case, so mom let me go. I told her I could not sit there knowing you guys are in the middle of a war. She understood and set me to get you. Thing is we are never going back until this is done." She ran her fingers on the back of the cow as she spoken.

"Edith are you scared to die?" I had to answer her when I first moved down, now she needs to answer me.

"In a way but then again I knew what we all signed up for. This is war Freddie. Not going to see how they make gummy bears. We need to get you a mask." She started to cry a lot.

"I didn't mean anything. Why didn't your wand give me a mask?" She wiped her face. The tears were so thick that it looked like it was heavy rain.

"I know only how to make clothing now. I still have a lot to learn." Okay that makes sense, I guess. The pocket mirror was shaking on the wooded beam near her. "Bloodied hell, what is that?" I grabbed it as she tripped a little. William was on the reflection on the other side.

"William!" I was happy now.

"Your voice is like candy for me ears. I am back in this time, but I cannot risk being seen getting to you. Do you think you can get to the castle for the ball?" I would do anything to see you again.

"Yes, Edith is with me." He smiled.

"Good I have Walt! The teams back together. Must go hearing footsteps. See you there. Love you." He was gone before I could say I love you back

"We have to go." As I started for the door, she stopped me.

"Mask Freddie. If they see your eyes that's the end of it all for us." I looked everywhere and could not think. Heard her scream when I went to look Walton was standing in her place as if they were switched. Good he can make me a glass mask. No, he was here because we were made and had to run again.

(William!)

Eight drawer dressers with an oak finish. Coal colored knobs with an attached mirror the same length as the furniture it sat upon. A photo of her boyfriend who just asked her to wear his pin safety sitting on the edging of the glass. Snuggled in her heart, as he was on her mind as well. A tube of red blush lipstick rolling on the surface of the wood as her lips were freshly wet. Baby's breath pinned down on her bouncing curly hair by her grandmother's old clip that she worn in her flapper says. Duck colored yellow blouse looking like a sweater that has short sleeves. Brown pencil skirt completes the look with a long necklace with a big charm on it around her neckline. Calendar of a 1943 March day on the wall behind her. The lace that travels the dressers face holds his weekend pass with his photo, and all the trimmings on the surface of the paper with his lucky blue marble he keeps in his pocket from his youth. He's going to fight as she goes to put on the show for the boys who crossed the seas. His uniform shirt on her bed as he sits up next to it. The fabric of his underwear in the grip of his hand as he jumps in the air pulling them up at the same time. Pulling them up looking into her mirror as he thinks about how he worn this before in another life like as he worn a pair like these swimming even though he doesn't know how to swim. Could just a touch remind him of a once that was? Tripping as he stumbles to stand behind her tucking his muscle shirt in the back of his trousers.

She fixes her hair as she takes her daddy's video camera from the top drawer. Both looking into the mirror as she cranked away listening to the clicking sound. He worn a giant smile, and she silently didn't want him to go. Happy, and laughing as they were together. The metal was now green like. As the opening of the camera was rusted shut. Walton was tilling the garden when he hit a metal box with their camera in it. Thing is it started clicking on its own. Walton took the rust off from the cap as we pointed it to the wall. Freddie was pulling in the driveway as it was going off. "Love you, Louise." He mentioned. She laughed as she said that she loved him as well, Billy Starr. My heart raced in my chest. As that was the day, she gotten pregnant with me. She was hiding her truths in a tin box in the earth not knowing we had found it. I locked the door as he wasn't to know what we have. This changes things. It sounded like a giant knock coming from the kitchen. Made me jump from my spot as it started to get hot in here. Walton grabbing the baseball bat near the front door, as he motioned me to walk behind him. With every step the knocking gotten louder if we stopped so did the sounds. Ghost was Freddie's thing, why was it happening to us. Walton took his boot and lifted it hitting the floorboards. There was a sound after a while of repeating that we knew it was coming from the wall of the stove. Looking over the wallpaper of an antique yellow with a pattern of a shadow. There was a fine line in the middle. Hard for the eye to see but it was there. Went past Walton with no pretense as he was trying to protect me, but there was nothing to harm me. Feeling the fine like a paper cut as it left a mark as my blood ran down the seams. There was a spot in the wall that started to shake. Stopped shaking when I bent to put my hand on the wood.

"Walt, give me those scissors?" I pointed to the table and looked him in the eyes. He didn't want to at first but we both knew we don't turn back. Cutting the paper on the wall like crawling a bow on a newly wrapped gift. The sun from the windows had just shown a blank color. There was enough to get my fingers through. As the door opened it made a sound that I didn't like. Walton held his teeth as the metal made them react to the vibration. As we investigated this secret closet like all we saw was this naked person from the backside. The back of the head had blonde hair that was sticking to the skin as the moister was making itself known. My eyes lined his spin as you could count the bumps of bones lining to his legs. He was in there as if someone put him there against his will. He must have been on his knees when whoever did this killed him as he was on his knees while his head was resting against the wall. It was if the person who knew he was in here used the body for other things after death as the body was still worm. Thing was if it has been years why had this been left like it had. For respect of the dead my brother and I pulled him out lying him between us. Now we are the ones on our knees looking down at him. His head was leaning on the wall ahead. His skin was the same color of a full moon, his fingers sat on his sides taking on the coloring of an old English muffin. Each point of his spin pocking on the skin letting themselves be known. I took my hand to go grasp the body to drag it out. The body just gave out, falling backward as if the feet kicked off the wall throwing him back. His eyes were red, he looked a lot like the same way my Freddie described Bradley being a frozen man. His hair was fluffy, as he was dead.

"Who is this? How long has he been in there? Did you know this closet was there?" Why are you asking me this?

"I know who he is? My father." Walton touched the face. I wasn't getting the feeling like you did when you see a dead body. A wind-up ballerina that dances when you open the lid music was playing in my head. I knew him from the home videos I saw as a kid.

"Walton, he looks like you, same age even, and when I touch him. He is still warm. How did he get in there after all these years?" My fingers hovered his chest as he was still wearing that same muscle shirt. His eyes open while he was now breathing. Walton gave out a yell, I didn't understand his words. He stood to his feet. Running from us as he was scared. Went out the front door past Edith who was waiting for us to answer her ring.

"What's going on?" Put my hands in my hair. As this was happing, I couldn't fathom it. My breath was gone as I was licking my lips.

"Follow him. Don't let him get out of your sight." The truck in the drive was a different person than who I thought. It was Edith telling us that she started her attack. My father got here the hard way, but I'll take it. Now find him. Take the photos that were stuck in the secret compartment of the camera and put them in my wallet. It was like I was out in space touching the balls of gas that we get the word star from. Looking down at the world just flouting alone in my own suit. Thinking that this is what it must feel being dead. Alone, looking down to those still having a meaning. Trying to speak but no here's what I say as you must be gone for it to sink it. A coffin you can pee in as they have their toilets built in. Still living yet alive at the same time. Must be how Freddie feels like every waking moment. That man we found in the wall must have been dead, but he had a tilted stage. See my mother was a Starr, so I must be more like his last name. Abplanalp, try saying that five time faster than the second hand on the clock. Oh, I forgot you had all the clock go to digital you don't know how. Thing is I never knew that last name it was just a name my mother would stop to the graveyard and have a beer with his stone every March seventh. While my mother would respect the man's wishes by having a cold one with his stone. She would tell me to go play with the grave taker's sons. If that was an unmanned grave, then who was really in there? How did my dad get to us this way, and if that's the case then why did he pick this moment? The moment I went to go and shut the light off and fall to sleep. The black lab was trying to get outside. I named him Shadow as he followed me around town one day. He didn't belong to anyone, so I took him home. He puts his nose in my palm when I want him to do something, he doses that first. "Let me open the bloodied door." He backed up, sitting down, giving me his paw. He never done that before. Opened the door as on the other side of the screen door there he was. Standing in the doorway under the light that was going on and off must get that thing fixed.

"Can we talk?" The dog made me talk to him as he put his nose behind my knees pushing me closer to the door.

"I don't know, you going to run away from me again?" He shook his head no. He lifted his muscle shirt up as he showed his back to me. He had the same birthmark on his back as I do on mine. Leaned onto the door frame not letting in until I could trust he wouldn't run from me. He gotten scared as the cat jumped onto the rocking chair wagging his tail as there was a new stranger at his house. Laughing some, but I didn't want to laugh to hard.

"You married the Prince of Death I see." I was hiding my fingers from him; how did he know this. "You are wondering how I ended up in the walls?" I showed my hands rubbing my ring, as I was standing there looking at him strange.

"You need to get out of my head." Gotten to the top step of the porch when it was clear to me now that this was going to be a new normal to be the same age as my father. It's going to take a while, but I was trying.

"She told me about what she was going to do while I was away. She knew that I was going to die that it wouldn't matter much to me as I was just a piece to her puzzle. I held the Tin Starr genetic makeup, she needed it for her final move." How did she know then what was in his genetics as I didn't even know?

"Must be hardheaded like you if I picked the good side not hers." Rubbing my face as I didn't even feel my hands dropping my glasses.

"Did she even tell you as a kid about the three-prince rule?" It was an old Germanic story that she said was passed down from her third great-grandmother.

"Yes, she said that Freddie was the death prince, then there was a Paper Prince which held all historical attributes, and the third prince was of magic, that all his descendants were the very magicians that we know today." He came over sitting down near my feet putting a chill into the bottom of my feet up to the top of my head.

"If she gets the wand from the third, the pen from the first, and the bottle charm from the second she will be most powerful. There is a way to stop her." Edith was coming up the steps as he kept talking. "There is a wand made from the heartstrings of a women who refused to answer a German soldier back in the 40's, she was hung on the spot for standing her ground." He looked down to her boots that she was wearing. "You found the wand." She took it from her boot, standing pointing it at his head. Put my hands up trying to stop her.

"How do you know that's this is her wand?" Well! Answer her!

"You found it in the walls of that stone house in the woods behind this house. Because I told Mary where it was." He stood on his feet. "Can I go in the house now?" How do you parent your own parent?

"Yeah, Edith and I have a lot to think over." He walked in as the outside light went out then on as he walked in.

(Freddie!)

It was snowing two feet up in my old hometown tonight. The children do not know that there will be no school tomorrow. Haycook High never left you home. You had to risk your lives to get there for them to keep the student two hours then make you go home. Yeah, it is okay to almost kill myself let figure out how I am going to die to get back home. Walking up the road to the bus stop because mother's car could not get out of the driveway. A half a mile with snow up to your knees. Walking the middle of the road as that part of the ground stayed the warmest. Wear bright colors so the hunters did not shoot at you. Freeze your legs off waiting for the driver to come up the road. When you gotten home you had more laundry than you did if we just stayed home. Here in Dickson we only mostly get rain. Heavy rain where you can't see the thing in front of you. The trees make a sound as the wind try to push them over.

The smell of one was hitting me in the face, getting its revenge from me cutting it down. The base of this tree was a strong ox if I had anything to say about it. My boots just kept melting into the mud as fast as the rain hit the ground. A man in a long reporter's coat started walking trod me. All he did was bend down doing something to the tree's base while standing back up smiling at me all bubbly like walking away with my tree in my hands as I stood there out of breath. "Did he just take my tree?" he did not hear me as my voice was so little as I tried to figure out why a stranger wanted my tree. Running after him in this mud trying to slide. "Mister, hey mister you have my tree." The tree lot was across the road from the head house where a two floored house stood with a barn and a stable stood nearby. He took the pine resting it on the table with metal rings. Netting it like a turkey. He smiles. He did not look at me just went on his working way.

"I'll put it in the back of your truck when you're done." His red hat with ear flaps, and scarf started to move as he spoke. My gloves that where in my hands had fallen to the floor as I could not believe that he was doing this for me. His eyes looked at my face then my feet back to my face. My eyes watched his teeth the whole time. "Ike Snow!" He was giving me his hand, asking for my name. what does one do in this moment? You knew the answer shake his hand Freddie.

"Fred! I like Freddie you can't spell Freddie without!" I did not know if I was to take his saying my name as a corny joke or an insult. Felt bad I had to keep him talking as Walton heard he knows more than he is letting on. So, Walt is hiding nearby as I talk him up.

"Die! Love that about you!" Was I leading him on, I cannot tell southern men have a female nature to them, so you think they are the way they are, then at the same tones of children then you question yourself?

"How much is the tree!" He was smiling like he was trying to get me to laugh. Maybe that was it. He likes to make people laugh. All I watched was his muscles stand the tree up.

"It's on the house?" Did I honestly just look at the roof of his house. Freddie! He laughed; he even sounds goofy.

"Are you hitting on me?" I had to ask. The tree is now rolling some on the ground as his hands lost the grip. His voice was trying to get around it.

"It shows ha!" I was laughing now also shaking my head. "Those wrinkles near your eyes made me fall to my knees. Liking boys in the south is the hardest thing, please don't think anything I wasn't meaning anything if it hurts your feeling."

"No! I totally understand, my ex and I haven't seen each other in a few weeks." He was thinking! He smiles every time he thinks.

"Are you hitting on me!" Did I hear his voice go deep then hit a higher note at the end? I know your Jeremy Quick, but you do not remember who you are. Not yet!

"Nice giving it back to me!" He is now sitting on the table the tree was on. Black tight paints with red flannel was a good match for him. "Thanks again, Charles!" He smiled at me as I took out my wallet pulling out a World War One soldier sitting in a wheelbarrow. Both men had the same smile. He was in the field hospital for a mass on his right lung after getting mustard gas in the face. He still had a wheeze when he walked. He asked me what I needed.

"We have some Questions. Not going to hurt you! We know William saved you from being killed. We need to know where he is." He puts his hands down looking me in the eyes agreeing to help.

"William is my father!" So, it is true. There was this man who came out to see if all was okay as he was taking longer than normal. He pointed with his eyes. "He is William's father." Yes, I can see that. All three-look identical.

"Where is William?" Walton asked again!

June 12, 1944

Last night another officer asked me to go to the picture shows. We see, "Percy Hopper Mystery's." Later we ate at a local pub. This Bernard guy sure is funny. Hint: never fall to sleep and let Bernard see your journal on the floor. This happens.

Chapter 9
Watered Down Gravestones

(William!)

She was practicing her needle point. As the needle points at her through the fabric it would make her nipple point on end as if it gave him a reaction to the point that stares back at him. She is begging her maker to reserve her soul as the needle mocked her. Her toes stopped the rocking of her chair as she needed the room to be still. The only sound you could hear was the sparkle of the fire. Her rocking horse she played as a child moved without her moving it. The mirror frosted from time itself. The rabbit mask she made as a teenager hanging off one of the posts attached to the mirror on her dresser moved in a circular motion. The tips of her hair moving just like the others were outside her window. The family inviting the town fold for a bomb fire after the harvest moon. She wishes now that she never retired earlier than the others. If you look up to her room, her red hair made it look like a flame was dancing among the place. Her eyes lock onto her bed. As the bedding sunk making it look as if there was a stranger in her bed. Yet, there was no one else in the room with her in the room. She let out a cry, as she saw a man walk trod her. Just to get drowned out by the crowed. Nothing was able to harm her.

Her heart fluttered when the doorknob moved as she didn't know what was going to come after her. Think about this it was her mother on the other side of that handle to say her goodnights. When mother saw her child sleeping, or what she thought was sleeping she left the door open thinking the room was hot. She stood to her feet lighting the lantern on the table near her chair. Looking back at the moon's light shining off the blue fabric to the chair she was once just in. The upstairs were cold as cracks of darkness surrounded the halls with only the light from her candlestick's flame making its final appearance. A man's laughter filled her ears it was coming from downstairs and that was odd to the girl. Why was there a man in her house?. There were only ladies amongst the household, how did a man get in here without their word on the matter. The girl was the only one brave enough to try and see who was making that laughing sound. Stepping on the cat's paw gave her a scare but she wanted to see the man. Each step made a sound as she tried so hard not to let him know she was coming. The wallpaper was strange to her as for the first five steps it was the same old chipping-away paper that needed to be replaced, yet the mother never had the means to do so as she never had to entertain inside the household. Thus, why the girl rolled her eyes as she now wonders why she didn't wed as she never let her daughters place a name on their calling cards. By the sixth step her fingers felt the new grass' green color. This one night, this one night she would never forget. As she stood on top of the wood on the sixth step the flame was gone off her candle. She was wearing her nightgown before stepping down, now she wears her day dress with the purple flowers on the blouse. A steampunk dress was her favorite as she was able to wear a vest like thing, where only before this dress was sold did men wear vest with their suits. Dark red fabric rustling around her legs. As she stopped looking at the wall that was near the stairs as the hall right past them. The entry table her father carved was still there but in a different stain.

The height charts her mother started were still on the door casing going into the living room. The floors were still the same oak wood. Thing is there was this strange little box that was under the table attached to the wall as a wire came from it. The wire if her eyes were right was attached to this odd lantern that gave off heat with light, but it never needed to be held onto. Nor light. All she could see was two feet. She didn't know what to think as she saw his shinny shoes, but her eyes went right to the boots with mud on them sitting near the door as that is what she was used to. Her eyes locked into his ankles as she never seen thin fabric like that before. The sticking wasn't handmade. It was as if a machine did it, but the only mechanicals she knew were horse powered. As she stepped trod him, she got more of his features. He was standing with his back trod her. His leg attached to his ankles were curved as she outlined them with her eyes. The back of his knees was bent as he was looking into this mirror on the wall near the door. The eighth step he saw the upper part of his legs. She stopped at the tenth step as she never saw the backside of a man before. She lifted her hands as she framed his bottom with her hands. Watching his hips move as she was shaking from kneeling from looking at him. She watched his shoulder blades pump forward and back as he was combing his hair. She saw his hair reflect the light as it reminded her of the feathers of a crow that could fly in the wind when watered down. There was a chain that was hanging off the bottom of his vest, but it was placed in his vest's pocket. Hers was hanging from the fabric of the dress. His ears flapped some as he heard it. Before stepping off the last step she saw his long fingers handling the comb. He was standing in front of the mirror so she could see his face yet.

"Emma, what in the world are you doing down there?" She heard his sister speak. The candle had a light on it once more, as the house was back to the way she remembered. She went back up the stairs holding her nightgown up to not get it dusty. Putting her sister back to sleep. Tucking her in best she could. "Emma, tell me a story." That's when she gave her sister the best surprise that imagination was the key to her soul.

"See I was walking down the stairs as I was acting out the best story ever, until you caught me." The sister laughed as she wanted to know more. "I was meeting the man of my dreams."

"Prince stories. You never told me one before." Her sister was getting more excited.

"Well, I am going to call him my paper prince as he hasn't been pressed in a book like those violets you forgot to press yesterday. There is another prince story I was working on about a prince that came from time. He lives in my pocket watch. You could see him if you sit still long enough, he will run past the face. Like the man they say lives on the moon." Her sister tiptoes her fingers on her sisters' arm.

"There had to be three princes. Emma you must go back and find the third one. Three is a good luck number. Tell me about him when we have biscuits in the morning with mommy. Hope they have cheese on top of them." Emma gotten a smile on her face. As she saw the tin near her sister's bed held a daisy. Her sister learned that you could take a tin type photo and rub the image off onto another surface if you work at it hard enough. That or it was just dim luck. There was an image of a young man smiling on the surface of this daisy. She was hiding this from her that she was seeing the boy that sits in that photo. Her prince that she was hiding from the world. That's when Emma heard the man's voice again. This time she went to the top step looking at the wall to make sure they both were there. The old and the new. As her feet went down, she noticed the frames on the new wall had colored photos he wasn't from here that she noticed. Looking at the back of his head again there was this bow like string on the back of his hair. When she stepped onto the floor after the stairs, he turned to see who it was. He had on this mask that matched his flowing hair in color that went only around his eyes. His eyes were the deepest blue as his lips were small like of one of her glass dolls. Color of a blood orange forms the stitching of the skin on his lips. It was as if they took the dust off the moon and blew it on his skin as he gave off that glow you would see on a full moon's light. She thought that she might be able to touch his face, and it would chip away at her fingers like the eggshell color chipping paper of her mother's that she will not replace as her husband picked it out before his death. Thing is this young man looking back at her has his face. She was looking at her third prince. As he was her prince of death. A man who can see her as she is in the past as he is in the future. A man who could understand how she thought as he too lives as if he is still from her time. She had never seen a bowtie as the ties men wear in her time were big and puffy his was around his neck and smaller. The only similarities the two parties would have was the bow tie pin. The same tie on that sits in her dad's old button box. He was her descendent and she knew before she had fallen in love with her. There was a knock on the door as she started to go back to her world.

"Wait!" She ran to hear his voice. It was a soft voice like her father's too. He took after her looks. She knew it wasn't her father's imagination getting to her as she always knew something was different about her, there must be something different about him too. She didn't want to turn around to see him. "Emma, Emma Ivory!" She turned to see his face once more as she knew her name. Of course, he did as he was her descendent. Right! He placed his fingers against his chest as he told her something else that would catch her ear. "My Name is Kipper, Kipper your second son. Freddie was your first." He reached into the breast pocket of his suit coat as he placed the daisy in between his fingers. The same flower her sister was working on. "This is my father. Thing is I never got to ask you something." She wanted to know more but she didn't want to tarnish the time yet to come.

"Why don't you ask?" She said as it was a thirst that was after all.

"Why did you kill father, and yourself? What lead you to it?" Her heart beating so fast that she didn't know what to think. As she stood on the sixth step he was coming after her as she was in her world looking into his, he was in his looking into hers. She put her hand out to stop him as he reached for hers. When their fingers touched it zapped them both pushing her down as he had fallen to the floor. She had broken time as they weren't supposed to meet. As she looked down at him, she saw he wasn't dressed the same no more. He was wearing what she thought was long underwear, but to him it would be shorts to swim in. The last time she saw an octopus was at the world fair while eating caramel popcorn. As she looked down to the boy, he could see his torso as it was now bare. She thought it was something how where he comes from, they can draw a realistic Octopus that he now had on his skin. The head of the sea creature started near his neck and the eight legs went around his body. He looked down to what she was looking at as now he needed to learn where she had sent him. He turned before forgetting to tell her it is something, they called a tattoo. She feared the boy now as if time could change that fast what is stopping time from coming for her next. She didn't know what that was on his skin. She leads down to her feet where the faded printed flower was on the wood. Before finally leaving his world, she looked back as he stood taking it all in. She wanted to come back, but he put his hand for to stop as he knew she couldn't belong there. She ran to her room as she looked at the stairs before shutting her door. The house was back to the way it should be now. She lights all the candles and just started to write until she fell to sleep. Writing about all that she had experienced. She woke up at half past four in the morning. To find there was a strange lady in her room with blond hair. The lady was reading her notes as she burned them all.

"Emma, my name is Louise. You are more powerful than I thought. Your three sons are not as strong as you are. Don't worry I'm not going to harm you. I just want to know where you sent your son you just talked to." Emma knew she did what she had to protect the ones she loved. "Your grandson has your abilities. Your husband's too. I have to kill him if not he will kill you." Emma was smarter than that. She knew that her son was sent by her to her grandson's time to protect him he went young to fit in. That lady was tricking Emma and she knew it. the lady left warning that she be back. That's when Emma knew.

"Go get them me boy. Don't let them win." She was now interested on getting started on her journey to merry the man on the flower that was in between her fingers.

Kipper found himself in an odd town to him. He had to take clothing off the line outback just so people didn't stare. To the kids now the lady on her porch next door is old lady Betts to him she was a looker that he would agree to sweep the porch to watch her through her windows. Her mail box read Betts for Fred Betts the boy that was after her and knew that Kipper wanted her too. Thing was Kipper was sent in the future. This was the price to pay for him if he wanted it all. As he walked onto the pavement of the sidewalk, she stood there trying to remember his name. She knew his face out of a line up anytime. "Kipper." She cried. Her voice was the same with some crackling in it now. She was different on the outside, but eyes never changed. "Don't go far Grannie wants to talk to you." She walked into her house as the screen door swung to hit her in the arm as she went and grabbed something from the closet near the door. Kipper went and walked up to her porch as he felt bad for her in a way. She came out with that red checkered coat he had left at her house all those years ago. She kept it in the closet all that time, and never let her sons wear nor her husband. He placed his fingers on it as if it was yesterday, he saw it last. "I chose it for you all those years ago, but your mother said you had left for school. I knew better than that. Your house was the odd ball house that no one wanted to be near as they said it was a haunted house and you played with ghost. I loved the idea of it." Kipper sat on her porch as he thought about it. he wished he stayed with her and grew older with her too. Then he looked at the mailbox near his house that he just came from. It read the Green family now. Her eyes followed his as she knew. "Your family moved from there the year after you went away to school. They never came back, they moved to a different county. When I went to visit you at their new address, they left with my parents, I was told by your brother you died while serving in the Navy. I knew better then too." Everyone he knew was dead. Kipper didn't have anywhere to go. "I had one son. I named him Kipper. He died while working on a car. They all called him Babe. I knew you were coming back I just didn't know when. So, I sat here every day until you showed up again. My granddaughters' bus is running late today. Babe had one child before he died. My husband died looking for him as we didn't know where he was for weeks. No one thought to look at his garage." The bus pulled up after a few minutes. As she gotten off the bus, he thought he was seeing things. She was the image of her grandmother if she ever saw one. The older lady on the porch saw the same look in his eye the day he fallen in love with her, now she sees it with him. He had a new home now as she knew her wait was now come full circle. Kipper put one hand behind his back like a butler as he walked the granddaughter to the porch. Once inside the older lady on the porch asked him to let her get to her homework as she had one last thing to say. "Kipper, this Freddie, your great nephew. Think it's time you two talk." What Kipper didn't know is that the last time she meets his mother she told her all that had happened as she knew that this day would come. You never know the roles people will play in your life until you live in it. Kipper looked at him with the childlike look.

"You have my mothers' hair, blonder than red." Freddie was shy as well. This was before William.

"I have to ask you about something. My Uncle Harvey, your brother told me that you knew the story of the passing bells that we needed to find them." He put the coat on over the shirt he was wearing as he knew what he needed to do next.

"To tell you is to show you. Let's go!"

June 17th, 1944

Edith sent me a dress pattern of a ballerina wedding dress; I get the hint.

Chapter 10
Corkscrew Lullabies

(Freddie!)

"The wind chimes were ringing in the morning as the air was slowly waking. The fish in the riverbed just singing along as they swim getting ready for the war ahead as they never knew if there were bears out there looking for them. Male fairies opening the flowers for their acting career was short but lush. Fog so thick that you could not see the hand in front of you. Top of the trees making a sound so grim that it put a chill down your spine. A house that was built with no one inside sits alone in the woods awaiting someone to find it to make its purpose whole again. Stone walls with a wooden floor inside all handmade. Just left there as if the people were running from something. Doors swing open with the wind like a child dozes when he or she has nothing to do. One soldier on each side of this empty farmhouse. One boy takes in the making of the house, the rock walls, the stain glass window in the sitting room. Wondering what it be like to own one of these one day and not have to fight a fight he did not want to begin with. The other boy out of bullets trying to figure out how to melt down the metal roof later when he starts his fire. Both at the same time, with the same movement make a sound as their boots hit something on the ground.

One hits the shovel almost hitting himself in the face, the other runs right into the clothing line almost taking his own head. When they got their footing, they look into the glass of their windows locking eyes. When the house was made two windows were placed so that way it could look right through the house on either side. They both lock eyes at the same moment when the one boy held up his gun with one hand and tried to keep his helmet on with the other. The other boy feeling the moister from the yarn uniform he was wearing, and the bullet-less gun he was holding tighter than anything else. They each walk to the back of the house. Stepping trod each other slowly. The one boy holding the gun could feel his legs getting weaker as the other boy felt the same. The one boy puts his gun down and puts his hands in the air. Telling him if he was going to kill him to do it already. There were no bullets for him anyway.

The one with the advantage was from England he did not understand his France way of talking. His eyebrows arch as the other one with the gun in his hands laugh. Asking the one with his hands in the air if he was hungry. His gun down rested right next to the other one. They ate day old crackers with some beans, told stories of their past. Wondering if they should go back. The one man asked, if he gave him a meal that he deemed something in return. The other man agrees as it was only fair. "Anything!" He thought about it, yet he knew what he wanted. When you're lost and alone going without for a long time you would want this in return as well. He had to throw out all he knew as a man to ask this of him, but he did. He asked for the other man's lust. At first the other man said no, but then he did say, anything.

The one man who was given the food stands facing the window he once past. Standing there telling the other man he was ready. The other man now standing right in front of him. Both men watching the other in their own eyes. He unbuttoned his pants down until he came to a stop. Letting it all fall around his ankles. Falling to his knees as the one who gave was getting something in return. Butterfly kisses on his legs around his calf of each leg. Behind the knee tickles a little. All the way up. Now the man standing puts a hand on each side of the window casing. Feeling the wood as there was now a tongue lining the cracks from the tip starting with the tail bone all the way down the middle. Feeling the heaviness of the others breath as he finished behind his sack where it was most tender. Only the glass, and I say only the glass heard his cries when he deemed. It was soft like cotton candy but red like a candy apple. Now standing himself, resting his hands on the others backside. Letting himself venture into the unknown. The one man placed his hands on the others backside letting himself feel the freshness that the other body gave off. How hard it was to break the skin. The other felt something going inside a place he did not know he could feel. Yet was both ashamed for it being there. One hand on the back of the other man's head forcing it back so he got a reaction. He liked it when his cheeks smiled as it made the letter C, on each side of his face. He laughed as he liked the way it was when it hurt him so. Liked it hard he did. Both wet from the workout as they switched positions. Two passing bells chime at the same time. As one sack hit the other would move. Once was done, they both went to put on their clothing going back to the fight once more. Leaving with the notion that their paths will cross again and they would never forget that night even though the fire was now smoke. War was done, now go home. Yet they pass the windows at the same time once more. Raising a family

116

of their own in the very house they meet. Still the windows line as they wait another's path."

We. I mean, Kipper and I were back in that old house that we had gone to as kids behind my house. It was here not the house I grew up in. Not yet as this was a different time. See the two men in that story he told were true men. That happened to them. There was one part where the story leads to the one man carving his name into the wood of the doorframe. Yet it does not say which one. So now we are looking at all of them.

"Kipper! What did that story mean to you?" He thought of it, whatever is in that stuff that we put in the tea, let it stay unknown. His skin started to look green almost like moss was growing. "You're an Orm! They are people born of one human parent, and one Orm parent. The child takes on both features of the parents in the DNA structure. Their hair looks normal but when you touch it, it feels like bark. On their skin in patches are glowing green moss. Most humans have body hair that is theirs. Every time they step, they leave a flower." He smiled as there's under one hundred of them left. Kipper covered the moss as he was scared.

"See my mother would tell that to us when we were kids. Not in detail as much but when I grew up, I investigated it more. She taught that to us so it would teach us that if we take something, we must give something in return. Then at the same motions we must pay our own way, and don't be mindful of the hand that feeds you." Some mother wish I had one of those. Mine just drank her heart out and slept with a man a week. Getting the only job, she could at the racetrack to pay the rent. She never told me grandfather's house was owned by Bo's family which she lost it on a horse. "Kipper! We shouldn't look any more it is getting dark." His voice kept getting smaller, and smaller as I looked. He dropped the whole Orm thing, but I was not done with him yet.

"In here, Freddie I found them." Where are you? Kipper this was not funny. Found him in the room where William and I first talked about where this relationship was going.

The room was different as when we redid things the rocks were not exposed no longer. His square like fingers lined the inlay of the name that were in the wood. I put my hand on his shoulder as he did a good thing. "James Grey, and Hunter H."

The two of us looked at one another as we did not speak. There was a voice in the back of my head looking for me to help him. This was another one of Ms. Louise's tricks. My hands got tense as I felt his breath on the back of my neck. "Help me!" His breath was scarce as I felt his fingers on my spine. As I turned there was a man standing behind me with a railroad nail going through his neck. Thing was I felt the tip of it in the back of mine. He placed his hand on my chest as he started to fall, I could feel them trying to grab at me to keep standing yet he was slowly leaving us. His hands grabbed at my belt. There was not much to do but lay him down. Begging for help. Put my hand on his chest now. As I looked him in the eyes. He was crying. Could still feel the reaction on my skin of his hands grabbing at my shirt.

"Go into the light as soon as you stand. That is all you must do. Don't let them try and talk you into anything else." He let out a notion of a negative. Just two letters to fill my ears. He took my bottle from my neck and opened it. Handed it back to me. When he closed his eyes, his soul stood. I stood too, but he wanted the bottle.

"With me you shall win, without me you will die." He had fallen backward like the lady ghost did before. When he turned to smoke, I thought it was just like what she did. But Kipper kept looking around asking me if I heard the knocking too. When I looked at my bottle, he was in there standing. They cannot get to him as he can't see them as the photo inside hide him yet I can see him from the bottom, and he cannot hear them as it's enclosed. Someone was coming I knew it he would not have done this if there was not.

"Take off your clothing now. I said, now!" He was looking at me strange. Really you had relations with the ghost I wear on my neck, and this makes you blush. Kipper took his coat and things as he stood there with nothing on. Just two hands to cover up what he did not want me to see. "Here!" I wanted his hand, but he would not give it to me. "Take this from me."

"What is it?" He laughed as it tickled him. Kipper do not laugh.

"A strawberry chocolate dragon he will dress you. Eat him!" Well he did that with no pretense. I bent down to close the eyes of the man who just gave his all for me. Still has more to give. We changed history, robbed it as if it was a bank.

"That's not the man I had relations with." Come again!

"Come again?" Kipper took my words out of my mouth.

"That's a man they found in the woods." He said, they! High heels lined the inlay of my ears. The smell of red lipstick filled the air. And a blonde youngish lady stood in the doorway.

"See I am not that mean. I let history be. For you anyway! Yes, it's fun killing dead soldiers before they know they are who they are meant to be." She was everything and more that William told me about her.

"What do you want Ms. Louise?" Yes, I know what you are thinking. William is not here yet and I am alone somewhat.

"I wish to talk with my son. Then you. Maybe we can get to a reason for all of this." She was meaner than my mother, never thought it was possible. "Your father was the best dead solider. Did all I said, and more. Think you do not know your father. Thing is I do not know him at all myself. That man you think was him. Is not him. They were good at hiding things from me. I want to talk to him in two days. If not, I will kill you Freddie Starr! You mark my words." She started to walk away. Yet I was letting her. She was gone like the ghosts do but she is the mother of the timeline, so anything goes. The man who she had pointing the gun at us slowly turned to stone. Just closed my eyes while he screamed as he closed his when I did.

"Hunter, that man in the woods right now his name is Hunter. He never told me his last name." He looks good after eating a chocolate dragon and all. Sharpe dressed if I do not mind me saying.

"He comes back, here right?" I said.

"Yeah, why?" Kipper added.

"We must stay and figure out the last name to Mister Hunter." His last name is my last name too.

"Freddie! Orms are rare because we can kill people who are in The Silver Leaf Society. Ask William who they are later, much later he doesn't know about us yet!" Will do.

"Tell me more about this society!" He swung his fingers in the air.

"See people in the society are called to hunt Tin Stars. They're called to protect history, and the timeline as much as possible. Your Ms. Louise has been at war with the Before because they are protecting the members of the society. The Orms have been sent in to hide the Glass Knight population until they are needed. You must know that her army is only after you to protect you. I know that, but your more powerful than everyone else in this war. So, they all have you targeted. I was sent to make sure you, Edith and William end this war."

"Thing is we are always apart when we are needed to be together." That needs to change.

Do I tell William what I know now?

Thanksgiving 1944

I give thanks to the underwear mom sent
in her package.

Chapter 11
Golden Silhouette

(Freddie!)

She was getting off Dickson if I was ready for it or not. She does not even talk of it any longer. Says seeing his headstone right next to the young cop who was shot in the head was just too much. As she knew both as deep as the water was in her cup when she brushed her teeth. Just yesterday she was taking our picture with her phone as I made a face holding up the peace sign with my fingers. There was nothing I can say to make her stay. See the police officer who was killed was her Scotts best friend from church. First day on the job and he was told to go in alone on a job made for several men. She asked me why everything gets taken away from her. There was nothing I was able to say as she told me I gotten everything. Yet with our love there came a price and I had to pay for it. This is a modern new world yet why is there a floppy disk on the top of my page I am typing on? Walton was taking her to London where she was going to become something bigger than herself. Thing was a week after being there we gotten a phone call saying that even the man who took her there he was staying with her. Mom took Kelly away from us moving him west with his family. I was fighting to keep my brother, but the bigwigs, you know the ones who know how to run my life better than me. The ones who get drunk most nights as their lives whittling down with time. They took her side not mine. Aunt Mary moved away as well, but for the meantime she cannot for the house still needed to be sold in the new owner's name. See, thing is, she thought everything was gone from her life when I was losing it all.

"Woken up and you weren't there. I gotten scared." Why did the coldness of your chest feel colder than normal? Your muscles on your arms flexed different than usual. You were just making my feet feel the metal bed frame. You were just letting your tongue do things you only wished for as you wanted our relationship to go there. I let you just get away with most things people dream of, yet here you are acting as if I was a stranger. You were not wearing a muscle shirt last time I closed my eyes. What is going on? Your hair was not that long before. I never agreed to a man bun before. My fingers ran up underneath that fabric you were wearing. There was something odd about your skin. You just let out a heaviness out of your lips and brushed my hands off your body.

Okay I will follow you. Hey, you are going into the wrong room. It is the second on the left. Why are you going into the first on the right? Was the bed always this small, and how come you put the bed in the middle of the room? Go along with this Freddie, he is going through something. You let my fingers under the rim even let me explore into your garden, but you made sounds as it felt good enough. There I was now sitting around your form as you let the fabric to your shirt lift. Never opened your eyes to see me. "William! When did you get another tattoo?" He had a tree with the works going up his right side on his ribs with a cowboy on his horse underneath it. In exceptionally fine detail. Your head tilted back as your mouth was letting all your reactions go into one lust timeless memento as you let my tongue ride down your Emotions. Start from the tope where the candy center starts and swirl down like I was waiting for my haircut sitting in the metal rocket as the man cuts the hair. Your hand on the back of my head as you really enjoyed the experience.

"Oh, Edith harder!" My eyes looking up to the bottom of your jaw.

"William, I know I sound like a lady, but you know that Edith isn't here." William opened his eyes. When he saw me, it was as if I was a stranger in his bed. His back on his headboard as he tried backing up, yet the wall stopped him. He feared me. His eyebrows were arched, and he regretted the whole thing.

"Who are you? Why are you in this room. Thought my girlfriend." I looked at him strange.

"William, stop this I am your husband." I put my hand on his foot, yet he ran to the other side of the room. I sat at the edge of the bed. I looked around to the room and seen what was in it. This was a different time. "What year is this?" He was not going to talk but he thought if he did, I would go.

"1944! Now go!" His face was blushed, and his hand over what my mouth was just around. I am going to sick.

"I was told that this might happen. Freddie, I was told by you are you are going to tell me to remind of Freddie." His mother named her mission after the person it was about.

"Freddie, what you know about this Freddie boy. I know him yet you don't." I was losing him too. It was like my life was crushing before it could hit the ground.

"I am Freddie!" He needed me to say something else. Could hear the back of his heels kick at the wall as he tried so hard to get an escape.

"Then if you're Freddie when was the first time I said it." It! Oh, it!

"We were in your father's 40's red truck. You reached over me to unbuckle my seat belt when all I could do was not scream over the smell of pine off your skin to your arm. Kept trying for the stick shift as you did not know where to put your hands. When your hand always went to me knee. So, we retired to the bed of the back of the truck, when you asked me not to say we were at the movies together. I asked what you were hiding from. You told me that no matter the time nor place I will always love the man who landed in the land of ash. As we must start again after the fire in our heart gets watered down. So, we ran into the future. Knowing that we were testing the odds. Yet time caught up to us. Aunt Mary, your sister at the time, used her magic to make us four again so that way we might love again. So, my brother and your mother had to raise us. We grew up again thinking they were our family in a opposite way. They say they killed a man, two men to make one trip to have a future they hope to fight for as we could not love each other in the time we were in. Yet the truth comes out at the end." How is that for an answer?

William gotten up from where he was sitting. Did not know my next move put him at edge but he went anyway. Put something on that would make him not be so nerves as I had to take heed of the situation that I was in. Gym shorts were not his grandfathers that day his father gotten drunk they were his. Green is his favorite color. I went over to the mirror he had on the wall. It was strange how things were now and yet when we come from the new now things really have not changed much. His mother was outside having herself a cigarette without a light at the end of it. Let it sit in her lips. Gets her fix, and not letting it kill her at the same time. He had a cigarette holder on his dresser too, but not be his as he never smoked. His was tin plated, with a cartoon sailor on the top. Another mirror was attached to his dresser with his wallet resting near that square metal holder. Underneath the two a small cloth that was hand put together by a loved one no longer with us. All I must do is stop this, yet I did not want to.

"Freddie, have you ever wondered why I tan so fast in the summer where you don't?" Why did he ask me that, he never done that before? "That metal tin square you keep your eyes on holds the answer. If anything happens tonight, then take it." That is was odd for him to say to me then at the same time he was trying to get his mind onto the fact that I am whom I say, I ought to be.

"How did I come to be here. I was sleeping next to you waiting for a sound of my brother getting up so I can help him get ready for school, yet I travel back into time. This don't make much sense." He was shaking as he was bent over the water basin letting his tears gather in its water. My finger lines his backbone as he laughed as they ventured up to his head. William then stood in place and turned letting his hands do all the talking. He wanted to dance. So, I went along. Trust was the clue here.

"What am I going to find in that tin mister?" Not fair knowing all the words to that old song we dance to. I knew the music humming it faster than the words came from your lips. He was trying not to say but I can tell he wanted to.

"My father's birth record. See when we travel into time, I have to tell you other information as we were hiding, but if you bring the truth into the future." It might just do the trick to stop this whole Dark Fantasy War. Why don't I capitalize on an important historical event you asked me that many times before, well this is my war not yours.

"I don't understand, yet I do the Louise I knew never talked about her husband before." That means William knew this whole time and now was trying to uncover the mission's core. He went to the wrong war before when he sent that message to Edith's phone. So, he had to let me come back to the only time he knew the information and kept it from his mother. He thought he got it from the horse's mouth, but he could not find that man. See he died when we were four just like my father. I think they were killed together. No! Now I get it. Michael is William's father. Why say that well the time frame gives it away number one, and number two! I would have to get back to you on that one. He must be his father. Why else would one try to help me by getting me this far and not the other unless they are trying to get her to not understand yet let me know in an odd way of thinking knowing I know how they know. Wow, that was a big thought.

"Freddie, my father was born on October 21, 1894 in Albania." Let me picture it he was about nine when he came here with his grandmother, and when he did the other kids did not take kindly to him, and she was the one who was the only kind. Taught him our ways and they loved one another and had you. Your story fits. Yet why hide him? She did not want William knowing the truth as it will hurt her in the long run. Why tell him of his father as he might take his side at the end? This whole time I knew who he was. That was not your grandfather in your compass, that was your father. That man who took over your body was him too. He was trying to get us away from her, yet I did not see it. Thus, why William made me come here. Knocking at the door. He let his hands go from mine. His hands went running in his hair. I felt sick.

"William, dear who is this?" She now had a soft tender voice. The man they killed was his father. Poe my son knew the truth and was trying to get me to tell him just as I now got the information the same way he tried getting it from me. William is in that Compass.

"Freddie, mother I did good right?" What? William!

"Yes, you did and early too." His hands were trying to tell me something. They talked but I did not listen. I went over to get his wallet and the tin metal square. Putting them into the back of my underpants. "I will deal with him; holidays came very early this year, must have been a good girl." Her hands grabbed my face as she was looking me over trying to figure out how to get my gift. William lips said like a silent film to sit on the ground. He taught me to read lips in school, his way of teaching me tricks in case of things like this was to come. I am bad at reading clues.

He was wearing blue boxer shorts with yellow rabbits. She was considering her lips in the mirror. Like my people always taught me to never have a mirror big enough to see your eyes. They were neighbors to my family I remember; there I was sitting on my father's lap reading a paper. This is odd even for me. I was reliving it all from this moment. His hands rose as he killed her for me. She fallen to the ground as the powder in her makeup case cascaded around him. I did not go near it, yet he was around it much more then I was. The dust went away and there he was four years old and all. That Powder was her magic. Took a blanket and ran down the stairs. Mary on the phone as Uncle Harvey was standing next to her. They were my age, this was scary.

"What happened here? Never mind! Give me William. Hey, you were never here. You understand." She asked me to give him up now that this needed to be. She ran over to the party where it all begins. When my father left, she entered. William's father came up to mine talking to him. As both had their hands on the hood of his car smiling and all. The three men who dragged me out from a dream I was not supposed to be in, silently put a round in each of their heads. I watched as the ghost came about. Uncle Harvey turned me around as I was not to see them take the bodies elsewhere. Hard thing is Officer Blue was the man holding the gun, as I watched Bradly witness the whole thing.

"You have to go back to your timeline. We will take care of things here. You go. We all have to." I grabbed the back of his arms.

"I don't know how?" He threw me off him as I hit the wall. My head hit a mirror as the glass went into my head, I fell to sleep waking up near William again. Thing is I had a sore neck where it went into and could still feel the sting. William looked at me as he thanked me for completing the task, yet I still remembered her as an older lady. The timeline changed for all but me and him as we did not get back here until after it all happened. Now we only had one more thing to find. What is it? Found my way to the sink where I found myself then sitting on the edge of the tub. Took my phone that was charging on the sink, texting Officer Blue.

Freddie: Officer Blue I need you to talk to me about something.

Blue: About what Freddie? I am working can it wait.

Freddie: I do not know can you tell me, why you killed my father.

Blue: How do you know about that?

Freddie: So, it is true than!

Blue: Yes! You must know it was to protect you.

Freddie: Who made you do this?

Blue: Louise Starr.

Freddie: Where is his body?

Blue: I did not kill William's father she did that on her own.

Freddie: What!

Blue: You witnessed her do that to the soldier not me. The soldier was his father.

Freddie: I saw his father's ghost talking to me dad then.

Blue: Sorry! (My phone started to ring. Halstead did not have a clue that William found his dad in the wall. He was lying.)

"Hello!" A female voice.

"Yes, who is this? My name is Alice, Officer Alice and my partner just killed himself by putting his gun to his head." My phone dropped as she begged for me to help. All I could do was pick it back up and push the end button on the screen. Took the records he made me bring with me. Taking a picture of them. Then uploading it to the genealogy website everyone uses these days. Now the truth it out there. William, I hope this is what you wanted? Now my mother's calling! Great! I let the phone ring as William sat there with his hands up wanting to dance as I returned to his arms. He sang and I hummed. Sick in a way yet let the song play. They say the truth will set your free, yet I witnessed all these killings again, and again with no blood on my hands. Why hide from something? All I know is that we stopped a war from coming or is it still here. You can kill the body but not the rest. Well you will have to see, I guess. His lips tasted like honey tonight.

Some reason William needs to have yogurt and spear shaped pickles about this time. I love those two together myself, but he never did. Must be a pacific brand with the big giant bird on the glass. Cannot be anything but the best I was told. Knowing Poe's birth date, I knew what was coming, yet I was not letting him know this information as he lost the last one, I must let him have this win. He thinks I do not know about losing the last one, but I do. Gotten his things, and I was alone this time. There are not many times I get by myself in both worlds that is hard to do. This boy found himself in the secondhand store. For technical difficulties I will not say the name of the store, so I do not get into trouble. Kelly in the carriage, it is strange how they call them buggies.

Each is own I guess in the matter at hand, but it is strange how we live on the same soil, yet we say a different thing for the item we are pushing around the store.

"Freddie! How are you it's been a while." She said that being I just saw her in the last place we were at. She is the best lady in town, never lets her older neighbors sit home, she brings them here to shop. She has salt and pepper hair, and she loves to joke around. Cannot remember her name but I remember her face. I was coming out from the dollar store one time when she saw me walking to me car and she blew her horn making sure she saw me. She always has a smile. She had a heart attack last year and I must ask about that every time.

"Good, and you! Moms doing well. Family's okay for the time being what it is, and all." We said our good days and went about our ways. My eyes watched as Kelly was watching another man in a curious way as he past her from behind. Thing is I seen it too. He was talking to a lady on the phone, Kelly and I laughed together as he even said his voice sounded like a cup of tea falling onto the floor. Cracking with every word. There was a piano on the sales floor. He keeps going to it like a fly to the lamp I forgot to plug in. He was wearing red jeans, and a light button up, not buttoned, and a purplish red shirt underneath. His hair was long but pushed back like a girl's in the eighties. His nose looked as if someone came up to him and broke it many times. It was as if the piano was calling him into its web. He was young like me, yet his soul was an old one. He has been here on this planet before with a different identification, and all the dressings to go with it. He was like asking for an ice cream with sprinkles and yet they were out of the rainbow sprinkles, and you leave knowing what you wanted will never be there.

To me he felt like those big named men you learn in class that created masterpieces with the pianos and now you learn about them in music class. He still to this day plays now knowing who he was, nor what he did. It was as if he was playing his funeral song. I get this old church basement feel when I see him. Bringing me back to my grandfathers' basement. I get this feeling he knows he is already dead, yet he still walks among us all. He was like me and do not know it as his gift has not been turned on yet. If at all.

"Freddie, I think I am going to be sick. I'm getting a bad chicken taste in my mouth like you let it sit in your mouth forever, and a day." I was getting the same thing. To me he was walking around in his funeral makeup as he will not let the lady put the lipstick on his lips as he was not ready to go yet. I was also watching his buttocks move, not letting William know. But I see him lying in his coffin in a tuxedo when I do. He was a dead man walking. "Freddie, I see him standing there behind his coffin smiling as all went up to it. He is waiting for that moment to come." How does a little boy see this stuff? Freddie, you did. He brushed me when he passed looking back to me. Apologizing! A few weeks later he was in a car crash, and his funeral was the next day. Kelly wanted to go. This was his first, so we did. The lady we talked to went as well as not many people were going not even his parents were going to show themselves. Dark as he was lost when he was here, but he was still like that any away. He was standing facing the wall not his body.

"Why do you face the wall Kipper!" There are two Kippers in school this one, and Kipper Gray. Too bad he was the nice one. Kelly was the one who asked him. Good for him I was not that brave with my first.

"They're coming this way. Have to protect you two." His hands were shaking as he investigated something even, I could not investigate. He was crying as his voice was telling us so. I stopped my brother from talking.

"Who is coming Kipper?" I asked. She went into the rest room we are alone.

"Ms. Louise and her army. Freddie you cannot kill her. Only I can. You have to get me close enough." Odd fellow.

"Why do you kill her not me?" What he said was not right, was it.

"She killed me in front of you before. Kelly let me out of the bottle to live again, so I can fall to your feet once more." The man in the past she killed he put himself into my bottle.

"Kipper, how can you kill her? We have been trying to figure that out this whole time." He looked back for just a single moment to smile as I saw tears on his face.

"Even you can't touch her without bleeding. Yet I am the only one who can pull her heart out." He told us to run somewhere quiet. The sound was gone because they were all around. I took Kelly by the hand as I was shaking. As he took his hand away from mine there was a chocolate dragon in his palm. I asked him to leave as soon as the lady with the gray hair came out of the bathroom. He sat on the floor near the restroom door while putting his hands over his ears. The doors were shaking as the walls started to crack. The windows busted falling to the ground.

"Let them come Kipper." William was in his suit, and he still has the cuff links I gave him last year with the bee on it. He looked at me. I told him to stay home. "What you think I wasn't letting you fight this alone. I followed your twos." Glad he did.

"You're making me miss the best play in years for this. London's that way boys." I was smiling. Edith always knew!

"Edith what are you? No, not going to ask, but happy you're here." She smiled at me too, as she grabbed her wand from the side of her heels.

"You are moving to London after this don't say no." I was not. She took my hand. "Walton's now coming." His heart was breaking I knew it.

"Oh!" No Glass Knight that is great.

"I mean from the front; He's going to attack from behind them with his buddies from London. There are a lot of Glass Knights over there." I made William form a metal masquerade mask for me to wear. With this suit I was ready. Let me die tonight in my own bloodshed. No one else. Kipper kills the queen.

December 1st, 1944

Happy birthday, Nanny Martha! Wish you
were here.

Chapter 12
Empty Lipstick Tube

(Freddie!)

There was a man who thought he was having a friend over tonight as his dog barked to get inside, the pug's head kept tilting as he heard his owner make sounds that he's never made before. The harder it got, the louder he got.

She was on top as he was on the bottom. His fingers felt the silk as she started to do more than dry out his liquor. Getting him to react to her before the party began. Her kisses on his skin from his neck down felt like sandpaper. Her hair was stiff like wood. She is stopped as he gotten up to let the dog inside. She screamed for him to get back there, yet her voice changed. Like when the needle goes to the next song on a vintage record. Before he opened the door, he felt his skin there was dried green skin particles all over him. He thought it was her makeup. Yet she was not wearing any. This was when he turned to see that his friend was not really a person but a shell of a once was. An empty body, no organs, nothing but the skin and hair laying over bones.

He started to get scared, but that made her come back to life so she could suck the life from his body the moment he let those monkeys land on the carpet. See what he wanted she was going to give him, but she wanted him to be with her until death do them in, he was young. She would be able to live longer as he would take her place. He turned to see an empty body as even the eyes were gone. She had been six feet under for a few years, but now she sits in his bed. Still dressed in the something nice. His tongue was just in her mouth as now flies started to come from his own. Good thing the monkeys on his boxers were covering their eyes as they did not want to see this very moment. When he looked to his bed again, he kept hearing her call for him to join her in bliss, yet he kept backing up to the door. When the flies were gone. She started for him, but then she crashed into a glass wall. They could see one another, but she could not touch him. He tried to get away to leave but he was now boxed into the space. Cold was just the start when he heard an elevator sound. He closed his eyes when I told him to open them.

"What is going on here? You are Stu's brother, aren't you?" He was breathing extraordinarily strong now.

"Yeah and you told her you were eighteen, so she brings you home. Good one! Going to bed with someone four times your age." He held his hat in front of him as he knew what she was going to do, and it scared him so bad that he did not know what to think. You could see the thinking going on in his head on his face as his lips were apart and his blush wasn't going away. His eyes didn't blink like a toy almost. "Look you're the only boy who was nice to my brother. Even talked him from killing himself the first time. For that you are like a brother to me and if this war is true more is coming. Not like her, but there is something else. You gotten away because you are a Glass Knight! Stu knew that, and never said anything to me about it. What is one well. The only other one I know of is now here." I threw over a bag of clothing in it. He looked to be my size.

"Why are you being nice to me? I had nothing to do with you before why start now?" He was trying to be brave he was on the right start. I felt for him as I could see his muscles get weaker as he spoke. He didn't know where to turn.

"Did you really want me to let you stay there and let her eat away at the one place your covering up right now? I can send you back. Oh, and one more thing." He smiled when William came in the door.

"William Starr, you gave me the courage to be in the play last year. You're a true person." He needed to be taught to never trust a person. William winked over to me.

"I think we should have let her eat him. All I have to do is snap and look the other way." I laughed a little and had to leave the room.

"No! You don't have to do that." He smiled; William always loved to get your goat. You got the boy to blush now William.

"Were you really his friend?" I stood there and looked him in the eyes. I never gotten answers to Stu's death. Why not get them now. He sat there thinking. He played with the rim of his hat as he smiled. His face red. "Worth! My name." About time I get a name to the face in the photo that's stuck in the corner of my mirror in my room that Stu was also in.

"Stu, he and I were going to run away together. He thought that he was not welcome here no more as your life was getting bigger you didn't have room here for him no more." He was my world. Then William came here and changed his outlook.

"What were you going to do when you got to where you were going?" Edith thank you for asking that. He stood as if he had to ask for my permission.

"He was going to ask me to ask you if it was alright if we gotten married." He licked his lips and rested his hands on his sides. His tears washed her green skin off. I went to the last person who saw him living, giving him a hug. His hands now on my shoulder blades. Felt like big bear claws that warmed with his touch. Worth gave me this vintage fifty popular kid vibe every time we locked eyes it was as if my brother knew he was an older soul. Maybe my brother was able to more than he was saying he could. "See, Stu got the okay to start having relations again from his doctor. So, we did. In that house you used to play in as kids. He was not supposed to die. We had plans. I thought maybe if I could get with her, then I be a different boy, but then who am I kidding." Edith stop crying, oh that is me.

"Just yourself." I whispered. You must act like them, be like them to fit in yet how come we must be them not our own person. In a plastic doll world always in a plastic doll world. If the parts fit, they say that is right, yet our parts fit in a different way how come that is not right because it doesn't have a prize at the end. I don't know about you, but we have a prize at the end too.

"They're coming! Five of them are approaching." Kipper let out the twilight bark.

"Five minutes, Freddie then I need to know that he is living. Freddie, Stu is alive." What!

"What" Thank you! Worth is smart.

"He is in the mountains. See he said he has the gift now and so he was now running so they go after him, but they must have found out." Edith stopped me from hitting him.

"Where do you think Walton is?" Her eyes never lie.

"You have to live for him. Freddie you can't die, and Stu did this for nothing." My brother was supporting my cause and he was giving himself up for me. Yet why did they play it like they did? They let me bury him for nothing. What is it that they tried to hide but everything from me? I was mad at them and I must take this anger into this war. I went to the front door as I opened it. The air was still. Just last year I was on the other side of that statement that Worth said to me. I know what a gay boy must go through to get the something a boy has who is not gay. To this day you cannot change a person from that. My feet gathered on the step of the funeral home's porch. Edith stood at my side. Let them come. I was done. Thing is why would Worth bring a date to a funeral home in the first place? Makes a person think. My blood orange red hoodie was missing, Stu was wearing it last. He was the boy in the red hood that jumped off the firehouse roof. Thing is where did they get a body to take his place? They were here!

"Hello their son!" My father, one.

"Where is my William?" Louise, two.

"You, don't have to do this." William's uncle, three.

"I get the one called Worth." The green skin lady, four.

"You see nothing!" The man who was there when my father was gunned down, five. I was scared, but I had to stop this before it begins. Heroes never truly wear tights and fly. Kelly's is a talking dog who reads books. Why couldn't I get a paper that told the future and I had to run around the city trying to figure it all out?

"How does it work? Getting my gift." Edith could not see them so there is nothing else to do but go inside. She was not happy with this. Her face said it all.

"Why do you need his gift for? You got what you wanted in life why do you need control of it all?" Kipper stay out of this.

"This one will die for you every time. He was good, wish I didn't kill him." She was sent in for more than the man with the monkeys on his boxers. I heard Kipper cry out about them coming, triggering the others. Maybe the gift doesn't transport itself to others, maybe it mirrors itself. Like when I was a ghost boy it was protecting the host it was in.

"It's what I gotten. I got to live longer than my dad. I gotten her son to love longer than she did. I gotten Worth for a friend. I was able to keep the happiness in his nephew, and I gotten the chance to save her dinner. They all have a reason to hate me. They do not want my gift. They want something else. They want what they cannot have. Being I have it." No, there is more.

"You unlocked something that no human has been able to without even knowing you did it. You weren't supposed to get this gift, yet you did." See that lady I told you about that her husband told her to get to bed. While giving birth to my father she died, but she was sent back. Her child did not get the gift like me, and it brushed into him, and passed to me. My birth was almost the same, but it was different at the same time.

"I have nothing for you. You leave now!" Then my father told me something.

"Run!" So, did I!

There once was a time where I thought my life was a place where it needed to be. Like it was something else but what it was. You would think a boy who sees ghosts would be a better person for it as he helps all those people. Well I cannot be remembered for being a drawing someone did then put it out as a cartoon. I ran the wrong ways. The boys whose funeral I was at he ran with

William thinking he could help protect me. Of course, William went after his mother who we thought was dead, so he is hot on her trail. Edith was finding where Walton was to figure out if he found my brother. Something tells me this was an end game for them as my brother was dead. See they, I mean those four ghosts who are after my gift will do anything to get me alone. I stood still for a moment when I thought about everything kissing my bottle at the same time.

There he was young man's ghost in my bottle. If I let him out what will happen? I know I get a wish and now I can stop all this from happening. Let us face it this do not end pretty this time. It took two hours to figure out there was a sound like when you make a sandwich and the paper going around it makes a sound. When my fingers gotten it from my pockets it was addressed to me. Open it Freddie you gotten nothing else to lose. It was a black and white photo from 1945.

"Edward Roberts eighteen, Sandy Fields age twenty." She was older that is odd. The photo went from being 2-D, to the two people when I said their names started to stand as if the photo was there stage. Recreating the time, the picture was taken. She grabbed his white T-shirt when he was tilting her to get a kiss. He was a sailor coming back home. Wearing his blue jeans, as she worn his hat. Young love right there. He was muscular as that is what those times done to a person. My bottle had tiny hands knocking on the glass. My fingers were cold, yet I still opened it. The photo of him let go of the girl as he looked at me pointing to the ground, so I put the photo on the ground while he walked onto the soil. She went back to her photo. Without him. Then his soul went and walked up to the photo version of him and they took each other by the hands and became one. It was snowing now as they did that. When I looked again, He was standing there as that gave him his life back. Kneeling like a man would to his prince.

"How did this happen?" I mean this does not happen, how do you take a photo and a ghost and make them together as one again? Edith! I know it was her as this was a form of time travel for her.

"Prince of Death!" What did he call me?

"Why did you say that to me?" I had to ask.

"You are the Prince of Death as you see the dead and protect them." He looked at his body as I did when William gave me a new one.

"How?" I was not understanding.

"That girl that you know with the pig tails in her hair. She came and took that picture. Had me mail it to you so in later years she could put it in your favorite coat. Then she told me to take my own hand at the time. When days later that lady killed me, I understood. She even told me to go into the bottle and how to do it." I thought we knew who you were.

"You don't know me yet. I feel as if I do." No this was not right.

"Bucky!" He went to my church when I was a kid. He was my grandfather when my real grandfather couldn't be there.

"Call me Deforest!" Ah, No! Bucky to me kind sir.

"What happens when this is all over then?" I asked.

"I am the only one who knows how to stop them all now. When it is all said and done, I go back to that year the day after I was killed, and they will never know. You and Kipper buried me in the backyard, so nobody was found.

"That story Kipper told me never happened." Well you would ask too.

"Yes, Freddie you need to understand when you think you are going to die no matter what you do things." He was right in a way he is right. Now what?

"We go to the nearest place and wait. Let the group come to you, and well talk than. They will come if I am here. Their leader tends to forget me from time to time." They dated I knew it.

"Lead on!" So, I went. He stopped in the middle of his tracks.

"There is someone in your aunt's house." Before I could talk there was a chocolate dragon in my mouth as he covered my lips with one hand. Did not think home was it. It was dark just like when the day Stu died, or he was supposed to be dead. No light, no stars, no moon just a hazel drag in the air. I did not open the door as it was already open. All I saw that was a light was his badge. I stood in face of the fireplace taking a fire pick in my hands.

"If you think for a moment that I am going to let you hit me I will put the bullet in you faster than your father's head that night." Officer Blue always nice to see you too.

"Mom said you were my dad." Well!

"She was not telling you the truth. Yes, we did things, but I am not your daddy." Then who is? The man you killed. "Why don't you ask that man standing next to you?" No! What! That lady in the picture was looking familiar. My grandmother was my mother? Wait! No!

"Yes! I could not be near you as they told me if I did, they would have killed my whole family tree going back to the first documented man. Killing you along with me." His eyes teared. She gotten pregnant the day you took the picture. The same day Halstead killed the man in my driveway. So, the lady who raised me were his daughters. My sisters. They had to protect me for him. William gave up everything to make sure it happened. His eyes gotten wide as he told me he had to go leaving me with Blue. My father is Bucky. I was tricked.

140

"Where did you send him?" He rested his gun, on the table near the sofa as he came trod me.

"Right now, you and that William boy are making love in the back of your brother-in-law's car. The same man you thought was your father." I could feel the coldness on my back as the door swung open. A hand grabs my shirt pulling me out of him. Making him get out as well. Forcing us to walk with my pants on my ankles to the middle of the woods. Lying me down into the dirt. Making William watch. Thing is that is not me. William went with someone else that night to practice on Duke Taylor's boy. All I could hear was a gun go off as his blood must have went all around my face. Who pulled the trigger? Stu! His body hit the floor I could hear that. He was asking for help yet why do I feel I should not. My dark side is showing. His hands were shaking from letting the gun go off. I put the gun in my hands. Police cried out.

"Hands behind your head," She told me. So, I did leave the gun on the ground. He died drinking his own blood. I looked my brother in the eyes. Saying my last thought before they could use it on me.

"Self-defense was going to kill me." Kelly was the only one who gotten me out of it. As his fourteen-year-old self was the one who pulled the trigger for me. Had to come up to the conclusion that my father made me witness my husband's first ever boyfriend's death. Thinking it was going to make me happy. No, he was making me see what happens when I try to find out the truth. That things get messy on the way. There was two men standing at the car when the man I thought was my father was shot dead. There was a fourth person and I just witnessed him getting shot. He was with William. Yet I remember a four-year-old William not an older one. Meaning that we need to figure out why we were put to a spell that made us younger. What where they hiding us from? My father was a member of the mob who made a deal with a witch. How does one swallow this?

December 2nd, 1944

Wrote to Conklin's folks last night. Had to tell them he died. He was my brother, and nothing will change that.

Chapter 13
The Devaney Estates

(Bradley Melvin Mason!)

Fedora hat tipping off his head. Fresh new penny loafers taking on the foundations of the woodlands. His green toe flouting in the wind as that deer shaped tie pin fallen off a mile back. Suspenders hitting the back of his lower legs like a screen door on a spring day. His flesh took on this glow like the light from the moon as his eyes were the deepest of blues like you see if you were looking down from the stars. His sister warned him to not walk onto the porch without shoes. Now he walks with splinters stuck in his feet. Hair gel dried into that spiked hair. A single freckle was like a dot at the end of a sentence at the back of his hair line. There was three other men with him. All dressed to the hill. One of them had a shot gun I did not know what to think. The other one dressed as if he just walked out of a Victorian novel.

The coloring of my long johns took on the color of midnight ink. The moon was full as the stars light up the night sky like each soul that have died was watching over us with their candles all full of light and joy. The wind was dancing around the trees to gather among my body. Arrow heads around on the ground as my feet try not to step on them. Funny when the wind hits the top of the trees, they make a sound. Fooled my sister when we were little ones that those were the sound of deer getting ready for the kill. The lake sure was something as the water called for someone to swim it in its wonders. Left my boots near the stump that my daddy left there last year. You wonder how we got a real tree in our house last year for December. The rings do not lie. Rolled up my legs to the top of each hip showing off the afterglow of each leg. We are always taught to not show your skin as he did not give it to you to show off and attract unwanted people. Each arm came out of the long sleeves and each button came undone. As it fell resting swaying behind me. Feeling the wind on my chest felt good not this heat that was trapped inside. Seeing that face of his before they shot him. Him sitting on his knees telling them they got the wrong man. He did not even know I was there. They gave him five minutes to beg as they laughed under their breath. I closed my eyes tighter than mama's cloth on a proofing dough. They ran off before someone came after the sound. Could see the smoke from the fireplace coming from the sky as it formed different animal shapes. My toes felt the coldness of the water wanting the rest of me to be in it. Slowly letting my body get used to the water. It was like water normally is yet to me it was not cold as much as it was worm. Too bad one day water will be no more than what. Splashing up water on my skin scrubbing with whatever I had. Trying to not scream as I washed off his blood. When I knew they were gone I went to him, his eyes were open as he looked at their faces before they killed him. Thing was he was not dead yet. Made something out of sticks and what clothing I could spare to get him off the mountain. No one was around so I let out a scream.

We need to start now thinking of that. Maybe by creating houses to sweat the moister from something to create water or gather rainwater. There was a voice calling my name from behind me. Did not think anything about it as it was the wind. There it was again. Turned and nothing was there. Had to get this out of my head. He was the only male for the Devaney Estates that is why he was targeted. Then I heard something coming from underneath the waters behind me, yet that was just my own hands. Wait, left than right. There was a hand over my mouth I do not recall having three hands. My elbow kicked at him until I was free running in the water until I hit land. I stood there near my father's stump breathing extraordinarily strong, my hair in my face as its structure was still compromised. My hands in the air as he gotten closer and closer. He had blond hair and a cat like smile. The back of my ankles hit the boy I took from the woods. I had to protect him.

"Don't come any closer. You hear me." My voice was trembling. He kept walking my way. "What is it you want?" I followed his eyes. He looked right behind me as I thought he would. "You can't have that. That is mine and mine alone." I was going to lose everything, and I have not even started. "One more chance before." Before what? He put his hand up in the air. I was just saying anything I could before he caught on.

"I mean you not harm. I need you to put on some dry clothing and come with me. You're in grave danger." Why should I go with you?

"Why come from behind me and do what you have done?" Be brave.

"The very thing you heard before I came from the water is still out there waiting to kill you. Now sir I think you need to come with me." There was dried clothing on my father's tree stump. Not going to ask how that gotten there. He had new clothing as well. He had this planned.

"You how do you know me?" Tell me!

"You're Bradley Melvin Mason. Tonight, your brother was going to kill you under the water. He was getting ready when I approached. You scared him off. After he killed you, he was going to cut out your eyes, so they think the fish ate them. My Freddie knew your ghost. Right now, my mother waits in the very woods for me. She is going to cross your brother and kill him. Give his body to Freddie. We need you Bradley." My brother was the one with the gun. I thought I knew that voice. Not my brother then again, he did say he wanted me gone so he could be the one to get all our parents' money when they passed on. My sister if she married him, the money went to them. So, it all goes to him at the end. My brother was part of the mob he will never come back from this. "Edith come on!" Who is that? There was a lady coming about the wood line as she had a hood on with a cape.

"Let me see your face." She let down her hood. When it hit me. "I know her!" She smiled I knew that smile anywhere.

"That was my grandmother. Lily Storms. My mother's maiden name." That is cannot be.

"She is the same age as you that cannot happen." I was right, wasn't I? She went over to the boy placing her hand over his bullet wounds. Her eyes and fingers played like a banjo as I watched the bullet rise from his body. She stood handing the other man the bullet. I saw nothing but a heeled man. What was this? She did this to prove herself to me.

"See we are from a different point in time come here to save you." I went to her and took her hand. There was something about her.

"With that smile I trust you. Not him! I will go." What was I thinking going with people I do not even know?

"Thing is we are going to have to get through the woods to get there. We might not make it. I need a wand. My powers are fading as I aged out of my childhood. It needs to be controlled by it." Let her hand go as I went over to my father's stump there was a little tree growing out of it. Took one of the arrow heads and cut it on its base. It was big enough to fill her hands, and it was part of me to be with her. Carved a pattern I thought he like in its beauty. It looked like the drum sticks they used in the wars. Love to see her smile. When I handed it to her, I feel in love once could I do it again? With her? "It's perfect. Your buddy there will be a new kid in town named Kirk Phillips. You are the Gray Brothers now. Your Gertrude, don't ask." She pointed it to the trees as she said something making the trees move. "Widow Coffin! Now the trees will look out for her if anything come of us, they will kill on order." A door came out of nowhere. He understood the door. "She wants him." The blonde guy reached into the door pulling out a ring the same color of my hair.

He was now the keeper of the door the ring will understand. The boy woken to say.

"Did you know that blood blossom is a flower that can kill a ghost, need to stay clear of those?"

December 3rd, 1944

Mother sent hard candies for the boys. They sure filled their pockets. Smile on boys.

Chapter 14
Mercury Top Hats

(Freddie!)

Ms. Louise, her army won over the globe. There was nothing for us left here so we ran into the future. One that we did not see coming. We went into the unknown to protect the things that she wanted. Just like the adults that helped raise us. When we gotten to whatever year it was the first thing, we did was find a person that was able to help us figure out it was 2134. Half of the humans on the planet were four planets from here. As they tried to find a new frontier their engines stopped. They settled there instead of coming back. There are very too few waters left for people to drink. So, the young man we bumped into in our stay here was a water farmer. He lived in the woods for a reason. He has buckets on buckets hanging off the trees so when it rains, he collects the branch water like they did not back in the horse and wagon days. They now have cars that run off air like the big windmills thy used to create energy where we are from. There are tubs on the roof of the cars where the water gets collected as well. Anyway, to get water. There are bins on the roofs in the cities, and instead of gutters in the roads they have collectors. Which are water boys who have long tubes on the sidewalks that collect the liquid as well. They run the water through these cleaning machines like we had filters. No more tubs just sponge bathing. Smoking is nothing of the sort. Drinking well it's used for cooking and medical used only now as they want a people that are clean.

They went back to the olden ways from before the 1950s. Cities of building torn down to make way for the trees and nature again. Earth is going back to the way it was slowly. But no thanks to us and the way we used it. They burn there garbage now. Not the things that can burn like metal cans. The young man we were with said to us his great-great-grandfather was an ice-boat man who went to the ice caps and as the ice feel they gathered it bringing it to shore for us to melt and drink. Away for the water leaves not to rise. Each house and business have their own unit for collecting the rainwater as well. All families go home and eat no more restaurants. Instead of the countries fighting over everything. They chose to come together as one. There was a fight that almost ended everything. So, when the wars were all over, they all just stopped fighting. Put the windows down and turned off the air conditioning so it did not harm the environment. Each state took upon itself to help the world. Like one was for rain gathering, the other for tree farmers, entertainers, etc. In a way they went back to the way of my great-grandparents. They are trying to redo the harm they first created by being great. There is no more money. Just a point card. Once you run out of points you work for more. The more points you get the higher in society you become. Your Nebraska is their fighting arena. Where once a year each state picks one person to come and gather. The stronger the better. It is like when the Romans cheered on the gladiators. This time it is for people like us. Each state fishes out their ghost seeker, their tin star, there whoever is different. They battle it out until only one is standing. They send the winner off to the breeding state where they breed the winner of as many children, they can have putting each child with a family in a state in which they belong to in the matter of test. Each state gives to the other. Canada chose to join us as well as one big united front. Where their states are the same in rules. We might be the best of the world, but then again, our system works. Everett Frozen was our young man who took us in as water farmers. The groundwater that is under the ground is being saved for it do not rain, but then it still hard to get it out of the ground. The young man has three green houses where they sweet the greens and the rocks for water, then there is a house for men. The scientist state has found that water off the skin off a man's ruff like skin has minerals our bodies need to survive. The water that drips off out groins is the best water in the world now. You get payed to produce water all day. In 2035, we were hunted by the rangers of Jupiter. Thing is we are not alone. Food is grown now, not brought in a store. You grow it yourself. No one person runs the world. Each state has a spoken for person and they all gather to agree. The Rangers run the other side of the world. Cancer is nothing to these people anymore.

They cured it by looking at dead cells and seeing how they can bring them back from the dead. One man found that vinegar can make the cells float apart from each other by a compound found in the vinegar. The things that made me smile the most is that people have found a way for men to have children with other men because they used the same theory William and I came up with all those years ago. We even have a state named after us in what was Canada. One man can get a change to get a lady part but stay a man. The baby grows on the back. Edith got married to the boy we are now living with. She was not going back with us if we find a way home. They do not have time travel here yet. They're working on it. So, I took a job to help the scientist find a way. As my tin abilities can give them tin that do not melt if they try their test. If your last name starts with A-L you can go out and work on the opposite days, the peoples whose last names are the other remaining letters. Except water people their job never ends. They even found a way for wood to be an agent in making water as well. Yes, so why are you looking at me with those odd like eyes. Thing was in the years my parents were in school they had big glasses like that and yet here you are my age still wearing that old fashion thing on your face. Face, I must watch all of them as I do not know who, who is these days. They keep growing as we get smaller. Here I am sitting on a sub train with my brother's boyfriend wearing these things on my head. William do not know that the two of us went back to see if we could get some control of the past with a hope. Girls now are wearing metal cat ears that are attached to head bands. Edith made me wolf ones to wear to this gathering we are going to. See it is just me and this boy sitting next to me now. Yesterday, William found that each member on their side owns a world that with a single breath can have the who planet killed. Leaving us as the only members from that planet left. His mother has Greenwood. My dad or whom I thought was my dad has the home where Tin Starr comes from. Cannot remember the name he said as I was told to run and all I could do was look at the top of Ben's hand. So, I lost Edith going after his mother and well you know where William went. The other two worlds are where people like Edith come from. I think Scott, and Kelly are on that trail. Walton if he found my brother is going to the world the Glass Knights are from. They just call his world Glass. His was the best for me to remember. Worth and I are here to protect Earth.

We win this planet then we might have a chance to get them all back. Hard thing is Worth, he is the one protecting this place not me. I have a world to protect that only I can see. The dead have a world too. Worth's knee was shaking up and down as that was a habit he did. Boy cannot sit still. Studying all the faces were all they come from, who are they after if there is anything they are looking for. Has it been ten years for Kelly already? Time went by fast if we run, I guess. The tin I took from the man who attacked us at the high school that night, William had made a masquerade make for me. We are going to an art showing where all the people going wear an animal type item and the host will give an x, amount to saving the wildlife for each person coming. This keeps us anonymous. I know nothing about him, yet here I was letting him guide me. Worth was holding onto a dried buttercup flower he took from his wallet.

"What is that?" If I was to trust you than I must know.

153

"When I talked to Stu last he gave this item to me. When I think of him strongly, I take this from my pocket, and it all goes back to where I need it to. It's like I was waiting for him to land after going into space." He put it back as he was done. William was in my head to and on my face as he did make this mask. The lights started to spark. The people thought it was normal. Under ground in the city. Yeah, this country boy does not know about that. It felt like the ground was shaking. Worth grabbed my arm, he was scared. The lights were out but not for me. Standing to my feet as Worth stood behind me. The man, with vampire teeth was standing there in front of me.

"I need you to give me the light. Or help me get someone into it." He kept looking behind him.

"What is in it for me? You sleep with my cousin, and she gave you her secret garden. For you to try and kill her. Why do I help you?" He was worried.

"Because she's carrying my child. Believe me, don't yet at the same time I need you now." He was sounding weak.

"Find Michael, and if you help Poe. I will help you. Only if you do that." The man who died at the piano last month he was standing there next to him.

"Take him with you." He put his hands on his hips. Getting mad yet he knew he needed to protect Edith.

"Deal!" They were gone yet back in a flash. The four of us looked at each other. Were doors were appearing where the normal doors were to be. One opened and William came from it. There were three doors, the second door was locked as Ben tried it. Someone was knocking at the other side. I opened the third. Edith stood in the woodwork. Handing me a blanket, as she fallen to her feet. Worth went to her aid. The blanket was crying. I looked at the man with the vampire teeth. He had a quiver in his voice. "What did I do?" the sound of a gun went off when Ben moved his shoulder. My eyes opened as that lady still looked at me odd, but we were at the stop. The door opened as we gotten off. There he was in a suit with a pink tie. This was just a dream that I just had. No wonder it did not make any sense of the matter. It was hard to look at the people as this was the last day for most of them.

"What did you do?" Worth said.

"What did I do? You ask as if these people who are walking around us are in danger." His eyes investigated mine as he never done that before. "You question your cousin, now!" He played the Edith card and I did not like it. All I could think of was walk to the stair to the real world. "Freddie, if you go up there without me. I am not going to say if you are going to come back. You have to think about your brother and what he would say." Funny! I remember the first time William and I dated. You think it was going to the movies, but you must think why I would go to the movies in a suit. That night was great coitus. I was waiting for something to happen. Like when the girl on the space battle movie lives and the battle was done that type of feeling. When you are the hero and when you are trying to get the courage to do what he needed to. I do not know I felt like I was going to touch the ground and stand up to be a Roman getting cheered on by the crowd. Feeling the heat from a battle, the heavy breathing. I was cold when he was walking me home. He did not know what to do but give me that flannel shirt he was wearing. Stu made fun of me for not returning it as it smelt like him. Thing is I was wearing that same shirt under this suit.

"Are you coming? What is your true name by the way? I just made one up when I saw you the first time." I made sure my cuff links that my grandfather gave me was still there. I was on the top step as I waited for them to come up to me. All I did was look at his shoes right up to his eyes. "Grass! Why is there grass when there is needs to be city under your shoes?" He was scared too. My hand felt for Ben's. When I found his he screamed. Thing was he screamed my name.

"Worth, you can call me Worth." There was a farmer's daughter standing behind him. Saw the barn so I guessed. She was pointing her daddy's gun in her hands. She was asking me why we are dressed funny. There is that word again.

"What year is this?" Ben asked.

"1909! Why you ask?" She liked him. He was using it to his advantage.

"Where is the city? Buildings, dog waste in the park the owners forgot to pick up." She did not know what we were saying.

"It's beginning she is changing the timeline. The City never happened. People never came from other places. We are here because our family must have come from different channels then the island with the green lady." Worth now is not the time. She forced us into the house, down the stairs into the basement. There was one chair in the middle of the room. She forced Ben in the corner under the stairs as her father I think tied me to the chair. The ropes on my hands. He forced cheese cloth over my face as he kept pouring water on my face. Every time he stopped the water I could breathe again. He said to her that he could not breath underwater. Could feel the veins in my neck as the pain was lingering there. Could feel the tightness in my chest. Could feel like I wanted to sleep. William once told me that to get into the military back when this was a test that no one knew about. My William was part of the dressing station, receiving a patient on a stretcher. He did not know how to drive so he tended in the back to the men. There was a lot of things back then they did that no one knows about as they did not tell. Thing is there is no such thing as fear as there is always away out if you deem it. Freddie once asked me about death.

How it felt when you are dying? The answer should not have come that fast to me. If you come back for a different mission, then we are forgetful of the past, so we do not mistake our mission. Thing is when you do remember, you try so hard to get it right, so you do not have to come back. Thing is the more experience you get the better you are. If you can remember your past the better player to this game, you are in. Dying is like a bee sting you; at first do not realize it is happening. Then you get numb as if you do not feel anything. Then you just fall to sleep. People who are still living think the way we die was not the way they needed to go. Thing is it do not matter how we die it is that our mission is do not. Everything you needed to do has been done. You might not get to say goodbye, but we do not leave them it is just you cannot see them no longer. Most people think that you must be at the grave to talk to the spirt of the person. Yet with knowing the person in my bed every night I wonder if that is right. The charming face of my dear Freddie keeps me going into all I have been doing.

The room was dark and cold. You could hear the dripping of water from the pipes over head as to me this was a basement. The mice kept the rhythm up of their feet in the wooden stairs that were to my right. There was nothing but a blank wall to look at. It was like when they put the sack over your head, so you do not think about the giant knife cutting off your head in France. That was the only thing about history I remember. There was another person in here with me. I think female as the coughing I was listening to be a soft noise. There was no food for days. The mice sound good with garlic sauce right now. The lips of mine the skin was peeling off that I could not say words as there was no water for so many hours. The last place I saw Edith was in a 1950s diner. She was in the restroom as I was at the trying to find a good song to play at the music machine. There were ropes on my hands that lead to a wooden pole. There was a bucket under my feet that had water in it. Think it was water at least. Thing was I could not feel my toes as they were in the water so long. I kept counting hours in my head. I gotten to the fifth one in my head for the seventh day in. When a light from the middle of the room started to come on. My neck was dried, and my brain was pounding. Heels on the wood now as the fabric to a dress dragging behind them. A hand grabbed the back of my head. Thought the hair was going to be yanked out from the skull. Forced my head back rubbing my face onto his chest. Thing is I did not see nor hear him coming in. Could feel the blood drip down my face onto my lap. The light bulb that was hanging by a string like the one my grandmother used to iron her laundry was swaying around the room. Blinking as the connection was off. Thought there be another person sitting crossed from me but there was not a chair. There was a chair on the pipes above. When the light would come trod my face there was this odd blue shinning object reflecting off its body.

Blue light! Where have I seen a blue light before? There was a blank in all areas in my brain standing there thinking about where this may have come from. Like millions of mini Williams were throwing around footballs to each other and no one could tell the other who could through it the right way. It was a tiny light, but it did its justice. Who had this light? Felt the tightness get to my torso as the breathing was a struggle. Astronauts without helmets in space could breathe better than I can now and think of the possibilities of that. There was a warmth in the seat of my pants as I thought about the person hanging there in the room on the other side of me. Urine trickling down the bottom of the wood from the chair as it traveled down to the top of the mouse that was hiding under my chair as he shakes it moved to the sand on the floor. My father hit me as a kid, but this was nuts.

All I could see was the veins on his arms. Or her there was no telling what I was looking at until the light finally stops. I forgotten about the heels as I was trying to get into the brain of the person that been down here with me this whole time. The hand behind me I could not feel the person standing there and all I had to do that was my intelligence. The heels started again. I was done with everything. If they want to kill me, I was ready for the bullet. My eyes were closed as I was trying to fall to sleep and get it all done for. I was watching film like pictures go by in the insides of my eye's lids getting ready to leave this life. A movie of when Freddie and I were at his birthday at four when it all started. A snap made me open my eyes to a lot of lights this time. I wish who ever this would just let me die. At least I can get to William faster that way. She was humming I knew who it was as she was humming the same song that I feel to sleep to as a child back in the depression. My hands were shaking for the fear.

"Now, now! You don't want to die before you witness this." I tried to see the face of her, but I linked to the man hanging there in front of me. I could not think of it. It was the blue from the light from his ring. His hair covered most of his face as duct tape covered his lips. He was wearing my boxers with the yellow rabbits on them, and the nightshirt with the pocket. My blood came from me biting my lips. His was coming from his back as they were using a horse whip on his skin. She whipped him again for the fun of it hoping me to see it. His body reflexed forward as his eyes tried to cry but his eyes were dried out.

"Let Worth go!" There was a man standing in the corner of the room. Dressed as a wooden solider. I was watching the red from the blood run down his legs. Her heels came trod me as I watched the fabric near her feet travel with a flouting box behind her. Her hands went to the box as she pulled out something. Letting it swing in my face like a pocket watch. It was the head of a girl I knew; we all know. She killed Edith swinging her head in my face until I reacted. Thing is I knew she was still living as the eyes were open and she did not have blue eyes. She had green like I do. In her hand with the hair from the head she was holding was a wand, but that was not her wand as it was with me in my boots under the fabric that I only knew about. Also, her wand has teeth marks in it where I bit it once. This wand had leaf marks all over it. Mother this was your wand and it has not worked in years once you found how to control the magic in your veins. You were trying to trick me, but a craft of a fake head was not going to do you any justice. "Let him go, and I will die for him. Let me take his place. Please!" She was wearing a black veil over her face. There was no part of her body that was not covered. A dress for a woman at the first world fair in Chicago.

"Dear boy, you make me think that I was going to do what you say. Thing is I have everything as it slips through your fingers. I get to watch everything you love to die before making you the leader in my attack on the living. I get the dead to make sure the light never glows again." I had to save the world. Tied to a chair even. How? "I'll let your Fred live if he chose to join me. Yet all I need is a drop of his blood to get the gift." She was right where I needed her to be in her mind.

"You're wrong you know. The gift is given to those who deem it. They obtain it for doing good in their last lives. We cannot remember the other times we were here because that is the trick. If you want it, you must be willing to give up something. You are given a chance to remember little things to help you survive in your lifetime now, but you must be willing to be open to the signs. Yet, people do not want to understand what is not taught to them. If anything, I have learned mother. I learned that things repeat and happen for a reason. That it only makes a person stronger than the next if he or she is willing to listen to what is being said. That we are here to get it right and no one person has ever gotten it right. If we did then there be contact from alien life yet there not from another planet. We are the game to them. Don't know who they are, but there watching." She was laughing at me. You do not realize what you have done until it is done. There is a moment in my life when someone told that what you say and how you act will come to it. There are some people in life that grow up to be nasty slugs sitting in their pink chair, the whole time never doing anything for anyone but when she or he don't get their way, there you have the threats of because they didn't get their way. You pay the bills and do all the cleaning so I can rule this household. Well it's time the slug goes into the grass where it belongs, and I wear this crown in this house. Being the responsible one stinks sometimes.

"Cut him free I want to see what he's going to do." The person behind me untied the ropes as she wanted. It is nice to get everything you want is not it. Some of us have to work the hardest they ever had to get everything they deem in life all you have to do is stand there and demand like sick twisted older sister who in childhood or in adult years don't know how to do anything because instead of doing her part as a child just sat in front of the television screen and as an adult there she is still sitting in front of the screen the way she's been taught. When the rope let lose my arms swung near my body for a while to get the feeling back in them. I felt sorry for my mother she will never know the truth in life as she does not want to live it. Just see the world in ways where change do not happen. My eyes watched as his fingers grasped the chair pulling it out from underneath me. As I fallen, she sat down on the seat I once was on. The ground was softer than the chair was. All the man who was with her wanted to see was she was being attacked by my words and actions that she never gets into trouble if he was there. My father always told in ways that I was never his son as I never think like he did, but my other sibling gotten everything because they cannot do things for themselves. Well, if you let that person try, they are going to have to think for who they are for a change. Maybe the comments that come out of your mouth should stay in there and never see the light of day. The thing of water my feet where in was spilling onto the floor of sand making it sticky. My thoughts were to get to Freddie first. She sat there making list of things she had to do repeatedly in her head because she ran out of ink and never went to the store to get new ink.

There was no feeling in my legs. So, I crawled across that floor until I was under his legs. My elbows dug into the sand forcing me an inch closer to where he was. Could feel the little pebbles that were in the sand glide crossed my skin. Felt my ribs scrap into the wood. My eyes forward. She moved her fingers to motion him over to me. I closed my eyes to get the kicking over with. When your faced with evil there is nothing like a sitting fool. Felt the coldness on my spine. My legs worm from where they were in the cold water. The man who was with my mother just stood there waiting for me to crawl past him. She was acting as if she did nothing wrong, and he was letting her get away with even murder. I was almost there when his boot landed on the back of my knees crushing down until the bone was broken. I screamed so loud that I watched Worth's scream for me. I could not feel my legs anyway, but I felt that. But like a good solider I kept moving on. When I saw I was under Worth, I had all I could do was flip myself using my hands on his legs to put myself up. If this was going to be our death then so be it, but at least we go together. She stood lifting the veil on her face. Her bright red lipstick shined the most. She tried to come after me, but all I could do was put my hands in my face. Closed my eyes as I watched Worth do the same. Her cries were the only thing I could hear as when I looked there was this glass like wall up between her and us. When her fingers touched it. It burned her. They ran as fast as they could when I put my hands down the wall was gone. My body lied there trying to scream for help. But there was no hope. Worth kept trying to put all his weight onto the chains pulling himself up to make the metal react together on the metal pipes. All that I can remember was falling to sleep.

December 4th, 1944

Santa came to visit! It was me in a hat and beard. It sure made everyone smile. I am a father; this holiday came faster than I thought.

Chapter 15
Forgotten Fairy Garden

(Freddie!)

I was finally here, on a stage in front of millions or so I thought. There was something about being here when I was only thinking about one person and he was looking and watching from backstage. "Are you kidding me. You liked him; I knew it. You didn't have to ride his guitar." The song called for a hot filtering show, so I gave them one with the boy playing the guitar. Yes, but come on. I just felt his hands in my back pockets, and the vibration off the wood of the guitar. Looking at his face as he reacted to my voice. Kissing me after word backstage. He tasted like sea salt as my lips were taking on his skin.

"So, it was time for me to have my turn at being caught by you with my tongue down someone's mouth." I walked away as I was trying to get him to leave me. I must win the war for all of us even if means hurting the ones I love the most. As I left the doorway, I heard his shoes from behind me come to a stop. He took of his hat as he was playing with it as I heard the bill of the cap start to fold.

His hat hit the ground as he gotten mad getting ready to storm off. "Fine I'm done with all your everything's. There was something I was hiding from him that I could do more then I told him that I could do. I think it was high time I told him what I needed too. Yet was it right? I turned as he was gone as the only thing; I saw was a door in my face. I did it this time. Alone in the big apple and all I must show for it was a used pair of another man's drawers hanging out my back pocket. Yet I did it, I made him leave. I turned to face the city as I stopped in my tracks when the door slammed on the wall of the building. "You know what I am not that easy for you to throw away. I will fight for you." Turned to see him terribly angry at me about now as he was holding a baseball bat. Where did he get that?

"William we are alone in the city. I let it get to me. Now I know I cannot live in a city type of environment. I did it to get you scared so you leave me. I

163

did it so you did not die for me. I saw what is coming and I am the last one standing. You think I want to see the whole planet fall to its knees to protect me. No! If you left me than you wouldn't have to see me give myself to them." You got me crying now and I hate you for that.

"You know I was in school this time last year. All I was thinking about is how did I look? Was Freddie Waters looking at me? Did he like me? Now I stand here with most of my questions asked, and yet here we are fighting over something that needed to stop then. I am going to look the other way as I knew why you did it as you can now look the other way when you caught me in the classroom." Wait you were in there for the same reasons, yet you told me that story. My phone buzzed.

Edith: Freddie, where are you two?

Freddie: Back stage in the city. Just gotten done singing with, (No names are mentioned for safety of copyrights. Singer is male.) Why?

Edith: Ms. Louise just attacked Utah.

William: What?

Edith: The population count is at zero percent now. They even killed the news guy right in front of the camera.

William: Are you sure it was her?

Edith: It was her face that was shown after he fell to the ground. This I am sure of. We need to get together and figure out a plan.

William: She is moving fast; she will not stop until Freddie is found.

Stu: Freddie, believe her as the world is now gone.

Freddie: Stu, where are you?

Stu: Do not worry about where I am at this time, I will find you. If the world is gone. She will go state by state looking for you.

William: Until I am the last one standing. We did not know about the world being attacked as she gotten to them before they could get word out.

Edith: The lady on the television just said all that is left is New York now. They're coming.

William: Edith can you stop them.

Edith: William dear this is your Mom; Edith cannot come to the phone right now. Hope you have room for some oatmeal cookies.

"William, what happened to her?" His face read Sadness. I was trying to hold all my emotions back. Edith was now dead.

Stu: Do not worry! Edith's with me. Do not move from your spot. We are coming.

"Oh, thank Goodness." I said in a whisper. All electronical devices went blanks as the electricity went with it.

"Attention people of New York City, we are not looking to kill any of you as now you are the last of your kind to stand. Yes, the people of the world are now dead. If you wish to repopulate this planet, you will listen to me. You have two hours to bring one Freddie Starr to me. If not, you will die. Fast!" She could not even say it herself. The man I was having a thing with came from the door where William was standing. Scared from what he saw. His hair all teased as his clothing was now tight to his body. Dressed in a black coat, white trousers, and a black bow tie, with a yellow shirt.

"Good thing you are still near." William was getting madder than a bee if you trap it in a cone flower, do not ask me how I know that information. If you hold the flower shut the bee makes a vibration sound using its stinger to make a hole to get free.

"This baseball bat is for you." The boy put his hands up.

"Wait I can save you." He looked at me in fear as William swung the bat near his head. "I can save you." He said, he was friends with my brothers. "Stu, I knew him. Stu, and I were part of The Silver Leaf Society together. He sent me to protect you. I didn't tell him that I would try and get more from the deal." He showed us a pin that had the society's name on the outside edging and a photo of a silver leaf inside it. There meant to be a bad people yet why was this happening. Was I given the right information? He took my hand as I took a hold of William's. He made me close my eyes as I could see the society's secret way of traveling.

"Where are we going?" He would not say. He would not say but all I remember was a flash of light when I walked back into the building. I kept my eyes closed while I was holding William's hand. "Wow! Freddie open your eyes." He was shaking my hand hard as it forced my eyes open. The boy was gone but now William and I are hiding in this bathroom. Tried the door but no luck. The advertisement for a man's swimsuit was pinned onto the glass of the mirror. "March 14th, 1925." Was printed at the top of the paper. I learned a new trick like I was told I had to do so I found the only frame in this bathroom and placed my fingers onto the glass. It let me beware of my surrounding. Walton taught it to me as he could do the same thing only better. Here goes nothing. William kept moving making it so I couldn't concentrate. William went over to the chair that was near the sink as it had a man's trousers hanging from it. He took the wallet apart as he was floored. "Freddie, this is your grandfather's wallet." Grandfather let's see what you got. Touched the cold glass, as I closed my eyes once more.

He had a sales ticket shaped dance card hanging from his wrist that were full of names. His hands placed so lightly on the headboard. The fabric to his muscle's shirt was teaching the strings of beads that were attached to the bottom rim of the Victorian powdered pink lamp how to sway with the vibrations that rippled off the mattress. His bowtie was in her hands as she tightened her grip with every puff of breath he left on her skin. Her cigarette girl uniform was on the floor waiting for her to put it back on once more. His gentleman's coat against her chest as the bottom of the coat split around his hips. Her lipstick was all over his face as her hand was cascading over the back of his head to force him to look down at her beauty. His pelvis would spring forward when she would move an inch more trod the wall from the reaction, he gave to her. When the clock struck ten after two in the morning he was done. Only a ten-minute call was all she wanted. Crawled his way back off her, as she stumbled to the floor gathering her clothing. On her way out handing him the tip money from last night. She took a cigarette that she uses to show the customers how to use the product and places it in his mouth. Lighting the end of its tip just like when she lights the end of his tip. He smiled as she left letting out rings of smoke in the air. He stood near the side of the bed with each side of his waist band in his hands getting ready to tuck in his shirt. When he heard something that he did not understand. It was odd to him but then again, this line of work would invite the strangest of people. Got all dressed back up slapping on a cheap thing of cologne and dressing the bed so he could bring up another one off his card. Don't mind the wrinkles.

"Freddie! Let us get going." William was right hiding in his hotel bathroom was fun and all, but I was ready to get out. See I can place my fingertips onto the glass of a picture frame and that person in the photo must show me what is going on in the room. In this case it was a man's add for selling soap. Well, the man in this add will have an odd dream about a calling card later. Just something new that the ghost world has taught me. William climbed out of the claw foot tube as I did not warn him that the penny tile was wet, he slipped and caught the edge of the tub. "You could have said something." Angry much!

"What's the fun in that?" See we came back in time to get answers from my grandfather. We were supposed to do this earlier, but we thought it was the right time now being my mother-in-law is killing all the people to get to me. There was something else. I stopped William from making a sound again. Placed my fingers in the same place on the glass as that is the only way it works. The cigarette girl was coming inside the room again. She was crying. An older lady was there too. She made the girl sit on the bed facing her. Asking her to tell her what she knew about the call boy she was just with. She could not answer much just telling her that she knew him through the halls. She liked him from his smile and she never thought to do things like this. Snapping her gun, and she rolled her eyes not seeing the condom wrapper that he thrown to the floor was stuck to the bottom of her one heel. The older lady reached into her purse as she pulled out a gun. The girl cried for her life, but the older lady did not care.

"The Silver Leaf Society thanks you for your words." I let go of the glass as it broke from the firing of the gun. William heard the door close as he ran into the room. There she was on the bed dead cold like this crystal doorknob I was holding onto. William closed her eyes as we had to move. He followed the older lady downstairs. She went to the counter and asked the lady for the boys next round. We were not in time as the lady behind the counter was telling my grandfather that she was his next person. William pushed me into the public restroom. Gave me clothing he borrowed from my grandfather's suitcase and we gotten a booth to watch him. Grandfather was going past us now as William reached out and grabbed his back-belt loop.

"Hey there kid why don't you sit down and join us." He smiled with the same high cheek bones I remember from the photos I studied for hours. "Come on, don't be a stranger." Saw the look on his face he saw the same look on my face. He handed the tray he was holding to the next waiter that passed by telling him that he was going to stop for a quick smoke. Even though he is never touched those things ever in his days. He was willing to take a seat near me as you gotten drunk. Good thing she is here to keep you for killing yourself. That is right sweet lips take his glass away for sure. Was your left pointer finger lining the rim of the glass like mine was or was I picturing things? Nerves! You trusted me kid even though you did not know me.

"Do I know you? Ms. Phillips did not send you to fish me out of here again. I know I am seventeen, but this is the best way to get a fast hundred in the hairpins. They do not ask for your papers. Look how much is it going to take for me to get you guys off my back?" Talk like him so it proves to him I was telling the truth. "Are you my next hairpins? This is going to cost you double or nothing." I was getting to see a side of my grandfather I did not like at all.

"Ms. Phillips is listing to her radio stories this afternoon. When she is her crawlers you do not get her to say a thing. In a while that gentleman is going to go up to room eighteen. Don't look back when you walk that way, he's three tables back." That key in your hand says what?

"That's the room I am in. Look I do not know what you are thinking, but I do not usually get trouble around these parts. The bar tender is my uncle he shares the room with me on the weekends, so I can work." Boy I wish I can master that red neck way for your voice. Put my hand on your leg hard, as you gotten the message. Your eyes said you gotten the code. "Your scaring me." He said for me to tell you truth well here it goes.

"Tell me something. You still living in the house with the old stables behind it. Think you carved your names in the wood of it when you got your first kiss after the sweetheart's dance. You never gotten in trouble as they sat you at the top of the basement stairs if you did. They kept the bodies in the basement before burial that is where they dressed the body and had the viewings. Back when that stables were really getting used." He was scared even more being I knew that. He was getting smart just like me.

"If you know everything. Then tell me the color of my cumber bun." Whispered, green in his ear. He looks like he just seen a ghost. I know I get the same look every day. Was I liking flirting with my grandfather?

"Thomas Waters! Yes, by the way you are looking at me I gotten the right man. That man behind you he is going to do things to you tonight that should never be done to anyone. You are the first. First of many men he is going to do things to. He like all the rest don't know your age, so he thinks it's okay." He put his fingers in the air to talk like a real New Yorker.

"Who are you? You know my name, but I don't know yours." Well here is a question with replacement.

"What was the name of the boy in your mother's stories she told you as kids. You even named your son this. He was born two weeks back." He smiled showing his buck teeth.

"Freddie! You knew my family. Did Billy put you up to this?" Took my first drink never thought I say it.

"Freddie Waters that's my name. I'm your grandson." He is thinking we are crazy. Those fingers of yours touched your chest.

"Your friend is gone. My key to my room is too. And if the image in this empty glass is right. That man three back is gone too. I can't be your father." He was right.

"Your right, but your wrong. Tin Stars are real. So are men who can see the dead after they are not on earth no longer. The characters in that journal of yours is all real. You were not getting a gold mine to write a book about as you're living it. You took me, and the family into the future in a few years." I scared him off. how do I get him to come back? The lady from the society was coming as we made sure he was with a different girl about now. William was on the dance floor as Thomas interrupted. I watched his feet going up the stairs by now, as William approached.

"If he dies tonight, so will you." He was scared.

"Tin Star!" I pushed William to the side.

"He is protected by The Orm. Right now, if you don't want to drown on moss then I suggest you go somewhere else." She handed William a white feather as she left for the exit.

"Ladies back in twenty-five would hand you these if you didn't sign up to fight yet." William, and I left this year with little, but the new clothing on our backs and some fancy soaps from the hotel's bathrooms. William had a chalk doorway of Edith's spells. You draw a doorway with the chalk, and you walk through it to any moment in time. William must have chosen high school as I was in our old classroom again.

"I don't think I have a student with that name on my paper." Mister Hand's voice. "Freddie, I need to know who you want to create a fantasy world with. Please pick, William or Walton?" I was trapped in my own fantasy. No ring on my finger, no ring on his back for what I can see. "Mister Waters Please." I did not know what to say. I was sent back into time to this point so I can learn my gift. He was letting me get a head start on her.

"Mister hand I can't do this project for you." I started to cry as I had to end this whole thing. He took his hand to his chin.

"May I ask why?" No! You did anyway.

"Because I'm gay! I want to choose William Starr, but I am scared that he might not feel the same." They were all looking me up and down as if I killed the president. He came back here to change time.

"William, why are you laughing?" William was holding his hands behind his back as his feet were dancing a little.

"I'm gay too." Mister Hand did not know what to say. Why was I back here? Did not matter I was given the gift to start again. I can change things. No if I get better with my gift, I can stop this from coming. Went into the hall as I had to gather my thoughts. William came after me. "Freddie, I remember the same things you do too. That's why I said what I did. We need to get back." What?

"Let's go!" I said. Then I stopped! "William, why did you tell my grandfather that the books he was writing were real. Did he know about us before we were born? He did write chapter books when he was younger about a boy like me. and mother named me after the character as she like the name so much." He was looking down meaning he was thinking.

"Yes, Freddie!" I need more information than that.

"William, why did he look like Bernard?" He did not want to answer.

"Because he is Bernard! He was living under a different name this whole time." He never died! He just was able to control his looks. He showed me the old man I wanted to see, but really, he was much younger than that. William knew that now not only did he raise his son, but he brought his best friend into time so he could protect me as he saw the world under her rule. No more thinking that she might be good, as she killed that for me a long time ago.

December 5th, 1944

Conklin gave me a locket before he died for Edith. So, I put his picture on one half then mine on the other side. Keep it in my pocket until I see her next.

Chapter 16
String of Pearls

(Freddie!)

Here we find our ghost seeker hero stuck living another man's life trying to get back to his reality, let's see what happens next.

Sailor hat sitting on the edge of the wood to this stall of mine. If you move your hands at all the walls shake and the other men would look at you strange. Ten men taking a shower together because they wanted to save on space better get used to that. My soap around my neck as the sand under my feet was cold. The only reason I stand here in the crammed stall is because salt water is stickie after a while. Tried to trick the nurses to let me take a bath where they are located after there all sleeping, but of course not. When I went to start the water, my hand was under this man's hands that he made into a nest like a bird and he was hunched over the stall letting the water hit his back. His face looked up as those eyes looked down. When I saw him finally, I blew a dry kiss? Made me laugh, but he did not like it at all. It was just the two of us in here, but he still looked to see who was looking placing his hand on the back of his head as if he was being one of the guys, and he didn't want that side of him to show. I did not care really, he left as fast as he could letting me lock the door and have this place all to myself.

The sound of a phoebe bird filled my ear drums. Made me think of home as one of those sat outside of my window. Her sweet song made me feel more at peace. The smell of good old cooking came in as the mess hall worked away. Did not see nothing but the insides of my eyelids as I stood taking everything in. The soap ran down the flesh of this twenty-three-year-old body. My chest acting like a shield to the drops of water, so it did not bleed through. The air kissed my firm bottom as my hands rapped around the manhood getting him all nice and clean. The touch of the sand under my feet was sticky, like bathing in glue. Singing a song that sat in my head from the other day listening to the radio. Boy that singer from Memphis sure knows how to sing. Watched my hair in my face letting the waterfall seeing the different shades of the moon in the droplets. The water ran cold as I found myself with my face in the towel. Smelling in the fresh clean linens before it got the smell of my skin.

There was a knock on the door short after the other man wanted to get in. I was drying myself off you can wait. My hand gave the shower its final bow. Towel hugged my body, dry cleaning the whole thing like a nice bear hug. The olive-green underpants hid the gift I was handed down by the last generation. And to top it all off dog tags swaying against my chest. Knock, knock, boy was someone waiting for a shower. I like to take showers for a long time myself, but I can wait my turn. Knock, knock yelling at me to let him in there were plains overhead. I did not know what to think. The air filled with loud noises. The ground shook making the shower head make a sound. What was going on? It was as if a giant was walking and everything was all over the place.

"Let me in, let me in." Do I save myself or do I save two souls? What do I do? I swallowed my pride and opened the door. Thinking to myself he was trying something. I do not like to be manhandled. What do I do? I opened the door to see a scarred young man wearing nothing but a white T-shirt and white briefs. Shacking like a leaf. Green eyes popped as the black waive hair was going crazy with the wind. Just a few minutes ago you left, did you forget something? His chest was breathing extraordinarily strong as his chest did not stop. He ran inside hiding behind me as he watched my back. Fingers pushing me trod the danger just a little. As I walked out of the showers there were plains lining the sky as dots were coming out of the end of them. There were too many to count. There were also a strange looking man standing in front of me. I did not understand his language it sounded alien or something. We both were frozen in fear as another man ran past the stranger. I watched as the stranger took a knife from his sleeve cutting the man who was running neck. I ran backward as fast as I could as the door was locked faster. He was strong as the door busted opened with no give. Really boy with green eyes you are going to wash that man to death with a plunger. Its better then what was in my hands, nothing. He stepped trod me, I did not do the same. The man with the green eyes stood still like he saw a ghost.

He smelled like a bad skunk. His hair was pinned back, but his hair was remarkably high pitched. Was I scared? There are no words to say how I was. It was like I took myself and replaced it with a braver man. He put the tip of the gun onto the side of my face. I did not have a chance with all those planes guess this was the next best thing. Was I ready? The green eyes man made a noise distracting him. I rushed him. Just letting and doing the moves I was taught to do. He was passed out in seconds and I was able to get his gun. It was heavy but I tried to drag the green-eyed man in the showers until I could think of something else. He was scared and ran outside but ran headfirst into the door. My feet tried to run backward it was. It took some time, but my ears could hear feet outside of the building. I was ready to shut until I heard the voice looking for living men. I knew I could trust it as I heard it before. I showed myself to them with tears in my eyes. Everything was going to be okay.

When he finally woken, he told me how there was no family waiting as he was an orphan. With open arms not only has my family gotten an addition, but I gotten a best friend. Sat near his bed side, refused treatment until he opened his eyes. Those boys I know were thinking before death, "Mommy I don't like this. I did." I lived his life through his eyes now it is time to go home. The man was awake finally he was awake. We stayed on the island until we heard that it was okay to go back home. Where did the others go? I came here with four, but I was just one. Where is my family, my real family I gotten off the boat to the state of New York?

Mother was somewhere amongst the people. She written that she be here, but where. My ears counted to ten, that is how many times her heels hit the ground. Lost count when other people started to rush the place. I found it odd that my pocket watch stopped at the twenty-five on the face of the watch itself. I was able to watch the top of her head until a man wearing a navy colored coat with gold buttons bumped into my shoulders. I just stood in place until I saw her again. All the other people in wonder from the framework that is history getting made. Something that just sank to the bottom of the sea that was made to do the opposite scares them. What if? Was all they were talking about. Names I didn't understand as there was so many getting there point crossed. Those people on the ship that was coming into port must have thought about all the people that where going to rush them. It was odd to me as I looked at the faces of these people rushing for the boat, and all I saw was death attached to them as if it was sucking the salt from their skin for payment of knowledge their loved ones are indeed never coming home. Yet, what is home. You have one here on this planet, and when you die there is one forever in a kingdom above. Are we truly home?

My brother Andrew was a man on the ship. He was the Morse code reader. Mother was here to see if his body was still at sea or if he was going to walk off the ship. She told him to quit as soon as he gotten here. The only way to get him here is if he worked his way here to the states. If he is alive, he did it the hardest way yet. Mother and I came here about three years back as mother gotten a job in button factory. She over sees her line of girls for sixteen hours a day, and still finds the time to smile when she gets home. We live two hours from here, and yet we still happened to be one of the first to get here.

Ladies crying out from the pain that they gotten news their loved ones where gone. Once they found out the news all I saw was a fog over their faces as they were done with the kiss of death. They paid there fair. The men who are with them all struggling to figure out where there money is coming from as now there money crop is now gone swimming with fish. The people who work for their money there family I knew didn't make it. the rich always comes first before anyone else. As money walks. I bet as the water was rising in the boat, they still wanted to unlock there jewelry as if it was a pet. Here I was pinching my hand on the top as mother always dose this when I say something that went against her better judgement. Betting was an odd she didn't like much. Looking at all these faces there wasn't anyone I knew. I only knew three people. Mother, Andrew, and Emma the shopkeeper's daughter. All her family was on that boat too. That's another reason I was here to see if they made it.

"Andrew Cann!" All I heard was a goofy laugh. Even though his underwear was wet and sucking up his bottom side he still found time to laugh. He isn't going to laugh later when he must pull the fabric off his skin. I couldn't figure out where that voice came from as I was surrounded by numbers of people.

It was as if time stood still for me. All the people stopped in their tracks and frozen in a memento of time. There he was my brother standing behind me. Wearing that hat with a white star on it, spats over his boots, with the uniform he loved so dear. To me it was as if that smile was a smile only me. I walked up to him as he put his arms up for me to hug him. "Up!" I forced his hands over his head, as I had to pull up his shirt. Placed my ear over the skin on his chest. Had to feel the heat on my ear from his skin, if anything I had to hear a heart beating in him. He stood there with his hands over my head as he didn't want the people to see me crying into my brother's torso. Could feel the vibration from his laughing. His fingers lifted my chin. How did he pick me out of this mess? We both looked over to our side as mother cried out when she saw the two of us together. She hugged her boys not letting us go. Thing is she didn't know him as she was a stranger, but my handwritten letters home made her want him added to this family.

Mother was in the front seat near Mister Adams who drove us to the city. Leaving the other people to sorrow on their own was a hard thing to do as I gotten the one thing, I wanted the most. I just sat in the back seat with my head on his shoulders playing with his fingers as he slept. What these fingers have seen and done just to get to this moment to let me play with them. My eyes were lining the print on each fingertip. Placed his hand under my nose as you could smell the rope burn from when they lowered the lifeboat into the water. His hand was worm, but it felt death and that will never leave him. When I look at him sleeping, I see father, as I took after mother. He came back to us, and yet it felt as if I was telling the other people that it didn't matter if your loved one was dead, I had my brother. His legs kept shaking as if the tension would not set into his muscles. The rest of the way I held his coat into my hands. In the inside pocket was love letters from a lady named Alice Ivory, Emma's sister. Do I have the heart to tell him that she was dead now? I gotten the first boat home; he was on the second one that was attacked before getting to shore. They wanted to hide the men in the ship with passengers, so it didn't get attention. Wish I was just on his boat too. Just think he didn't want to be my friend at first now we are better than that. When he woke mother handed us a few sandwiches, he just put the whole thing in his mouth at once. Wish I could have done that. In the back of my mind I knew I was Freddie, but I knew that I was reliving the moments before William's father meet Ms. Louise. As she was on the side of the road with a nail in her tire. That's how the meet as he changed the tire. What I couldn't figure out is that if she puts him in the wall during this time, then why did she bring him back to nineteen eighteen to raise him, unless she really wanted to make sure they never knew each other. Yet at the same time she knew I was there; she was training him to kill me from birth. What went wrong?

December 6th, 1944

Ate two apples today, forgot how they tasted.

Chapter 17
Rabbit Tracks

(William!)

England 1919

The postman was taking longer than usual. People in here packed in like a bowl of nuts waiting to be eaten on a holiday. The wind was coming in from all the corners of this building as the toll of the war was showing itself. Old man Witherspoon was in his later years but as a true fighter he stepped up to run the town's post. Thing was you had to wait half of your shore leave just on him getting your letter out saying you are coming home. In my case I was trying to surprise them. Trying to get the letter before they make me out. They are meaning my loved ones. By the time it gotten to me he was about to close. So, I put the sign up for him as he was itching his head on were the key was to lock the door. "He's the last one boy after he lock up the place." There was a man that came into the place not showing his face as he kicked off the snow from his boots. Locking the door with the key that I found under the welcome mat the young or older man went to the counter. Why was he here? Guess even the rich need to get their mail. His shoes had golden implant enclosed around the laces. That walking stick he held has a finishing to it with a pug head on the top of it. White gloves that has been bleached many times even these times gotten to him as well. His pants were tight to his legs as his coat at the end came to a point. Looked like someone took their scissors to the end cutting it halfway up the middle. There was this top hat on his head that was a darker green more than an emerald shade. While he was breathing, I could hear it in his lungs. In a way I felt bad for him. On his waist band was a chain that had a little watch attached at the end. When he was done getting his mail, I was next he even left without showing me his face. But I had the key he could not get out. "We are closed! Come back in the morning." He waved his hands at me to get away." Cannot believe my luck.

"Wait! I have been here an hour and your still haven't gotten me my letter." I was getting ready to leave and give up on getting him to get back here from listening to his shows on his radio.

"You know blue isn't your color sir!" The stranger went behind the counter as I looked up to the back of his head, to the letter wall trying to figure out my name. He was trying.

"Sir!" Okay let us see where this goes. Those eyes the boy from the tea shop followed me.

"I'm more into red myself!" He turned to let me see his face. He had curly brown hair and blue eyes. He had this freshness to him. His smile made you smile back because that was just the way he was. All he had to do was look at you and he had his hook. "If you give me your name, I can get your letter." I do not know you sir, but you and I are locked in here for the moment. You have not hurt me too. Guess it is alright.

"William Starr! The letters addressed to me mom Louise." His fingers danced over the opening of the boxes. He made a noise when he found it. "Thank you!" That is what you say to young man who was standing there doing a thing that can land him in jail? He bent over on the counter wagging his bottom like a dog to his tail. He looked my face over like it was a letter unread.

"What are you doing later solider? My folks are having a party to recognize the end of the war. Why do not you do me the honor of letting you come with me. Plus, one!" He smiled.

"I have to think about it, and for your knowledge blue is my color." I turned to unlock the door.

One moment I am finding myself falling to the floor with everything going blank as if my eyes closed and I was sleeping for a long time, then to open my eyes as if I was a different person like everything from my death to my next life wasn't real. Like I was stuck in a void where time stood still until I was ready to come back, but everyone was older in the case I was in they were all dead. To me life is strange the way it happens. The moment we leave we come back knowing the people we knew in the past. Like growing up in my house I would hear myself in dream say, "Man I can't believe I have to come back as my brother's grandchild." In a grumpy voice. Yet the wife I had in this life is very mean trod me if she only knew who I was. Then at the same time so I know who I was? We play different roles in people's lives to give them something to grow on. Thing is we lose a part of ourselves as we gain. That is the reason we cannot move on. Life is a game, a test to see if we are ready for a bigger role, a more gifted life. Yet we keep failing. I know the moment my mother made me grow up again I gained a lot more know how. That it makes me a double trouble case. See it's strange being married to a young man who can live here with us, yet he knows the can talk with those who are not here and get help in that way too. See thing is he is not going to remember this in his next life. If we are chosen for a reason than what is life if we must come back? If I do good in this life, have kids and all that good stuff then my next life I do not have kids then how does that work? Freddie was breaking down a wall that no one wanted to be torn down, but he is saying that it is time for it to be broken. Do not fear the fear inside as once you face it there is nothing left. But what life has in store. In away preserve the history and the woods so when I come again, I can learn it again and odd to it. Plus, I want to see a deer in the woods, not a building for my health to crash and burn as you take that away. I think about death as I cheated it twice, but the next time if he goes with me, I will welcome it. walking and thinking lead me to my house.

There was a lady I think sitting in front of this mirror dusting her face with powders. Could not see much as my glasses were off my face. Nothing but bubbles of colors in my eyes. "Your glasses are in your right boot." That was her voice I knew it. Boots! My hands looked for boots, but I was having a hard time finding it. "There on the table facing you." Glad she was there to tell me!

"Did you change me!" I was not wearing what I was wearing when I went to sleep. A white nightgown felt more like a dress. How did men walk in these things? Edith was breathing very heavy while watching me in the mirror.

"Stop tripping over your own feet. We have a meal to get ready for. Take off the nightgown and put on the clothing I set out for you." She pointed, I started walking. "What is it now?" Was it the half smile of the turning red of the face thing that had thrown you off?

"You see me naked!" She rolled her eyes; I saw her in the glass.

"Please I've seen you before. Nothing to write home about. I mean I don't know how my cousin works miracles with that thing anyway." Did she just! Let it slide off the tip of her tongue William. Let it go, and fart in her face later when she is not looking.

"Well at least my boyfriend doesn't die after dating me." She had it coming. She stood with her puffy dress on walking trod the door knocking on it. Did I say something? There was tension in the air. When the door opened a man dressed in high class poor boy clothing came walking in with a powdered wig on his head.

"Lady Edith!" Did he stand tall like a wooden solider for her?

"Yes, my husband needs you to dress him. Please make sure he gets what is coming to him." She left without looking at me. I take that as a good thing. He shut the door. Walking over to my backside. Lifting the back of the nightgown making me feel the wind on my bottom. This was his job to dress me. I quickly put the fabric back down. He breathed in heavily as if he did his job wrong and I was going to get him fired. His eyes gotten bigger too. "Sir, my job is to dress you and that is all. If you like I can be your waterman as well."

"Can I ask you something?" He stood there not blinking. I knew him he was the man from the post. Why act rich knowing you're not?

"I am here for your every need sir." What does one say? "Yes, I know you see that I am who I am, but Outside of here I think to be more like the chap you saw in the post."

"Be yourself for here with me. I do not want this man who stands like a toy. We are alone be yourself. Now it does not bother you to bath another man while he stands there facing you. Nor testing the odds of seeing him dress." His face started to laugh giving me the lines of his smile.

"Well if I to be truthful they're kind of funny looking. They do not look like mine and I know that is not right. I just thought where they used them so much or not at all." I do not know who was laughing harder me or him.

"See you can be yourself with me. I know she is waiting to go the ball. I make you a deal I will go play nutcracker solider for her if you be my boy. No one else is to tend to me." I think, I can get used to this time period. Sometimes I feel as if there was something missing. Like I was standing in a giant snow globe. Dressed like a wooden solider from, head to toe. Dancing a show in one spot for whomever comes by, but the thing is I am in the woods where not many people walk these paths. Waiting for someone to come set me free so I can see the outside world. That must be how he feels never getting to see the world for what it is as he was born in lower class. Yet I am never was supposed to be here in the first place. He leads me this dining room as he pulled out my chair.

There was a man with a toothpick making kiss faces as he picks the food out from his mouth. One lady trying to balance a book on her head as she puts the spoon to her lips. One man looking at another winking as they had a secret code for something. Me, I am trying to figure out what spoon to use at what time and trying to not touch the napkin on my lap. Poor thing the girl I am here with blushed and called me names. Then she even knocked the finger bowl out my hands. I just want to know why men must wear corsets too. Feel my ribs going into other parts of my body. The table full of fancy crystals, and all the people silk fancies. The host of this party was an old lady whose money was bigger than her ego. Her nose could be in the air more she could teach me to back flip. We would not have been here if Edith did not get a tip that Ms. Louise had visited this family just the week or so before. Making me stand in for the son. Each seat had a butler, mine was quiet, and new as he spilled the first course on my back side. Fine white gloves, and a tuxedo to boot. He places a long candlestick holder with a blue egg sitting on the top. Only one hand of the butler goes in front of the guest. This time he places both around me. The other hand placed a little bottle with a cork on. It was full of water. No one was looking at him, so he took the chance.

"I know why you are here." I patted my lips as I excused myself from the table. Every time you leave the table to go anywhere the butler follows. The bath was not that far from the dining room. You could still here the music playing through the walls. He stood with his back to the door with one hand at his side and the other one behind his back. He was looking to the other wall not even blinking.

"You wish to explain this bottle to me." His neck reacted as he swallowed extraordinarily strong. "Do you wish me to tell your head boy that you have been sleeping with me and there will never be a job you be able to get who don't know." His eyes widened as breathing went weaker. "Okay, I think you are the cute one out of the bunch, so I guess you're getting paid to take care of me. Then let us get started." My fingertip to my ring finger moved crossed the top of his hand he had on his side. Flirt with my eyes, he did not like that. He went from a wooden solider to walking to the sink looking at the bottom of its bed. He through off his coat, his vest went the other direction as his pocket watch busted when it fell to the floor. Tearing the buttons off his white nightgown as he pulled it off over his head. Lead myself to his side as I put my hands on his back. His skin was cold with all that clothing on him that was strange. His breast pumping faster than he was breathing. He had freckles that is lined his back making the shape of a turtle on his lower back.

"I'm not a fairy!" He thought. "Whatever dollar you spend on me the higher the level of work I'm supposed to give you." He thinks that I am after him to, no! He stood there with his trousers at his ankles looking as if he did not want him to be here no longer. There was one thing keeping him here and that was the money in my pocket.

"I just wanted information from you, that's all!" His eyebrows were up to the top of his forehead.

"Once alright, I was given a drink and didn't know it was happening until I was walking out of the son of the Duchess of Tottenham. He was carrying around a sack of balls that he did not win in a marble game" took some fabric as I placed it in water washing his face while he dressed himself. What Type of things did this family make him do? His fingers started to scratch at his skin. Tried to stop it but he kissed me thinking that is what I wanted. Pushed him as Freddie would not have this. "Fine!"

"Let's get you dressed and back to the table." His shirt was torn. Took the hat pin from the top hat I was wearing and some thread that Edith made me carry as a modern thing in 1887 was not something that needed to be shown. I learned to sew a long time ago, points for William.

"I didn't mean to put on a show. It was a hot day last week and I retired earlier than normal. It was that hot. I was in my room alone, so I put the uniform and all to hang dry. I was in my closet getting ready for the afternoon rush of it. The door slammed behind me as if the wind pushed it. When I saw her walking near the door. I put my hand over my lips, so she did not hear my breathing. She just walked up to my long underwear. And started to squeeze the fabric. Bottling the moisture from the cloth." I have one of them he stolen the bottle from her. "She didn't even think of me being there. Just went on her way." Biting the fabric with my teeth as she put his vest back on.

"Let's go back to the table." He pulled out my seat as I sat.

"You took forever!" Edith leaned into me to speak.

"My Butler was telling me how she time travels. From the moisture off a hardworking man's cloth." She took the bottle from my hands.

"I heard of this! A different water from a man doing different acts will be a base for different spells. The only other one I know of is after the man has a relation that water gives the wizard the ability to change their appearance for a few days. Must be how she became the old lady you knew on Sundays." She was speechless a first for everything. Even a cat had these days.

"We need to talk to the host." I mentioned as I picked up my spoon.

"Quail eggs, how divine." Who was she?

"Who is that lady Edith?" She looked at me like I should have known.

"That's the Lady of Tottenham, Why?" He ties to her son, yet her son is a mad man to them as they do not have his kind here. The butler was dragged into that world as he was his aid. The money thing makes sense now. "The tie pins your wearing of the man with a smile form each ear and brown hair, looking like he's smiling is your chaperon." How is a man's pin I ordered offline and brought here lead to him unless Edith knew that too? I need to be here to help him. "William you need to talk the butler to coming with us. He can help us with her wear about. As the last thing she hates more than a living person who saw her alive is someone that can tell us her spells too. He is with us if he likes it or not."

(William, in modern times.)

The icicles were dripping down near the screen splatting down onto the ground making a dripping sound if dripping made a sound. Berries growing nearby as the kisses they make are in the air for one to smell. Cherry blossom petals falling against the grass as it tries to shy out of its winters coat. Boots gathering the mud from the trail to the house as the water was gathering in socials to make puddles. Rabbits running in the woods as it makes a smile on this aged face. It is been five years now since we found a way for my mothers' powers to be taken away. The yeast was rising in the proofing drawer as I gathered the eggs. The sound of a child trying to get out of the glass from the windows was getting trapped in the fog that was taking heed. My first true love waiving from the window as these boots hit the bottom step letting the mud drop to the ground. My hands shaking from the sound and the echoes from the halls this households. Forcing me to drop the eggs as I hear the men's screams from the war the swallowed the late nineteenth century. A bit of ginger cake will hit the spot and get this out of me head. The stone pathway that was laid down last year a sound of a fancy stick was hitting one of the faces of the rocks. I did not want to turn as this was a trick was not it.

There was a fancy dressed man from the city. A bumble bee tie pin with a tinted yellow tie. With a penguin suit with an hourglass like coat and a tall top hat. His eyes were like jumping into an ocean so wind and deep and you would get lost running in that hair of dried weeds as the browns mellow as you run throw its beauty. Lush eyebrows like two boats flouting on the salt of the sea. A slender build as his lips bounced from the brush that powders his skin. I thought this was behind us and I was able to get my house in the woods with my family by my side. Yet the past was right behind me. She let him out of his cage. The one man I was keeping from my love is after all the love I loved the most. That red scarf was all I was wearing when we first made love. Was I being haunted from the past because of this life I chosen for myself? The jaw line if you looked hard enough was shaking like a leaf. It was mine! He always knew how to show up when the first frost hit the meadow. He smiled with the line on the side of his face as he saw something behind me that made him smile. As I turned the house was gone, Freddie was gone, our life was gone. Standing in the mud with him at the other end of the trail and nothing but grass and trees surrounding us.

He told me he was going to fight for my hand as I was the only person he ever loved. There were many nights he cried that having a chance to get me back he had to take it. I was hitting the rain as it feels as if he could feel it. Screaming out my pain as it brought me to my knees. As I stood there were a black ribbon in my pocket on the left. The other on the right held a purple one. I had to choose for myself. Do I get the past that I was trying to get back to, or do I spend it with what I came to have it? It had to be good one as it was meant for me to choose. Who was I truly in love with? I dropped one to the ground as if it were nothing but something that should be there. I buried him a long time ago. I chose!

December 7th, 1944

Took a bullet in the hip. Doc says I might be able to walk again. This hurts more than the time I stepped on mother's sewing needles.

Chapter 18
Invisible Headstones

(William!)

Last night I sat on the toilet seat looking at myself through the glass of this old fashion doctor's cabinet that Freddie brought home. I sat there as my finger's tips cascaded blood tips around my face and the back of my ears as I was trying to brush what hair I had behind them. Sat there as my nerves done all the talking. It looked like I was running but, yet I was sitting still. What is he going to say? Freddie, pause as I look him in the eyes. I lost the baby! He gets up and starts to hate me then love me. No! he's going to throw me out in this snowstorm as he doesn't want me no more like a toy you bring into the pool and forget in the waterbed. The surface to the seat was colder than normal. Red was running down the inside of this seat as the water was stained. Tears targeting my toes. Stand up and put the suspenders over your shoulders Starr boy. There is nothing left for me now. It took all I had to let him go. Holding this undeveloped baby in my hands. Rocking him to sleep. "I'm sorry was all I could say!" I was alone, but this was a good thing right! The cat is now scratching itself behind the door as the little bell was giving my child his wings. His name was going to be Stu, not his name is Stu.

"Hello!" Walton picked up the phone. Finally, as it took me an hour to get him. "William stop crying and tell me what's wrong." He was at work as the cash registers were making a noise in the background. There was a burning in my head as this was too much as my tears were stronger than my words.

"It's a boy!" He was happy as he thought he was an uncle. "Walt, it was a still born. I need you!" He was not there. Where did he go? A girl at the other end picked up his phone.

"Yes, hello. He just ran out to his car he be right back." Sorry to say it he was not. He was on his way here. He was faster than I thought. The baby was cold now like a turkey you get from the frozen section at the store. Never will I to eat meat again. The car door was left open as the key was yelling for him to come back. The front door swung open as fast that Mary lost her flowers. Walton took his corps and rested a sheet in a shoe box. Stood at the sink as the skin from my waistline down was pink as the blood ran down my legs. The cord was still hanging around coming out from my tail gate. My hands resting on the sink as my eyes watched this tired-out face. Walton helped the sack come out as I cried, I did that a lot lately. It just felt like a hard poop.

"No, let me stand here." Walt tried to get me to sit down, but the last time I did that this happened. "Walt, what do I tell my husband?" I looked as him throw the mirror. "first thing we get a coffin. Burry him with Harvey. Freddie's not to know." Slammed my fist on the countertop. "I failed him! It is my fault. I ran to hard last night or something. The doctor told me not, but I had to it in my nature." I was blaming myself. It was my fault. Walt took the back of my arms and force me to look at him. Did I fight him, but he did not let go?

"It wasn't your fault. Billy it was not his time. He was not meant to come here and do this purpose. They called for him to do another task. There's someone else coming, waiting." I took his hands as they were cold and wet.

"Thank you for being my brother tonight." He looked as me strange.

"Always! I think I lost the job, but that is their fault. Your more important." Walton was trying to get me to have some type of reaction, but it was not working. If I felt bad for him then at least I was not thinking of that child. "Do you still have that old dish that grandma ate off as a baby. It was yellow with kids playing on it." Tears were gathering on my face once more. Took his hands as he stopped talking. He was the only thing I had left.

"You know the first time I saw him, I thought he was the one. There was nothing else I was going to do with my life if he was not in it. Now it is falling at my feet." He looked at the window thinking if Freddie pulled up, but he was not. "The night I was in room eighteen with him. I know this is not something you wish to hear." Getting the tears away from my face. I was testing him.

"Tell me! Too late for it." He said it like I wanted him too. Even men have feeling even though you say we don't.
Your daddy always told you that this was just an illusion. Put on your glasses even though you are not smart boy you look the part. Yet why does life have to be a wonder behind glass walls in front in your eyes? Your daddy told you that the world was out there to take it as it was to fall on your will. They did not know you. Well he also told you he catches a grenade for you, but we found out what happens when they say they would do that. He taught you to shave, to throw a football, to laugh when time gotten to you. The thing is we do not know what was going to happen, if we did, we did not know the whole picture. You can dance for him as he played his musical box. Thing is you would walk a tight the tight rope for him, but you walk it for me instead. Human is what

you are. That is all I can ask of you. Your daddy made you human, but you did much more than that. Never letting them push you down as you stand back up. You have what it takes to do this. Whipped the water off from my hands as I was nerves. It was worse than the time I went to take the test for my permit. It was worse than the time I went to court for my speeding ticket and I didn't even feel safe then as the cops in this county were on their phones texting each other making fun of the people as they came to the counter. I was better than they are they might have a gun, but I have bravery. Sitting here as there was an old time turn style phone sitting on the surface. Each cell has another person talking to another person on the other side of their glass they were sitting front of. The door behind me was locked for safety yet all that protects me from the bad parts of this world is glass. Officer Gary stands near the door watching all the men sitting there. Making sure they do not get out of line. But he stands there as if he was plastic waiting for his boy to play with him again. He did not too much older than I was. He was spent, he had it with this job.

But he had to keep it as there was a family of little ones at home. He did not want to let them down. You know it was bad when the first letter in his name was miss spelled and I noticed that. Masquerade for now Gary. Get out and live a little sir as you do not want to go home lie in your bed thinking you dug your grave early. There is more. Here I am telling a cop to live his life behind glass without my lips are not moving. Change the world, what if it cannot be done? People are set in their ways there is no turning back. His breath took hold of the see-through material that is made from sand no matter what you do. My heart was pumping me harder than the night I was with your son sir. Again, nothing was coming out of my lips. It was cold in here my cardigan has not made me feel any colder in here. Freddie was there in the doorway as my brother called him. He wiped off his backside as he went to get something from the kitchen. He came over to take my hands. Forcing me to my feet. I did not want to get up at all but what he said made me want to. Nothing, but he did not have to. He was going to sing our song. He was wearing that royal blue suit coat that I loved so much with his black pants with matching tie, and that white button up shirt that I ironed last night. I didn't know he was leaving the next day until I read the letter he left under my glasses.

December 8th, 1944

Got to meet some good men here in the field hospital. Someone should write their stories down. Will I be forgotten with time?

Chapter 19
Drummer Boy

(William!)

1. Earl J. Clark, Oakland Oklahoma, Teacher
2. Steven Kirk, Illinois. Farmer
3. Andrew Cann, New Hampshire, Car Salesman
4. Gibson Wood, Charleston Tennessee, Singer
5. Pip Pfeffer, Alabama, Forest Ranger
6. Thomas Franks, Peachtree Georgia, Hiking Guide
7. Wiley Boone Craft, California, Producer
8. David Rose, Vermont, Iceman
9. Pymm Jordon, Texas, Cattle Rancher
10. Gordon Nichols, North Dakota, Lumber Jack
11. Bennett Peters, Utah, Historian

There were a field of eleven men lying face deep in the wet dirt all lining a trail like logs into a cranberry bog. Each man missing a different part of their uniform as if whom ever did this was collecting one thing from each man to remember there kill. Each one had a different name on their dog tag as my eyes read the names, I was thinking about the mothers in waiting for their return or the somebody they were to a pacific someone. Freddie once told me that if you think it through that each man died in the war. Any war you want to think of. With each war they bleed into the ground well if science is writing and most of the time what is in the blood breaks down to make underground water. Then we are indeed drinking their blood. I feel as if I just blown the mind of millions of genealogy nerds right now. When the body count stopped in its own tracks there was a canvas tent with a red giant cross on the side. It smelt like black garlic and vinegar. No, it was the urine that just left all those dead men on the ground under my feet. Each man was different. Todd Franks was tall and slender with a firm character and no wedding ring. He also scratched himself when he was nerves as there are scratch marks on the back of his arms. Wiley Boone Craft had blond hair that I could look at for days I even have the same hair type and still get mad at how closer to white his hair was. He had a long face with a nice curve to his back. As I am crossing over each body Freddie was not far behind making sure their souls went to the light. For some odd reason, each man had drums around the grass and sticks on their persons.

I did not want to know who was behind the tent flaps, but what I wanted to know if my thoughts were right. There were eleven drummers out here if this person going based off the song from when we were kids then where was the other man. He was missing and I wish to find his footing. I heard something like when you break a chicken bone in half and give it to the dogs. Looked back and there was Freddie taking off the uniform from the one man. "What on earth are you doing?" He looked up me like a face stuck in an old locket that a woman worn until her loved came home yet he never came home.

"William dress like one of them that way they think you from this time and they will not kill you as fast. I felt dirty. Taking off my pants so I could put his on. Freddie made me put on his tags to play the part, but I was trying to hold back the tears as there was a fingerprint on them made from the man's own blood. "You know at home I have letters that men typed and delivered to their loved one's home saying there not coming back, ration books, and letters. Trying to figure out where the families are and return them to their families. Now I must face the fact that I must witness the events for myself. Thank you very much." I whispered to Freddie as if he were listing to me anyway.

"Look at me, this is two thousand ten not World War One. They are here at the same time we are and there is no play battle being held here today of so millions of people would watching big belly men running on a field dressed in clothing that don't fit them no more." He was right we had the right to let them die for a reason they thought they were sent here for. I did not think, I just went into the tent. There was a cot with the bedding on it to my left. A table at the end of it with a wash basin. On the right a single chair with a man inside of it. There was a man sitting there staring as if he was lifeless and he was waiting for the kid to come home and play with him. A lady was on the other side of the tent getting a needle ready to put in the man's arm.

"Happy holidays to me! Twelve men drumming away on me until death do, we part." There was no question to who she was. She was my mother. The voice is all I had to hear. "William darling wearing his clothing isn't going to fool me. I knew it was you from the smell your body give off your skin smells like pistachios." She must drink blood from a man's blood who was pure. That has not been with another person because they were not wed yet. See the warms of her basement gets them inside her basement it is getting them to walk down the stairs that kill them. Once faced with a door opened to a darkness not knowing what is waiting for you is the hardest thing as they never see it coming.

"Mother let me have this one! I have to learn the family trade sometime now!" she played with the tip of the needle thinking about it.

"You got the one I wanted. If it was not for you, he be dead, and the gift be mine a long time ago. No, you don't get." She read his dog tags as if it were a tag off a gift you get during the holidays. "Walter Stalter!" Sounds like a candy flavor. "I had a change of heart and you can have him. I will kill him later. Just remember my dear son of mine that when you take one another shale takes his place!"

"I can tell you that time is nothing to play with. Yet, you did! We are paying the price. Freddie do not have the gift no more it was taken away from him the moment I saw the dead police officer in my tub under the water. I still have the bullet he made me take out of his head. He was a ghost mother. Tell me how I still have the bullet when it supposes to be in the evidence at the police station? You read his tags wrong that's not his name." She dropped the tray that she was carrying with the needle and what have you on it.

"You have the gift now too. No, you have it from him as it hides in people if it knows it is in danger. Killing Freddie is not the key. You got the bullet being you are a Tin Starr and can-do things with metal it combined the two powers as one. If I kill all the living things on this planet it will still go into the stones." Her lips were fading like a watered-down painted barn in the middle of a winters storm. I bent down as if I was going to pull up my bootstraps, but really, I was looking for Edith's wand. She went to find Freddie outside she never thought I was telling her the truth. He made his way in from the back of the tent like I taught him. Knowing that my Freddie could get the two of them to safety using the man's sweat I had to go and find Edith she is here somewhere the wand will tell me.

The metals from the ship was buckling as it was taking in water. The only thing that is not frozen in time was the air surrounding us. I was looking a sailor in the face who was in a running pattern. His one foot trying to step down on the floor as the other in the air. Not wearing any pants as he had just enough time to get on his shirt and hat then run remembering the other men sleeping underneath not knowing the attack has happened. His eyes looking forward as all he wanted to do was save lives. "Do you wish to tell me why we are helping save this man. He was supposed to save lives." Edith's hair was in her face as we ran off the deck onto the land. The silence of man was there in the air. All these men running from the bombs coming from where they did not know. "Edith!" I yelled! As I ran, she stopped short. She was scared as she looked me

199

in the face twice in the same moment. It was Strange to see me running from this, but if they moved me from this moment, I did not save my best friend who married my future wife in my absence. Trying to catch my breath. "Edith, I was in England when I heard that my Father's family wanted me to stay with them in the states. I spent a year with them before signing up. I ended up here not knowing a thing. Those two mates get to the nurse's station then was found hiding in the cleaning closet with one man's gun pointed at the enemy. There were so many men who died whose screams we heard, and I returned home a hero for hiding." She came over after kissing my frozen face taking the man's arm. Leaving a letter in my coat that I did not remember at all.

"We need to get him to safety!" I asked why! "He's my Brother. After you told me what you told me I did my digging too. He gets to the door that will not open and he goes under with them. No matter what those men died." My arms were getting weak from the dragging. Felt the mud from the spats on my shoes I took from another man's belongings. I stopped as my vision was taken from me. There was a time when Freddie told me about this happening to him. My eyes made me look at a soldier on the ground as bullets were flying, he was trying to move backward as he could not move. It was if he wanted me to see his darkness from the fear. There was no way to tell it to you as I did not know myself. It was as if he was a log and I was hiding in his body looking out. Turing into this ball of gas that released from his death. "William!" my vision returned with her voice as there was sailors all over the place. Standing watching me. One of the men came out from the line of them looking sad.

"Man, let us die just get time going again so we can get to it." He was sadder than I could even try to think.

"Where the ones who die protecting you. We knew that Freddie was supposed to save us all. We cannot be ready from him if you do not let us get to the light. Now take this man save him then put time back ticking." There was a fifteen-year-old who said he was of age that came about this time. Edith did not know who I was talking to.

"How do you know about Freddie?" I stated.

"That's why we signed up to fight knowing we were going to be here to waiting to die. This is bigger than all of you, but you five are the only ones with boots, and heels on the ground in the future. You five where chosen to stop this. We were told at any cost." I looked over to Edith as what was going on here. "We all want to be on the right side of history. You need to know that the light will be blocked not letting anyone in soon. That is her last stand. We need to be there to help stop her. Freddie needs to be ready for this. He needs to be the one to bring peace to the dead and the living. It all leads to that. You need to be there to help his do that."

"Yeah, but if we stop her there are going to others out there who will want what she is after. All the control." He heard my heart beating faster than what I needed.

"Yeah, this war isn't going to end, but at least we have to try." I rather be getting drunk on the mountain with Thomas Conklin then take a swim about this time. Yet we went on running with John W. Cotton under my arms. When we gotten to the safe zone. Edith used her wand letting time resume. Edith and I walked with him after he ran into the wall when time went back into place. He rested on the bench in the hall.

"Edith, what is my sister doing in Pearl Harbor!" I shrugged my shoulders as he was her brother not mine.

"Mother didn't know I went after you signing up to be a nurse. When I heard you were going to be here, so this was my way making sure your safe." Why was he so important as he can time travel? He went back in time to get a letter a letter that changes the playing field. It proves that there are people planted in time that know the future who are on her side.

Mister President a symbol for all boys young and old to look up to. To try to be like him a nobleman. Everything we all want in life is to be noticed. I might not be on the money like he is today, but I will make myself known as I see fit. When they notice it, it is too late you got pulled in. The Civil War went a calling for me to come. One day at church the third Sunday of March Father Booker gathered the three remaining boys left of this small town. He led us into the woods when he stripped us to our birthday suits and told us to find our way home. He took away the boy and replaced us as men. On the way we all stuck together making us brothers now. When we got to town Father Booker moved the town east to New York. Said if we get back alive to meet him back here and he will help us out. We got dressed in what he left.

Washington did not get to see much of it just old buildings. When we listed up the men took us by wagon to a farm. In the barn Mr. President's men gave us our orders. Fred got to stay behind to take care of the children who were now orphaned. It fit him being he was our town's schoolteacher. The other boy was my older brother, William the last thing I remember about him was seeing the back of his head, his black waive hair leave the barn doors. Mama gotten the news of his passing as soon as I retuned. I was the only one out of the three of us that made it back. My brother went to go pick his gun back up, while he bent down a solider from the other side stuck his gum up his butt and made him beg for his life until he took him. I miss him. One of Mr. President's men stood, he handed me a gun. Did not want to even know how to shut it. To look a man in his eyes and shut his soul out. Cannot do it. He told me to shut him. I could not shut him ever. The gun hole pointed at the man, then my hands put the gun down. I told him that it was not my place to do so. He did not say I was weak, but I was different than the other two boys that came in. He could tell as I was the shortest. So, he handed me a drum, and made me a drummer boy. He handed me a red drum with two sticks on it. Then he told me something I could not forget. I had a message for Mr. President, and I had to give it to him. It is in the drumsticks there is a copy in each of them just if I lose one on my way. The letter was to end this war just wish I gotten there sooner than my brother might be alive to this day.

We walked about eight hours without resting for a spell or two. Boy when they decided to make for the night my feet gave them a thanks. These men knew I had the message. It was there job to make sure the message gotten to the white house. I sat outside of the flaps of my tent. There was just an old trunk sitting in there. I oversaw protecting the food supply. That trunk was bigger than I was. Just sitting there looking at the full moon wondering if my kids would get there someday. One of the men pulled out his violent, boy did not that sound good that beats the quiet. You could tell that they were getting started on the moon shine. They sounded my daddy at Sunday dinners, singing along with the song of the sweet piece of wood he was holding. Yankee songs, I guess. I gotten to know one of the men he was about my age and he had red hair. He grew up three hours from my town. Did not know it but we found that we were related his mother was my father's sister. Small world once you think about it. He looked like my brother so much. It filled the emptiness I had. His name was Dalton. He grabbed my arm and pulled me toward the others. He let go and started too dance. Shaking his head and just letting the music in before I knew it, I was dancing too. I found I could trust my new friend. Away from home, but I made a brother in a short time. Got mad at the violent player said I was the wrong drummer boy to go. Dancing not worried of what was going on. He knew I could not even shut a gun. I just ran back to my tent ripping everything off my body that scrammed war. Took my journal, my drum and bag and took off I stopped for a voice.

"Leaving so soon." Walton cried; all I could do was stare at him. "That's all you can do is stare at me. Those ladies do not let them in that head of yours were chosen for a reason. There's a river for a bath if you like it is a few minutes from here." His Irish way of talking was confusing, but I knew what he was trying to say, get away for a while. We took a tub and filled it with water and brought it back to the tents. He was the first to take one. Dalton called me out for my turn, but I did not want a turn as we heard leaves crunching in the wood line. We did not know what to think. The two of us linked hands to make sure if there was an attack, we would not be separated. We ran into the tent as fast as we could. We took the trunk and emptied the food out of it. Took my green blanket and put it in the bottom. I hid my drumsticks under it all. Walton laid down on his side first. Then making a Z pattern I laid down as well locking us in. We gotten in the trunk to boys laying sideways in a trunk what was I thinking. I did not know how to shut a gun, but I knew how to hide. While in the trunk we could hear the other men fighting away. We knew the mission we were here to do.

"I don't like being man handled here, boy." It was the man who played the violent they brought him in my tent I watched through the whole. He would not say where I was. They took him. We gotten down as flat as we could as the southerner approached the trunk. He shot four times through the trunk. Thinking there were men inside of it. You need the key to open it, so he did the nest best thing. We gotten lucky it was a big trunk and he was a bad aim. I took the bean that Dalton had and torn off some of my red long johns and mixed it in my mouth and spit it through the whole. That was not a taste I do not want in my mouth again. He saw it was red and thought there was no one else so he took off. We then took ourselves out of the trunk. I gave my hand to the man they shot; he took his last breath win in minutes. He told me to make sure that this end. He told me were to find the fresh clothing that the troop had. His eyes closed with the memory of his wife laying in his thoughts. When I left the tent there, he was the only other one still standing. Standing there holing his pride as he was bare after the bath. Shacking like a leaf. Now I have the image of what my brother would look like naked in my head. I found the clothing where he said it was along with a picture of his wife. Took the picture with me maybe one day I will pay my respects. We only put on the long johns we found. Did not look back. Two boys walked the river without bare feet, long johns and a drumstick.

We walked and walked to the location we had to be at. Eating berries and we had plenty of water. We gotten to the house with dirty feet, and we sweated right through our long johns it stuck to our skin. The way we smelled made the people hold their nose. I did not get to meet Mr. President I did not have an appointment and was underdressed to speak. I was presented to his wife. Lady President, she took the note. It was done faster than I could even speak. The two of us were heroes. I did not want to be a hero. I just wanted to go home. Sure, there was a big party for ending the war. I had one more thing to do. We were giving new clothing, and Mrs. President gave me a locket with my brother's picture in it. That is when she gave me the bad news about his death. All I get is a picture? I went back to the spot; Father Booker was there like he said he was going to be. We started a new town named after my brother. Walton and I token a wife and together are raising our families together. Took a job with the United States mail. I wanted you to know my story, Mr.

President. Someone rather knows. This letter was written by Freddie and Dalton the man I left him with. They ended going back in time as my mother was on their heels.

December 9th, 1944

Thomas Kyles did not let me sleep last night poor fellow. His right lung was hurting him again as his wheezing was loud. He gotten blood everywhere. I felt for him.

Chapter 20
Pressed Flowers

(Freddie!)

Today would mark the three-year anniversary when I started the cashiering job I gotten back in high school. You remember the one where I was trained for a day and fired that night when they were locking up. The only reason I handled the register was because the girl you had training me was inside the bathroom stall texting for an hour and there was no one else scheduled. It was that night I was able to cross over my first ghost. Did not know who was happier to get the news the mother or her daughter. Her daughter was in high school at the time as she was a tired over worked mother just trying to give herself something to keep her mind off him being away, so they came shopping.

Mother: Hello there how are you today: (I smiled at her and asked the normal questions until I felt these few fingers tap me on my left shoulder. That is how my boss always got my attention. Instead when I turned there was a whole new room like I was in. I could feel the mat under my feet they give you, so you do not stand on the concrete so long. Felt the coldness surrounding me. There was this boy standing there where the first register was meant to be. He was smiling so big that only he could be happy about being dead. He asked me to tell his mother something. When I turned, I saw the daughter's eyes roll?)

Daughter: That was mean. (I tried to apologize but she wanted me to just cash her out and she will talk to my boss later. I had to try and figure out how to tell her that he was here without her thinking I was nuts. Put my hands on the counter with the nails only hitting the counter.)

Me: Do you get any discounts? (I name them off one at a time until she told me she did not. she was waiting for the total, but I was not telling her the amount yet.) Do you get the military discount? How do I out this dose anyone in your family belong in that line of work. A boy with blond hair. (The mother looks at me strange as her daughter put the screen of the phone down.)

Mother: Just tell me my total please! (I had to figure out if she was the one for the message as if I did not know as she was the only one here in the middle of the last hour of being open. I looked down to the counter as I thought. Then looked over to the pocketbook wall. Buying myself some time.)

Me: Your son was in the military, wasn't he? He went missing. (Her lips where going to say the word, what. But she kept herself from saying anything else.) You can still use his discount as he died only a few weeks ago. It only goes until a month after his passing for you to use it. Ten percent is not bad. (Oh, if I was not fired by this moment.)

Mother: What are you talking about? (I was scared but I had to say it for him.)

Me: I Do not know how to say this, but I can see things not many people can see.

Mother: That was him was not it? You were not trying to be rude. He wanted to talk to you before I left. Your connected to that side.

Me: (I smiled as I went on to describe him.) He has blond hair. He is short, and he smiled so wide that, that was his most thought of feature when he was created. He was standing in there with his hands behind him with his uniform on. He smelt like and old book you take off the shelf and flip through the pages. He told me to tell you he is okay he is where he was meant to be. That your I forgot the nickname he said. He has round eyes like oval.

Mother: He knew that he wanted to do something with his life. So, he joined the army. I did not want to be a worried mother waiting to hear of him dying. That is all he wanted to do was help people. He was big church going boy, and always respected his elders. Your described him to the blond hair. He knew he was going to die young.

Daughter: We were waiting on the word as he went missing in action. His plane went down. Now we know. Wow! (I felt this wind coming from behind me. It even brushed on the mother's face.)

Mother: That was him was not it? He crossed over, good boy. He could have come through anyone, but he chose you he did not trust a lot of people so he must have trusted in you to tell me. That makes you family. (She had his military card in her wallet as she showed it to me. She wanted me to have a photo of him, but I told her that I did not need it, it was hers. I had his name and everything, but I forgot it.) I remembered his face. Also, his sister friended me online.

(William!)

The trumpets started as his feet come onto the stage. He held his hat at the side of his face, so you did not see who it was. When he stood at the microphone his hat was now in front of his head. The people in the audience whispering about who it was up there. When the trumpet made a different note, he would move his hat as if he were going to let us see who it was. They all were floored. He put the hats rim under his eyes not letting us see his lips as his eyes made a funny surprise. Then his hat went up to his eyes only letting us see his lips as he licked them. Then he topped it, his hat was in front of the mic as we still could not see his face. But he started to sing. I knew it was my Freddie's grandfather's voice, but they did not. yes, I was back here in 1909 but I had to see him again. Freddie did not know I was here. Kipper was killed the last time I saw Freddie, so now I needed to play this game. He was my card holder.

"There's no drinking on the moon,
Just me dancing without you,
Reminds me of times you said,
Mister moon loves you too,
What do I do?"

He sang that song in a jazz way with his voice. I sing that sometimes. I did not know it was one of his. The last word from each line he held the notes that made you feel the waive the song gave off. He was a funny singer too. That is something his grandson gotten too. He walked off stage as they wanted more but he was just the opening act. The lady in a green dress came on who was not as good but she will do, I guess. Had two glasses of some drink on this table. I told the waitress to bring the bar tenders best. Thomas Waters was passing my table as his eyes looked down to mine. The tips of his fingers wrinkled the top of the table I was sitting at. He stopped as he looked around him. He sat, but he was not happy I was here. He took that hat he was wearing as he leaned over the table and placed it on my head.

"That blond hair of yours is going to give us away. Do you love death wishes?" He took in a heavy breath as I had to think.

"Well I married into the company!" Took a sip from the glass and spit it right back out. What was in this glass. Thomas drank it looking for more. I think this ends up becoming a bottled floor cleaner in the future.

"What do you need? Can't be caught talking to you for long." I scratched my chin.

"The Silver Leaf Society members are here, tonight, aren't they? I need you to get me into the meeting. The one happening later tomorrow night." He looked up as if he just swallowed a goldfish.

"Did you put a radio nurse into my room that I couldn't see? How do you know that I know about this society?" I had his card up my sleeve.

"Freddie's grandmother is a member, isn't she?" He hit the table as he did not want this information out. I took a modern photo from the future as I showed him the photo of the lady and daughter that Freddie helped.

"Yes, you need to know that Freddie's brother wasn't supposed to die. It was to teach them a lesson. Freddie gotten in the way and did not know about it. Your mother's a member too you know." Freddie's brother? "I already told you too much." He was playing with tie pin now.

"My mother's the president. See Freddie and I are not part of this society. We chose to side with The Orm." He was smiling and I did not know why!

"He chose right! See now Freddie is the rarest of them all." He kicked me in the bottom on my knee cap. "That was a member I had to hide your face." Getting the feeling that hat trick on the stage was practice. "Seekers are a threat to witches. As they can do magic that they cannot understand. They can talk to the dead and much, much more. He is the last one left. You must have this baby to keep it going. One more thing. I have many children. At least one in each state, still that have grandchildren by the time you come from. You need to find them. There might be more seekers." He handed me a list of names on the back of a napkin. With their addresses. I think I got the message.

"Where do we start?" He knew the answer.

"When you are stabbed in the back by your best friend. He puts a bullet in your side. That's when you start." Sounds like he has done this before. He reached into his pockets. Hands me a necklace with a bottle charm.

"What's this?" This was odd.

"The one he is wearing isn't working no more. Give him this one and his powers will come out with every day." He paid for the drinks as he stood from the table. Looking at his dance card again. Looking for Alice Cook from table eight. My hands were shaking that I knew this information. Now I must find a way to get a pin.

December 10th, 1944

They're sending me home! Thing is I walk with funny now. Do not know if I could do that to Edith.

Chapter 21
Swinging Bird Cages

(Freddie!)

The clock said it was nine after two in the morning when I looked. Eyes so heavy yet you still wake to a sound. The bedding was all messed up in a ball on his side of the bed. Buddy the Cat was shaking hiding in the closet watching to see if he was gone. The dresser drawers where stacked on top of the dresser itself. All the videos in his collections where in piles around the bed. All the photos on the walls where turned backwards with a single letter written on each one in red. It did not make sense as they did not spell anything I could think of. The bathroom light was running as the shower was going crazy. Down the hall there were these little items he gathered sitting in between the railing like he was going to use them as little bombs if someone came inside the place he was hiding. The clean clothing where shattered all over the house. He was cutting up the cloth to make something. Walton's room was the room right down the hall. The bath sat in the middle. Edith was downstairs. Did not have to look far as Walton was sitting on the stairs all puzzled in his thoughts. Opened the door to Walt's door his room looked as if we had an earthquake. On the back of the door was a pocketknife stabbed into the wood with a green bandana tied to it.

"He's downstairs!" Put my hand on the side of his head as he was hitting it against the handrail. As my feet were walking down each step his voice kept getting higher in pitch as my hearing gotten a better drink of information. He must have done this before as Walton just gotten up to start cleaning the house back up. In the kitchen the table was over the windows as he had pots on the chairs to catch the water from the roof if it rained. How long was I sleeping for him to have the time to make a wind chime out of the cooking spoons? The living room light was shining onto the pots. Leading me to him. My feet felt the coldness of the floor as I went to the door. "No!" He cried out. It made me stop from opening the door. It was a sliding door as it was sliding, I saw. He was standing there near the desk we had behind the sofa. He had gotten his old radio from the closet thus the upset cat. He tied the wire from the nonworking radio to the end of my purple headset. Holding the side of the one side writing down something on the paper. His fingers were bleeding that explains the letters on the walls. He turned the dial trying to get the right station. Where did he get his old army green muscle shirt and his original boxers, he came here with those the night he woken on the floor? He bent his face to the face of the radio. He was writing in dots in code as if it were still the time he was from.

"Hello, hello! Repeat that." He yelled at the radio as if it were telling him something. Now I see why the house was turned upside down. He found his dog tags. I was hiding them in Walton's sock drawer. He heard me somehow as his face turned. His eyes where a gray with a mirror glaze. "Freddie, you are supposed to be home taking care of the girls not here. I came to fight so you wouldn't have to." I had to get him out of this. How did I do this last time? He grabbed my arm trying to get me to safety.

"Private! He stopped in his tracks. War is over. You can come home now. Hand in your tags and get packed up to go home." He acted like I was his officer. Standing straight with his hand over his forehead.

"But Sir the see bees were going off madder than a hound dog in the spring. There flying over dropping birds to the ground." His body was shaking.

"You have another mission son. You need to wake up now. The wars over." His hands were out for me to reach for him. So, I took my fingers brushing them against his palms. The gray to his eyes where slowly going away as he started to look around. This was not the first time I had to bring him back to bed. Is war the answer! Why not give peace a chance? This is what happens to the men after they come back.

"What happened? Not again!" He sat at the desk looking at the mess he made. "I was sixteen telling them I was older by two years. They sent me home the moment they found out what age I really was. It was too late as I was already among those who saw way too much. I got home and all went to hell. I woke up in this strange place. And then I was four. I left them there to die Freddie." I went to sit on the desk near him. Swaying my feet in the air.

"You didn't do that at all. You came somewhere where you can protect their children." His eyes turned gray again as he stood. I stood trying to get him back again. He put his hands up I did not know what was going on as I just felt the wind. Those hands pushed me to the wall where I felt the impact it left. Felt his hand grab my neck as he lifted me in the air. Could not feel the ground. Gotten my fingers in his dog tags with an inch of my luck hanging in the air. It was the tags controlling him. He fallen to the ground as I did. He was gone when I was able to get my sight back. The ringing in my ears didn't go away. Walked to the end of the stairs where Walton was pointing to the bedroom. He was frozen not even blinking as he stood at the top of the stairs. I kneeled in the opening of the doorway to the walk-in closet. William was petting the cat as that orange pet loved it all.

"I can kill you anytime. Her spell affects me most nights anymore where I cannot control it. I thought it was the dog tags too, but it is not it. I am gathering my things to go back now. Trying to get back there so she can have you and I am not in the way now more."

"Where is your trunk?" I put on his oversized boots for my feet. As he said it was where we park the cars. Just started to walk. Walton following me asking me what I was up to. I did not stop nor answer him. He even helped me drag that trunk into the middle of the driveway. Took the gas for the tractor and gave the trunk a bath. As I throw a light match to it. "You need to get gas in the morning." Walt was cheering as I did it. William thought I was mad. That is all he had from his past. "I'm putting an end to this spell now." Took the muscle shirt right off his body myself forcing him to lift his arms, even pulled down his underwear. I did not care if he was nude in our own yard standing. Everything needs to go.

"What about your ring?" Walton asked as he was right.

"No! When you said you marry me the spell was broken on that." That he knew. The spell was gone, and his nightmares where gone with it. William took the clothing he had in the truck and joined us as we danced to this song he played on his phone around the fire. We all just started dancing not thinking about why we're doing it, it was just three of us having fun. Thing is will this ever be over. I had to stop dancing as these men all surrounded the flame. All men form different times. Some gladiators, soldiers, sailors. One of the sailors walked up to me.

"Can you break our spells too?" How do I answer them? I was not looking at him as he spoken. As my eyes were on this boy behind him. The boy with the red hood who jumped and killed himself before we moved. All you saw was his hood moved through the men like a maze. The sailor noticed him too, but he needed my attention. "He has been following us like a kid to his older brother and his friends." His hand rose as he pointed over to William. "I have meet other versions of the two of you. Time is a mystery. There are many different versions of earth. You two are very well known in all of them. Thing is those other Williams are dead. Yours is still living. You help us I will teach you how to get to those other worlds. Only if you help them. We have been trying to find the right Freddie to help and that hood is with you no other versions of you. So, we stayed and waited." Your telling me that in all the different world that we are living in there is only one William. I do not think I can tell him that.

"What do I do?" I was scared about what is going to happen more than if it should happen. It was like I was getting shoved into the wall by William all over again.

"Get William to open up more about his mother. See we are all the sons of his mother. He was the only one who lived. Why because of you. We are not going to get even, but before they leave this planet, they need to know that he knows her. More than he needs to. He is in the house and its cleaning itself. You might want to get in there." I did not know a ghost can clean a house without me knowing that they can clean a house. How is that a possibility when they cannot touch anything? He was not kidding the house was as if nothing ever happened. I will get how he did that later. Make a mental note people. Ghost cleaning business idea.

"This is never good gooseberries are in a glass bowl and flour is in your hands. I smell tarts getting ready to be made." He rolled his eyes at me as I started to laugh. What, I thought it was the funniest thing I had said all day.

"Freddie, that wasn't me. You know that." He was stress baking. Nothing new here. I took the bowl of berries in my hand as I was playing with them. It was getting the thoughts out of my head if I looked at him, I could not say it in full strength.

"I thank you and I need to talk." What he was holding hit the surface hard as he did not like what I said. "Nothing bad! Just you and I!" Would it kill him to let me finish a sentence? Yes, yes it would!

"Your leaving me aren't you. Freddie this was not me. You know me." Your standing there in front of me trying to make me stay. I just put one of these berries in his mouth. Smile and I hooked him.

"Look I have news. A record label rang me the other day, and I was going to let you know on your birthday, but I must tell you. I have been signed onto the label for a five-year contract. It is my start. Look happy." Cat like smile he was happy. Why was I waiting to tell him this for so long? Oh yeah, this war thing.

"Why didn't you tell me? I mean sooner." He took the bowl out of my hands so he could kiss me, but he ended up talking instead.

"Because I had written to a school and you gotten in. I was willing to give up my thing for your thing. You're going to baking school." I was getting this angry cat face now. Do not look like that. You stress bake and school is stressful you will ace the classes. "I was thinking if I sing that money can pay for your school." William stopped what he was doing as he put his back trod the counter and held his belly button. Looking down at his hands.

"I can't go back to school. I just last week was told I have to eat for two."
Looks like we both are hiding something for each other.

"Look you only need a few classes to get you into your own place to bake
for a living. We can work around a baby." Now I was leaning in feeling his
belly button.

"I have been taking classes behind your back online. I am in the last class
to pass for my two-year degree." In the middle of a war you found a way to go
back to school and save me too. What I did was for nothing. I had to take
myself into the other side of this room.

"Why did we keep things from each other? William you and I are better
than this." Guess we were both trying to make it a better future while at the
same time does not think about it as there might not be one. "William your
mother had a lot of children in time." He stopped me with his famous way of
getting out of a topic by not hearing me or trying not to hear me.

"I know! I was going to tell that you too. Edith and I have been in time
meeting some of them. They weren't supposed to tell you so soon." That
explains why he was gone during spring break. Also, why all these younger
men have been making appearances.

"You two did what? William you and I have not been together in a while.
Whose child is in there?" I had to get out of here. I just ran into the closet in
our room. I was the one petting the cat now. He stayed in the kitchen not
coming back. He was in love with someone else. I felt numb like the astronaut
who was in space waiting for his help to come. I just took myself up on my
feet. Put the cat in his carrier and walked to the door. William came from the
kitchen with a towel in his hands. Looking down at what I had. "I will be at
Edith's if you like to call or not. Yeah, do not even come near me anymore.
You cheated with another man in a year I do not know. Maybe I should have
let you just snap my neck tonight." With tears in my eyes clouding my
judgment he grabbed my keys. Getting in front of the door with his other hand
in the air.

"I am four months along. The last time you and I were together was that
same time frame." He took my hand and placed it on his belly button area. "He
or she is yours." Something was sad at this point he made my favorite baked
good. Cheese biscuits with a hint of extra on the cheese. I ran for the kitchen
for the baked good as he ran trod me stopping me in my tracks. "I'm sorry!" I
turned placing my hand on his chest.

"Me too!" Freddie said I mean, I said.

There is this flattish plastic box that is baby blue with a flip up lid. It had a
gold pattern on top of its lid. It was a girl's jewelry box from back during the
early seventies. It was my aunts then now I got it as we found it in the trailer

upstate that my mother grew up in. Now it's a blue box, I put my necklace in every night and place William's glasses on the lid. A box passed down yet forgotten. Last night was like most where William went for a run as I picked a movie on the television. Something was wrong yet I shock it off after you see ghost as well your world is shaking all the time. Heard the front door shut when he always strips down throughout the house then sits on the bed half wet with his suspenders hanging down his pants and his trousers unfastened. Goes into the shower as he comes into the bed in his boxers with the yellow rabbits on them horny as a bee most nights, but not this one. Falling to sleep as it does not matter, he came into the film halfway throw. Me getting up and fetching his glasses from the floor and placing them on this box.

When I opened my eyes the next morning his hands were over my chest so if I get up, he will wake. Thing is I always wake to seeing that box. This morning was different. William was on the floor sleeping as he rolled off the bed and it did not wake me. Everything was a blur as my eyes needed to catch up. Cut my hair yesterday it felt strange as I was used to touching long hair. I cut the sides and the back of my head and kept the top long. It was a new thing man were doing. The box was there and all the works as I gotten up and picked William off the floor put on his glasses and forced him downstairs to start the tea. It was going to take him awhile as he had to have fresh raspberries thus why there's bushes outside the kitchen door. Picked up his clothing as there was a new box sitting near the blue one. It was small and powdered blue with a purple ribbon around it. put the clothing on the bed when I took the box in my hands letting the ribbon hit the floor. Inside was a card stating, (Read me!), underneath well, after a layer of tissue paper.

Inside was a vintage lady compact powder mirror. It is round with a brass siding with a glass finish. It opens from the middle inside was soft pink powder and a mirror. On the top of the glass inside between of the glass and mirror was a photo. It was a round original that was taken in the early forties in the middle of the war looking as this type of paper was given to the men fighting where it was rare for the other people. There was a married couple, the lady with her hair in old fashioned curls and the most beautiful dress on. In her hands she is holding her man's hat. His left hand is on her arm as it shows his long fingers. The other hand in his pocket as he is in his morning jacket and all the fixings a man from those times would be dressed into. They had some of this photo colorized as you could see the green of the grass and the darker shade the tree on his side gave off and mind you that there is only one tree. His suit coat was a royal blue. You could see his hair combed back as he was trying to smile when the photo was taken. His ears cute ears as they were like elephant ears. Lush eyebrows with eyes that would kill and get your attention from the moment he was looking at you. his jaw like a seagull strong and just.

"William was keeping a bin of his old things at my house. I was snooping in it as I found this. Freddie did he ever tell you about her. That or did he tell you that was me." Edith was coming in the room as I was looking at it.

"How do you know this was him?" I asked as the men in the photo was not him. It looked like him, but I do not think it was.

"It was one of the Gunn Brothers, see he was with William when he came home that night. His mother mashed their souls together. Freddie, he chooses to be William, but when the other man comes about you need to know who he is. He's just trying to get back to the way things where." Somehow, we need to change things.

"That night that I trapped the other William in that compass was your Gunn brother. Then we must find a way to pull them apart. Can you do it." She tried to change the topic. "CAN YOU!" I yelled out of turn. "Sorry, didn't mean to make you tear, but who is in my bed. That's why he tried to sleep with you as one half wanted to as the other part said my name."

"I have my old love letters from the Gunn brother. If I burn the pages, it will give us a wish to go back yes." I looked at her as I did not want to. She knew it had to be. "Yes! Let us get it done then. Freddie you must know. You both have been looking for the Paper Prince, but the whole time it's been inside of him." Your telling me that the man in him was the man who did all that bad stuff to me trying to tell me what she just did. Why shadow it away? Unless he was trying to protect him.

"I'll be ready tomorrow please!" She agreed as there was something, she needed to post in town later.

The clock was reading two after nine at night. The hands frozen as if there was ice gluing up the gears. The outside light was showing the snow coming off the roof. Do not know why there was this thought in my head to put this oval frame with my dead ancestors over the headboard. Now all they do is stare at me mocking me that I let the Starr last name end with me. Don't they know that I was different that in my case I can keep it going as my ability's let it happen. Fingers crossed it still can. A foot upside down on each of my shoulders and a sound off his vocal cords fill my ears as I take the thing those people staring at me gave me jousting it inside what I trusted. Pushing him trod the wall making that frame shatter with my anger. His lungs were breathing letting me hear his wheeze from his asthma. His skin was wet as silk. His fingers cascaded over the birthmark on my right hip. Well, it is not on my hip its little over the hip do not know what it called but it is there. Freddie looked up to me as he didn't understand what I was doing. Kept seeing myself in a

First World War manhole, then I was back here near him. In one spot I was dressed in my uniform, then I was on top of him with nothing on but our blanket. It finally took me in fully where I was looking over the edging the whole, we were hiding in. that's when I was shot from behind. The bullet went right through me. I knew I was dying so I begged the man I was with to give my wife a letter I had written. I watched at her photo until I closed my eyes. The last thing I could feel was him forcing the photo out of my hands. All I remembered was going to sleep then waking up on my bed after my nap when I was four. Is there nothing after this until we get to the next life? Or is there only a darkness? Thing is Freddie was the man who forced the photo from my fingers. It's a circle, going around like an endless loop.

(William's play)

Took one of my father's ropes he had in the shed and hung it up in a line. Great-grandmother Phoebe's hand put together quilt making a homemade curtain. Hurricane lamps filled with fresh oil and light to set the mood of the play. Freddie standing in the middle of the curtain peeking into the audience. The freshness on his face of splendor that await. Eyes widened as if there was a gift outside of the other side of the fabrics. His hair all messed up after fitting that crown over his head that we made from tin foil that his aunt had in her crafting tools. A golden crown for a fiery waive love seeing his hair look like his heads on fire in the light. "Stu, can you think of it tonight a living room full of neighbors, and tomorrow who knows what stages we will get to see us acting on." Stu was smiling at his face as that was what he wanted, and he be any brother to get him what he wanted. His aunt's tights on his hips as he pulls at his crotch, but he does it if that red headed boy wanted him too. Against the wall there I sat as my brother was painting a fake mustache under my nose. I laughed so much he had to redo it repeatedly. His play had to be placed in 1607, and we had to wear all these heavy clothing. Only Walton would come up with this. Did not know Walton wanted to write until he came up with doing this for the kids in our community. "You two ready over there?" Walton put in my hair, so the wire did not show these antlers that Edith made for this play. I was to play the deer that the king wanted to kill until he saw the beauty of the animal when he chose to let the deer live. There was more to the play, but I remembered the part where Freddie loves me. "When I die spread my ashes. On the stone my grandmothers sewed. Let the river bend when I get there. The lonely angle bleeds again. When I die let it sorrow in your blessing old. Let the lonely soldiers follow me into my light. Pray for my halo let the bells ring for my flight." He even writes songs, oh man I hope I did not forget the words.

"Do you remember sitting in Mary's car waiting outside of that two-floor house near the high school? There was this man who gave music lessons and Edith was one of them. You would tag along every time as she took us to the fast-food place to get the meal with a toy after she was done." Walton made me laugh again. Man wish there were not paint under my nose.

"Yeah every time the teacher hit the piano keys we would joke as Peggy Sue hit the wrong note again and he had to start all over." She went onto play the county fairs, but after that we did not know what had happened to her. Just a memory between brothers for now. The play was fun the kids laughed and that was the key. I think coming up with the lines and getting to be different people for a little while was the best part of this whole night. It seemed that each of our brothers where outside with the others as we were left to clean up the place. Just kept my eyes down as there was not any words I had to say. There was so much at the tip of my lips, but I could not get them out. "I'm going to go bubble dance for a while." His eyes looked over at me as he was not trying to figure out what that was, I said. I stopped before hitting the stairs.

"The hot water comes out cold, and the cold water comes out cold too. You might want to bubble dance over at your place." He was shy not looking at me just refolding that blanket in his hands. Went over to the table he was working near as I sat on its edge. His eyes moved against the line of the edging as his fingers moved along on the blanket.

"Bubble dance is Sailor talk for dish washing. Are you saying I was going to take a shower in your house?" We had to stop what we were doing as this man walked into the room with Freddie's uncle.

"There you boys are. William me boy your father asked if you sleep here so you can sleep on the floor upstairs. If you do not mind the pull out. Freddie, this man is here to see you." There was a man in the other room talking to my boy, well he is not mine yet. Then how come I was needing this dough, and how did I make fresh bread so fast.

"Okay, okay I think Freddie talking to someone else is getting my kitchen dirty. William deer you have to breath." Freddie's aunt touched the top of my hands as my face was red and the dough did nothing to have this happen to it.

"What do you mean? Freddie can talk to anyone he likes. Why? What do you know that I don't?" This was getting to my head.

"I know that whatever Freddie is getting told he is wondering why you haven't asked him out yet. William all he talks about is you. His videogame character is Sir William of Starr. You know this kitchen is a food place. It is like they do not know I am in here half the time. Yet Freddie watches your house to see if you pass your bedroom window standing right where you are now. I am inches from him you are almost a mile. He's not telling us, but you two are cute together." I was sitting on the floor while she talked. Sitting on the floor usually helps me think.

"What do I do then? Every time I give hints, he looks the other way. Or if I try to talk, he changes what we are going to talk about. My heart doesn't know love yet." She put the dough in a bowl to proof as she through some flour at me.

"Go upstairs! Freddie is dancing around his room about now. Give him an ending to a night he will never forget." As I stood, I stumbled some. She was right he was in his room in a nightgown one he gotten from England fashion magazines and he still had on that crown. Spinning on his heels as he was humming. He was starting a movie as I saw the bag of chips he had on his bed. He stopped as he saw me watching leaning on the door frame. His aunt had put two bottles of pop in my hands before heading up here. He was smiling as he was still somewhat childlike in a big teenager body. I licked my lips as I was trying to gather my thoughts. If I say the wrong thing then I lose him. But if I say the right thing then what do I do? My hands were letting me show the nerves.

"So, what was that man talking to you about?" I said it almost under my breath, yet his ears heard me say it. I was a fool for being up here. Boys like me do not get the prince. Being gay in a southern state I rather just go into the middle of the woods and let them kill me know. Yet I was getting a smile out of his face. He placed his hand on the back of his neck as he asked me to shut the door. This was really testing the waters. A shut door and him standing on the other side of the room with me in the middle.

"Are one of these for me? Root beer! My uncles favorite he thinks if he yells at the television holding one of these the sports players will magically hear him. Funny right!" I handed him the bottle as he made me laugh and make a sound doing that too. Now he knows I sound like a geek when I laugh. Was it getting hotter in here? "The man was cleaning out his grandfather house and his relative saved all the clothing from his brothers then himself from the forty's my favorite decade to learn about. He wanted to know if I wanted them as I can still fit in the clothing." That was mine too! Mom put my grandfather's navy photo in a bottle charm and I never take it off. I have his complexion she said. My frames of my glasses are reporter themed from that decade as well. "Cool save me a cardigan!" My eyebrows are up in the air and this smile is not doing anything to you. I was sinking in my own footprints.

"Is that all you be wearing?" What! He said that to throw me off. Didn't he? My eyes looked down as I was nerves. My brain was thinking about if I react to him then I will be dragging him out on the carpet too, and we both be bullied until one of us kill ourselves. "You know if a person likes another person back, they look at that person. Did I do something wrong?" my mouth was wide open or so I thought I had to put my fingers to my face to make sure. I was frozen in spot! He put his hand in his hair as he sat on his bed. Rolling his eyes. A boy once thought I was different and wanted to beat me up after school, the girl next to him talked him out of it. I think I was having my fear take heed. "Forget about it. you can go. Man, I knew you did not like me! Why would your brother tell me that you did?" man my hand was on the doorknob and he had tears. Starr Boy get over there. Sat on the bed next to him.

"No! No! No! I do not like you, but I love you! There I said it now. Let us wipe off those tears." I stood as there was something, I had to show him. Did not want to take off my shirt, but I had to prove to him I was willing. He was scared as I could tell by his face. I was not even looking at him yet as I was trying to get my shirt over my face. Walked over to him as his eyes socked in my body. "My father is a bad drunk he hits me with his belt and well there is nothing to hide it now." I had to show him I meant what I said. He placed his fingertips on each line the belt left as he ran the tips down the links. My tears fallen on his hand when he looked up to me. He stood as he wanted to say something, but I said it for him. "I love you too!" He kissed me faster than I was able to say those words. It was better than I thought it was. Butterscotch with a twist. He was eating candy being it was in my mouth when we stopped. We ended the night before falling to sleep in each other's arms to a song where we slowed danced. It was an older song that was now our song. Now only if I can get him to not dance on the tops of my feet.

December 11th, 1944

Something was off when I got home. Mother was there but she said Edith took the baby to her mother's. Mother told me that she was a witch tonight. That I had another mission to fight.

What is going on here?

Chapter 22
Chipped Garden Gnome

(Freddie!)

Here I find myself in a world without my William. Edith ran after him in time hoping to find a middle ground. So far to me it has been four months. Walton needed to teach me things for when they get back. The attack will not be long, but it will be there when they get back. I knew they were trying to get into her head. Louise is the hardest person to read so if you get to her in her weaker state like she did with me then maybe there is a chance. Walt said we need a solider. Walton was the solider! I have been sleeping in his shirts long sleeved or not it still smells like him. With all the superheroes that are made up and people try to repeat in dressing up like them to online chatrooms it does not matter none of them have the only power that I hold. Many hold this power, but they do not say nor try to save a planet or people. Man wanted a hero to fall for a lady as history teaches us that is the way it is needed. Yet, the unsung hero in this case loves a gentleman. My love interest, and scenes in a book might be different then there but the only thing they have that we might have is that the lady can have a child. William almost did so we are halfway somewhere.

I have been doing my homework. There was a boy we went to school with that I knew and became friends with. He did not ask questions about why I was the way people like me were. After school was over for us all. He called on Edith, but she was with Scott. So, with a broken heart he joined the army. Took on the act of a brave man. He was sent home once he set his boots down on the ground. He stepped on underground bomb. It was planet there in the 1950s where people thought that the bad guy from the war before was not dead and they wanted to make sure wherever he went he would be dead. When he came home, he had no left leg from the knee down. Sure, he can walk on one leg. But there are many dark days for him.

"Honey, there is man here to see you." His grandmother was the nicest lady ever. Loved her wearing flowers on her shirts.

"Send him away!" She turned on his light.

"He is here to give you a chance." She turned to tell me to leave. But I did not knock on her door for a half an hour for me just to leave. Placed my finger on my lips for her to not say a word.

"I have something for you." I leaned on the door case as he went from looking at the item outside the window to my face. He was a solider down to the shaved head all the way to the boots near the door. "I have a titanium leg for you out in your grandmothers living room for you to stand." He started to wheel himself, but it hurt his fingers.

"For what! Get out of here I don't need you." He did!

"You need to try and help save the world I need you to train me." He was getting mad as he rubbed the back of his hands like he did in grade school.

"Look I can't!" He was lying to himself!

"I see a man who wanted to do something good for his people. Yet he let them down the moment he even tried. I get that. But I am trying to give you this chance to do that. That person that lady on the news is after is me. I need you to get the gift out of me so I can use it. William is doing his part. But we are not together as he is in time. You are the only man he trusted with his life, so I am asking you to trust me. So please help me and I will try to get you together with my cousin." He was going to save something, but he did not.

"What is in it for me?" I smiled.

"This leg can make you faster than a speeding bullet. With some of William's tin gear you can save people again." I am from the start I was in his world and he did not welcome me. I left in his terms he would look at the legs and think about it. His grandmother let me stay the night on the sofa. Thinking it might bring him to his terms. Yet, I fallen to sleep instead watching a 1990s drama about a man, a paper, and his orange cat. The crackling noise woken me as that orange cat meowed for the man to open the door. My body needed to pee, but my brain did not want to stand. Stood up as something just told me to go to his room and look after his wellbeing. I knew who was telling me yet no open else can see what I can.

There was a whistling sound coming from the room like a tea pot on the oven. Her hair gathered in his face, so I did not see it. Her nail from her right pointer finger road his body from the tip of the bottom of his neck, down his midriff, then stopping at his waistline. He was awake as his leg was moving from his nerves. Thing is the bomb he stepped on changed him. He can do things no one else can. "You can join me boy! You can be stronger than you ever imagined. That Freddie might want you all for himself, but I can do many

228

things." She sat up sitting herself around his hips moving back and forth until she was exactly right where she wanted to be. Until the prize showed itself. Now I see where William gets it from. When he was seen by his eyes, he looked right to her. His finger rested on her upper leg as she screamed from his touch. She jumped up on her feet faster than I ever saw. "You're the titanium elk! The rarest of them all. There is only one to be known to man. Freddie's gift bounced off you back to him and somehow a little of it is still in you. You can see them too. Thus, why I picked him. When I found out William kissed that girl in the classroom. I lost it and kissed his best friend from the ninth grade. That is the trouble from the people I love they become seekers of the dead too. He gotten the form of not being able to die. He lost his leg from being stuck in between rocks when he woken. William told me once that I can never love anyone but the one person, I do choose to love in life has to be it. No shopping around and I must make sure that I know that is the one. William was the one they say I saw him running. I know I slept with pam too. Thing is nothing happened to her because the gift was not activated yet. See William's body is the only one who can penetrate the pain. Being hit by a belt all your lift he was used to it. She turned into smoke he told me. I just saw the door open when I heard a big popping sound.

"You get me the leg, and I will do anything!" Now I was smiling. Wow, his grandmother was happy as well as she was watching from the toilet. Do not shut the door.

I sit here now on train going I do not know where. The door locked from the outside so I cannot get out. A dead wizards wand sits in the candle stick holder as ever three hours glows and for appears. The wood for the wand laced with teeth marks as the man must have been a writer and kept the stick in his mouth. The walls are green, somewhat green as the paint is chipped seeing the original color it was first. Next to the door is a seat with a hole in the seat letting the waist go on the ground as the train moves onto its tracks. When you are sitting on that area there is a little door that opens and there is new clothing you put the dirty in open it and its clean with a snap. There is no knob to the door, just a little hole to put your finger in. a mirror on the wall the is dirty some from the money men whose backs rubbed against the glass from pretending they were wed. the window the size of shoe box. The bed of fresh linen every night that have flowers in the inlay of the body of the fabrics. The only thing I have that has not been taken is a notebook under the matters. The muscle shirts here are tighter than the ones we have, and the underwear are like modern briefs, most socks go up to the knee and there are bands that go over the knew so your socks do not fall to your ankles. The suspenders are thick, and they keep the trousers on your hips. The vest is worse, do not gain weight.

The pants are like lady's capris. Love the hats if I were going the gulf. There is a bowl under the bed with water, and metal shelves on the walls with towels. See William was hiding me on the train until Freddie needs me. It's been hard in a 1940's world. Waiting for a knock on the door. When a single knock comes on the door than it's time for Freddie. It is now going on the one hundredth day on this train when I was writing in the notebook hearing the rain when a knock came on the door. Stood as fast as I could and put the want in the back of my pants feeling it in my crack on my backside. The door opened as I had my hands up to fight. A gentleman in a giant coat. Before I could speak, he put his finger over his lips. Came over to me whispering something I wanted to here. We had to get far from here as it was hunting day. It went from every day to a few days now. When they do not find me, they stop to see if I will show myself. He has his leg now we run.

(Stu!)

I sit here now on train going I do not know where. The door locked from the outside so I cannot get out. A dead wizards wand sits in the candle stick holder as ever three hours glows and for appears. The wood for the wand laced with teeth marks as the man must have been a writer and kept the stick in his mouth. The walls are green, somewhat green as the paint is chipped seeing the original color it was first. Next to the door is a seat with a hole in the seat letting the waist go on the ground as the train moves onto its tracks. When you are sitting on that area there is a little door that opens and there is new clothing you put the dirty in open it and its clean with a snap.

There is no knob to the door, just a little hole to put your finger in. a mirror on the wall the is dirty some from the money men whose backs rubbed against the glass from pretending they were wed. the window the size of shoe box. The bed of fresh linen every night that have flowers in the inlay of the body of the fabrics. The only thing I have that has not been taken is a notebook under the matters. The muscle shirts here are tighter than the ones we have, and the underwear are like modern briefs, most socks go up to the knee and there are bands that go over the knew so your socks do not fall to your ankles. The suspenders are thick, and they keep the trousers on your hips. The vest is worse, do not gain weight. The pants are like lady's capris. Love the hats if I were going the gulf. There is a bowl under the bed with water, and metal shelves on the walls with towels. See William was hiding me on the train until Freddie needs me. It's been hard in a 1940's world. Waiting for a knock on the door. When a single nock comes on the door than its time for Freddie. It is now going on the one hundredth day on this train when I was writing in the notebook hearing the rain when a knock came on the door. Stood as fast as I could and put the want in the back of my pants feeling it in my crack on my backside. The door opened as I had my hands up to fight. A gentleman in a giant coat. Before I could speak, he put his finger over his lips. Came over to me whispering something I wanted to here. "Freddie needs you now, Stu"

(William!)

There were plastic wings hot glued to the rims of my penny loafers. Cloth diaper around my waist as Edith was kindly to plaster a tissue paper four leaf clover on my face. Freddie had found a metal head band that had golden wings on the corners to be placed in my hair as if it were hiding. He always told me that he was going to be the last one standing in the land of ash. It was written for him that it was meant to be. Blue glitter splattered on my skin to give me a shine. They were getting me ready for the Halloween party that we were to have. Yet I find myself standing in the land of ash in the middle of what was the woods. Everything on this planet but myself was burned to the ground, but my mother and her followers. They stood on one side of me in a line stretched out that lead to a point my sight could not see anymore. On my other side stood, The Before. This war was not going after Freddie. My mothers' side was using us this whole time to get to them. The Before trusted me yet I let them down. I was holding Freddie's crown. He was standing right behind me trying to catch up as I was following this flouting glove. That lead me to this spot Infront of the house in the woods. I stood there between them just standing. I placed his crown on my head when I started to run. Just ran until the faces ended. They never ended. Just this morning Edith had put a spell on the mailbox to play a trick on the mean mailman. The mail in his bag chased him down the road. We laughed so hard. Now I stand Alone. I hear Freddie say my name, so I know there is a place where he and the others are still alive. I must run until I get there.

December 16th, 1944

Woken up on the floor. I was not in the same house I was yesterday. When I saw myself in the mirror, I was a little boy again. I need to wake up now.

Chapter 23

Gardeners Skull

(Freddie!)

Her fingers grasped the handle of the lantern harder as we walked. With every step that she took another notion that this battle was real was getting to her thoughts. Eating at her as if she was a duckling looking up at a field of wild pigs and not a way of getting out. She didn't wasn't to be in this hike whatsoever. But this was for me, so she walked on. The smell of the metal from the old rusted lantern lined her hand and it ventured up to skin. The tips of her hair cascaded over the sides of the hot pink hood she was wearing. That soft pink dress in the other hand as she didn't want it to get dirty. Thing is that might give us away as girls back during the fifteenth century didn't mind there dresses dragging on the ground if the work got done. The path was in the woods mainly following the man-made stone wall nearby. The closer we went down the trail the animal would run the other way. If it wasn't dangerous, they wouldn't move, but to move an elk there was a powerful more than they could imagine. Twilight was taking heed of the morning as the flame on the lantern went out. She didn't understand why the fire was gone as there was enough lighter fluid and the fabric that it was light onto was still long enough.

The trail leads us to these two giant rocks bigger than the tallest man alive. Edith didn't want to go on the tail much more as she didn't want to past the rocks. They might crush us or something. A white rabbit ran on the path running in-between the rocks as she saw this, she indeed followed the rabbit. They say ladies first for a reason. Each rock had these exceptionally fine detailed figures carved into the rocks that went from the top of the rocks upward. The stem of the figure was the hips of a man's waistline all the way to the man's head. All young men from around the world. Five one each side. They have been carved into the rock for a long time as moss had gathered on some of them, and there was a bird's nest in the one man's hand that he was holding out. Their faces read fear, thing is Ms. Louise feed off fear for a quick pick me up before going in for her kills. As she passed each one on each side it would magically turn into these rock girls. They turned into the last person their eyes last saw. Each one was a different form of the lady in question herself. Thing was it only did that for Edith. As I passed them it was different, they all just would come to life as they watched me. Whispering in my ears to turn back that if I don't, I be there with them. All talking in different languages that I didn't understand. She exited the rocks, but I had the hardest time. If I walked right though and keep going them, I was a ghost. I had to show my ghost boy to her. That I can be a ghost then return to my physical form. Edith saw me that is what counted, but this way my gift felt stronger. I felt like I was standing naked in front of the whole world as the people stair at me like I was riding in a parade on a horse. My hair isn't long enough for that show.

A mile from that rock I was able to be myself again. For some reason, those men that was carved into the rocks didn't want me to be seen until now. They were naked carved into the rocks I had to show myself too. I kept hearing my name as I saw a girl running in the woods. Must have been the youngest witch to die they say in Massachusetts. We were on the same land they were burned on. At the very end of the trail was this sod house on the hill and a cabin. The cabin was made from trees that were freshly cut, and the windows were very thin as glass wasn't quite easy to get where she came from. There were cows, and all the works to make a working farm from this land. Edith stopped me by putting her hand out. We were hiding behind some trees as we watched Ms. Louise's younger self leaving her house. William couldn't be here to help us as he was the baby that was in the basket she was carrying. Our mission was to retrieve the child and kill the witch in question.

Her door was a modern door as it had a lock onto it. You could tell not many people came here. To them it would look like a door made from wood, but to us it was an iron door with a glass window with flowers incased into its structure. Edith stood near the door as I walked behind the house. There wasn't a way in from the back. Ms. Louise knew what she was doing. Knowing that this might catch up to her in this time. Her magic was weaker now, and we knew it. she went after poor Edith when she first learned about her power. Being the granddaughter to a witch it skipped her mother and went to her like mine did. It was funny how she figured out she had powers as she pointed her fingers at buddy the cat, she wished to turn him in an orange. Well, for a brief ten minutes the cat was some fruit. What was funniest was that his face was still there and reacting to what we were doing. There was no hope on getting in here and making our surprise.

While she was trying to think of a spell I was worrying if Ms. Louise would return to her house before we could make our plan. The plan was to get inside and hide somehow then make our attack when she was in her deepest part of her sleeping. Having a child Edith said was the weakest for them as it took a while for their powers to charge. Edith looked at my boots while I was walking back trod the woods as my eyes saw something coming out of the glass on the door. The flowers parted to the sides of the glass as a clear hand came trod us holding a single key. Good ole Walton was on the quest and we didn't even know he was watching us. His job was to keep my William distracted until our job was done. The key was thin and had a seahorse head at the top of it. Walton's glass hand dropped the key as the head of the seahorse sneezed. Never heard one sneeze before, so it is hard to describe what it sounded like. Looking back to make sure she wasn't coming back to the house we made our entry.

The house was just as if we walked in our house back home. Nice clean walls and even electricity. We were not able to put under her spells as Edith's magic put us on an even playing field masking us from the jester's touch. Edith found there was a door on the floor that lead to the basement. Their version of one anyway. There was this young man pocking his head up as she lifted the wood. I knew that face anywhere. It was the man that William saw in the butler's pantry that day. He knew what her magic was able to do and warned him the best her could. Wish we understood him more. Edith started to light some candles as she let the boy free. Maybe he was able to get to the town folks here to help us. Thing he had to talk in code if she made her appearance. He told us that he was forced to take hot baths for her to get the moisture from his body. This wasn't a boy he saw this was William's father that she used for his genetics. Later after his death she found him again all those years later putting him in the wall, so her secrets weren't exposed.

Edith called out for me to gather into the bedroom. The walls were covered in blue flowers painted on the wall. If they were real, I wouldn't be able to cross as I was allergic to those flowers only. One touch would kill me. I don't understand the lighting of the candle, but she had something up her sleeve. There was a bed and a nightstand, and she never fails to have a bigger television then we do. These people must really see a different inside then what we are seeing. Edith didn't make a sound as she looked at the wall the was on the right-hand side as soon as you walked into the room. She asked me if I knew these men in the photo. If there were any similarities I saw.

1. Photo number one was of a man who had coal dust over his skin as he stood there with no shirt, just hi suspenders over his shoulders and pants up to his belly button. My eyes linked to that old reddish hat that William wears upon his head to this day.

2. Photo number two was of five men swimming in the creek all looking at the camera. The forth one from the left and the one second from the right being the same man had that cat like smile I saw every morning. Behind them on the logs were the men's clothing. They were in eighteen sixty-something as there was a hat that gave it away hanging from the branch off the log. A bugle boys' metal was on the tip of it.

3. Photo number three was the cherry on top of the cake. It was a blonde boy; it was hard to tell the hair color as it was an older photo it was taken around the same time that the secund was. In the room that this young lad was in was a vintage sleeping cot that had four legs attached to a three-square frame that you could fold up and take with you. it had springs in-between the frames and a thin mattress on top. You could only see one side of him as his foot was wrapped in bandages. There was this pillow hanging off the side that his leg was pressed against as his leg was hanging off the side. His leg was bare as you could see the indention of his kneecap as he had it arched. Being he wasn't wearing any trousers you could see the line on his leg that connected to his hip. His left buttock was exposed as the tail of his undershirt wasn't long enough to cover it. One of the dreams that William written about in his diary was that he kept dreaming that he had no right leg. That he woken up and from the hip down there was no leg as he lost it from the battle. That he could remember being on the front line not wanting to fight, but he had no other choices. Why do men have to go into a fight they didn't want to? If they don't want to die, they should have the right to say. If you're running the whole thing then here's a hint give peace and try and fill your pockets later. His but was arched into the air as he was lying on his stomach. Looking at the camera resting his head on his large fingers. His left arm was even hanging off the cot some. The wall was full of pictures of William. Each a different point in time. There was one even of him, and me on one our date nights. She was following him, and he never knew it. Over on her nightstand were these old vintage lockets that lead to our timeframe as well. Now I knew where Edith was getting these lockets. She was trying to collect her powers while Edith thought she was getting somewhere with them. Ms. Louise had the upper hand in this whole time. The other wall was full of creepy dolls yeah, I didn't stay in there awfully long. William knows those things creep me out.

There was a sound at the door as we came from the bedroom. We didn't have much time, so we were hiding under the countertop in the kitchen. That's where I was, think Edith was under the sofa. In that dress I don't know how she did that. Every part of my body had been touched by the nerves. That it was hard for me not to make a noise. My fingers were knob, as my face was hot. Couldn't feel my feet. Knees buckling. It wasn't her. I didn't want to look at who it was, but I knew that humming. I chose to come from where I was hiding as I knew the face to the voice.

"Stu!" He looked at me as he didn't know I was here. He took the toothpick from his gum line and thrown it to the floor. "What are you doing here?" He took off pigskin gloves as he placed them in that long coat he was wearing. He was looking around the room as he knew I wouldn't be alone. This was a trap he said.

"Edith, I know you wouldn't send the only seeker we all are trying to protect in by himself." She showed herself as the other two men that Stu had with him looked her over. "Now, The Devaney boys and I are only here for the same reason you are. If we kill the witch today, life will go back to the way it needs to be." When did Stu start talking with his hands? This wasn't the Stu I remembered he aged very well. I was still in my teens and he was in his late forties. "When I saw the door was open, I knew this was a trap, but I didn't think it was yours." He talked like an old coon hound. Stu, what happened to you?

(Freddie, remembering back!)

Time must have past fast as sleep took over my eyes before I could figure whom it was who came up the stairs. It was not his mother. It was not the dog. the pads on his paws would give that way. It was not Walton as he bounces a bouncy ball at night where he fears the darkness. The smell of hay filled the air. Did not want to open my eyes as now I was sitting. Last time I was remembering my body was on the floor near his bed. The air was cold as it passed by. Colder this time as moisture sat in its wake. With my eyes closed I could feel my hands behind me with wet ropes holding them still. If I was not social phobic then I am now. My legs where split open on the chair as my stance was not set. Boots circling the floor as it sounded like dirt when it gets disrupted. When it stopped behind me fingers grabbed the top of my head forcing my head back by my hair. Pulling tighter as those fingers forced me. Oil form a car's motor on his fingers. Still did not want to open my eyes. Cloth over my face when it rained. Tried to catch my breath but the cloths made it feel like dough over my face seeping into my mouth cocking me. It took a good chunk of time when it finally came to an end. The fabric was taken off letting my head lift. Thought I was getting the worst of it. It stung worse when the hand slapped me crossed the face. The force moved my face to the right side

239

of my body. That is when these eyes opened. Right in front of my eyes was a cage a metal cage like one you put your dog in when your away. Small, square, and William set in its rusty interior. Kneeling on his toes. Not letting himself sit on the floor as it was mud. holding onto the sides so he does not lose his balance. Nothing on but bright white boxers shinier than his teeth. His eyes gravitated to mine once my lids opened. His eyes said it all that he has been in that cage before. He did not go to camp, as he was trained here. This was placing to teach him how to a perfect boy if he was not, they made him sink or swim in a wooden chair. The man all I could see what the curve to his back. dragging a chair to the front of mine. William's daddy was not the face I thought would be looking at me now. My nose started to bleed as he leaned his chair trod me filling his shot glass with the substance, sipping onto it as if was the best spent dollar he earned.

(Bernard and William, nineteen forty-four.)

I was sitting on a bench outside of the Yellow Rabbit Medical Training School for Military Men and Women. Most of the time the ladies were getting trained as field nurses, and if they came with the background then they got to train as a medic. Not many men medical into this field as the women made up most of this field. About time they get there just deserts. Bernard Conklin was one of the men who learned here. The trouble we gotten into here was nothing to write home to mother about. Every afternoon around 1:12 he would be sitting here on this bench for lunch. Never fails as the time came and the aske is, he could sit. He sat like he always did plucking his pants up near his groin, so he did not get the bottoms of his pant legs dirty. He never took that hat off either. Even when we got a weekend pass to go to a beach. He still worn that hat with his then in style bathing suit.

"William! Knew you would follow me. I don't know where he is." He knew I was coming how unless Freddie was here already.

"Bernard, we have been friend for years. I know you more then I know any other person than my Freddie. Whatever you know would help. Please!" He bit into his sandwich as I could hear him swallow hard.

"You still get those night dreams? The ones where you thought bugs were crawling under your skin. I still remember Sir Pfeffer Oswald was our tent mascot as you couldn't sleep without your childhood stuffed octopus." How did he know about that? Don't smile when you say that you know it's embarrassing.

"You were sleeping the whole time! Your snored louder than me." He laughed under his breath.

"Who do you think stayed awake to make sure you were okay. More than one of us love you, but you never let us." He loved me.

"You're the one who took my son in. You never died! You knew that my mother was evil. You took him to Holland to keep him safe knowing this war was coming, but he found me anyway." I remembered a man who gave me a letter and a photo after he passed on, I took it to give to his parents. He looked at is loves photo until he closed his eyes. Yet I find that he was saved. Here I find myself in another life of my own remembering who I was all the way back then and yet I was not supposed to.

"He was here, he brought your brother in to get treated." Walt! He put the bag down as he stood and asked for me to follow him. Lead me into the giant room of rows of beds. They had him behind a curtain.

They had his legs arching in the air. With that nightgown on him it was like they were using his legs for a tent for a view. That nightgown was an older one. It had blue, red, and white strips and three buttons. Water build up on his ankles and going up his legs. When you lifted the fabric from his groin up to the base of his neck was red patches of a rash. His ankles were the size of soft balls and yellow patches going up his legs. His chest beating for air. Took the water basin getting the cloth wet cooling him down. As he saw me, he spitted up blood as then heart was trying hard to keep up. his heart when the water in around it is almost in a whisper as its faint to hear with the human ear. Running to his side feeling helpless just holding his hands. "There must be something you can do." Looked over as he places this glass bottle with tubes attached to it. a giant needle on one end of the bottle to the needle.

My brother was dying right here in front of my eyes and I must put my trust into Bernard, and I did not know if I could. He took the needle getting it ready by cleaning the tip first. When in war together he was getting ready to pass the medical board as I was trying to get into the ambulance driving course. He knew to puncture the skin from the bottom of his breast. I watched as he looked to make sure no one was looking. Walt his eyes kept looking down at it as he grasped my hand harder. He muffled at the pain when it went into him as I watched the needle tube. His eyes went closed as his face sunk in, he was too weak. The liquid coming from his heart was yellow and bubbled. Bernard said it was normal to see it look like a glass of bear. Even this glass knight could not tell me he would not drink beer after seeing that. It was seeing through as you saw his fingers on the other side of the glass. Once full the liquid was released into the container until he could not draw no more. I was going to be sick, but Walt was not moving he was not breathing that when. He put in this substance into the tube to shot through the needle. I could feel his heart stop as I counted the beats in his wrist. The beats started to come back

241

after a few seconds of nothing. his chest started to beat again, and his complexion reacted to it as well. A nurse came about the curtain as he placed the evidence into a box and handed it off to her. Thing is she vanished as she went past the curtain, she was gone thing was she was supposed to be there. Then I remembered her ring. She was a lady of the Silver Leaf Society. "He's going to live an exceptionally long life now. Thing is he would not have lived if you didn't get here."

"How did you know to do this surgery?" He looked the other way from me.

"Who do you think taught me while you were off fighting?" He went over to the sink nearby as he was trying to get out of this conversation.

"Who?" I asked.

"Freddie knows more than you think you just have to get him to remember." Freddie knows more than I do. This does not make sense. "He chose you to protect him. Freddie is part of the society mate." He pushed himself from the counter he was leaning on with his back. I watched as his shoulders moved when his hips did as he walked. This was way too much to take in there was no way. Bernard turned to tell me something else as I was in wonder. "Freddie went to the future after visiting me. He was trying to find you and he knew my photo sits near your bed. When he went back to your timeline, he found out that you were not being a good person as you turned on him and went with your mother. He asked me to get to you before she did. You can't blame her." That last boyfriend his mother had before getting married was a paramedic who taught Freddie the old fashion medical treatments. That is why he knew this. I forgot about him as Freddie has not talked to him in a while.

"That's why Freddie was in New York for three months." I went to the darkest side of my mind during those three months I must have turned worse off ten I was thinking. Freddie was my hero.

"You can still stop this war. Freddie, Edith, and you can still win this war." I looked over to Walton who was just hanging onto his life. Edith's wand is broken in my boot. And I am here trying to get there. Our team was weak. Bernard and myself locked eyes. If anything, I was going to end this war now.

"How?" Let us get started.

Bernard reached into the back of his pains as if he were going to truck in the tail of his shirt. My eyes followed as his hands flickered into the light that the window gave off. He licked the taste off his lips as he only did that when he was not sure about something. His arm rose as his fingers gathered around the trigger. Now I find myself staring into the tip of a gun. I know this was a field hospital but as I looked around once more all the beds were empty. What did he do to all the other people? I did not even see it nor hear the metal ball coming from the tip of the gun. I was shot. When I felt the impact, he pointed behind me as I stumbled backward throw a door he had conjured up with his wand. That broken wand was his. The rims of the frame of the door looked to be looked like a sparkler. As the door shut, I saw a lady standing behind him. She shot him right in the head. When I was yelling out for her to stop, I saw her pin on her blouse. It was a Silver Leaf Society pin. I had to look around me to figure out where I was sent. The stone walls that lined the woods behind my house. Put one hand on the wall as the other was on the wound. Turning on a dime like a spinning ride at an amusement park. It stung worse than the time I got stung by three bees I sat on. Just dropped to the ground as I heard something.

"He's over here!" Freddie was running up to me. By the time he got to me I had my shirt off and my suspenders crawling over the back of my person. It was nice to see his face again I was shot in the same place I was before. It was not long until I die. "What happened?"

"Bernard shot me! He did it to protect me. Whatever this society is, he is with thinks I'm dead." I took Freddie's shoulder. My words were not making much sense this time. "Take it out. The bullet Freddie." His fingers hovered my skin. "Just push the fingers in and pull out the first thing you feel make sure it's hard and small." I sat there screaming in pain. My stomach kept waving as I was trying to breath, but it hurt. Felt his fingers inside me, then looked up to see his fingers red covered in my blood. Edith finally showed herself. She found that book bag that Walton got me. She told me that they had him, so I sat still. Freddie took some loss thread she had found in the front of the book bag. Leave it up to my brother to pack everything. Always knew that Freddie would have fingers small enough to sew skin back together. Tried to make a pain face, but I didn't help I kept pushing his shoulders away when he pushed into my skin. I wasn't ready to move yet, but there were these people in hoods walking the woods, and Edith didn't trust them. With one hand over Freddie's shoulder we ran not knowing if we would make it.

July 29th, 2008

Meet Freddie Waters for the first time today. Think I ran countless miles just to get a peak of him. There was something going on here I could not explain. Journal. I think life as I know it is going to change. I found my purpose in life to protect him. Oh, Journal remind me to look up, how to be a gentleman. If anything, he is getting one.

CPSIA information can be obtained
at www.ICGtesting.com
Printed in the USA
LVHW021219011220
673102LV00009B/159